72|9

ben barka

ben barka lane

by mahmoud saeed

translated by kay heikkinen

Interlink Books

An imprint of Interlink Publishing Group, Inc.
Northampton, Massachusetts

*For Congresswoman Jan Schakowsky for her courageous
stand against the invasion of Iraq* —MS

First published in 2013 by

INTERLINK BOOKS
An imprint of Interlink Publishing Group, Inc.
46 Crosby Street, Northampton, Massachusetts 01060
www.interlinkbooks.com

Library of Congress Cataloging-in-Publication Data
Sa'id, Mahmud, 1938-
[Zanqah Bin Barakah. English]
 Ben Barka Lane / by Mahmoud Saeed ; translated by Kay Heikkinen.
    pages cm
"*Ben Baraka Lane* was written in 1970 and immediately banned in Iraq. It
was published in Cairo in 1987 and by Dar al-Caramel in Amman, Jordan
in 1993. After it won the Ministry of Information Award in 1994, it was
reissued by Dar al-Carmel, Jordan in 1995, and was later published by the
House of Arts in Beirut, Lebanon in 1997. This is the first English language
translation."--Title page verso.   ISBN 978-1-56656-926-2
 I. Heikkinen, Kay. II. Title.   PJ7862.A5236Z2613 2013
892.7'36--dc23   2013000043

Printed and bound in the United States of America

translator's acknowledgements:
I would like to extend my heartfelt thanks to Farouk Mustafa and to Kitty
Burns Florey, for their support, their skillful critiques, and their shrewd
observations.

All the characters in this work are fictional.

chapter 1

The vacation is defined in my mind by an event that seems at the very least more important than the usual. During the days of that tense summer I spent in Mohammediya (Fadala) in 1965, the weavings of chance made me feel I was confronting the experience of a lifetime, the excitement every young man pictures in his dreams.

A year before, I had found an apartment in a building of three floors belonging to a Chinaman. It was pretty and pleasant, and blessed by the warm rays of the sun at about twelve o'clock, after the last fragments of the midday call to prayer rasped from some worn-out throat. The sound was not far away, as it came from the Casbah, behind its wall of reinforced brick. Storms had played havoc with the wall, turning its strength and form into red earth, constantly eroded. That had brought those responsible for monuments to think about protecting it, for fear that it might collapse and leave only the Casbah Gate, that exemplary historical monument, to bear witness to the grandeur of an ancient edifice adorned by rare arabesque designs.

The building belonging to the Chinaman, M. Bourget (who had confused me at first by his multiple names and his origin), stood at the head of Zuhur Street, as Si Sabir calls it, or Ben Barka Lane, as al-Qadiri calls it. It is a street that divides the small city in two, beginning from the Bab al-Tarikh Square and ending in the new port and the fish market, passing by the most important and beautiful features of the city—the lovers' garden, the nature walk, the large casino, and the Miramar Hotel—until it nears its end and the space is allotted on every side to the Samir petroleum refinery, to canning and printing plants, and to the unending farms stretching left and right, until the city ends at the rocky sea shore, on which one looks down from a great height. The lethal rocks had once brought a Spanish steamer to grief by night, destroying everyone in it and leaving only a small part of the frame, rusting and still bathed by the ocean waves.

A Bata shoe store shines on the ground floor of the building with its refinement, its gleaming glass and modern décor. Across from it is a row of modern, elegant shops: a bakery that made my mouth water over its delicious displays every morning, a store selling stamps, another selling lottery tickets, a butcher, a *brasserie* serving everything from bottles of soda to various kinds of drinks, then the largest store, for luxury goods and furniture, belonging to Si l-Wakil and his brother, and another *brasserie*.

At the head of the street the new city begins, splitting off from the old Casbah, proud of its radiant youth and smiling at the future, after the last vestiges of domination had disappeared and the French would no longer burn alive any Moroccan they found wandering in their streets after dark. This city embraced the newcomer as soon as he stepped off the bus from Rabat or Casablanca.

More than anything else, my heart was gladdened by the presence of a busy coffee shop, where grains of idle time dissolved in a singular haze of pleasure, melting in the aroma of fine black coffee and visions of the past and of time yet to come.

From the first moment, I fell in love with this unique apartment, its floor a single expanse of gray and soft yellow mosaic, rising on the walls in every direction to the height of a yard, attempting to rival the colored arabesque tiles rising to about the same height on the walls of the Casbah. What more could I ask for? Could the stranger ask for more than to find everything he needs no more than ten steps away, from the bar to the butcher? After twenty-five years of deprivation, persecution, hardship, political struggle, prison, dismissal, and unemployment, I felt as if I had stumbled on a paradise that Adam himself would envy.

What attracted me to this spot was its peacefulness, as well as its beauty and its history, but also the pigeons which clustered in flocks near the wall and its gate. They paced serenely and securely, delving in the cracks of the ancient brick for some stray seed, from time to time fluttering over each other, descending calmly or rising noisily, at times bestowing on the observer a pleasure akin to the early, eternal pleasures of sex.

When I gaze in the afternoon to where the sun immolates itself in a strange calm over the sea hidden from my sight, I feel a strong longing for something I dream of without attaining, wrapped in a captivating, wine-like pleasure flowing through my body and numbing my limbs. I am barely aware of anything in my surroundings until the sudden, daily reversal occurs, and all at once I find myself in a light gray darkness which pushes me with gentle fingers stroking my back, driving me to where I can find all the small pleasures I dreamed of.

Others might consider them trifling, but in my particular situation they are enough to justify a happy life.

The Chinaman lived in the adjacent building, on the other street, which formed the second side of the equilateral triangle, in which Bata represented the main angle, across from Bab al-Tarikh. He rented the rest of it to a Jewish tailor and peddler, and to a few French and other foreigners.

One warm, sunny morning at the end of April, Si Ibrahim motioned to me, so I crossed the street. Si l-Wakil caught me and asked me to please take a rare stamp to Si Sabir. Si Ibrahim spoke to me, proudly raising a box of strawberries in his hand:

"Do you plant them in your country?"

"No."

"A private farm ripened them three months before their time."

"What are they called in Arabic?"

He began to look for the Arabic word, and I thought his head would explode before he found it, so I said first:

"*Shaliik.*"

He nodded his head as he repeated: "*Shaliik.*"

"Put them on my account."

I was on my way to the school. It was a vacation day, and the guard at the end of the hall raised his right hand in greeting and picked up the broom with his left.

I saw no one but Si Sabir. I held out the strawberries. "I brought you breakfast."

He laughed. "How much did you drink last night?"

I put the small box on the table. The red heads of the berries glowed enticingly.

"Please have some, Si."

But he stood back and said, "First, let me present to you… Si l-Habib."

4

I was surprised to see the man, sitting calmly off to one side, and looking at me searchingly. I shook his hand. He got up a little and bowed.

Si Sabir threw away his cigarette and took one of the strawberries with the tips of his fingers. I urged Si l-Habib. He took one, and I burst out: "One isn't enough. Have more."

Si l-Habib had been forced to stay in Mohammediya after the stormy events that had crushed the country at the beginning of the '60s. He had been fleeing to the east when he was arrested. All that saved him from the noose was a severe heart attack that flattened him for a long time, leaving him suspended between life and death in the prison hospital, in the care of doctors and nurses who hid their sympathy behind the frowning mask of someone doing a duty. When the crisis ended he was encompassed in the supreme neglect of the authorities. Afterwards he played the game of living with a weakened heart, under strict orders that warned him away from any exertion or activity or shock that could lead to his death. His illness cut the hangman's noose but left him in bitter banishment from activities he believed he was made for, without which his life was no more than death itself in slow motion.

The arduous struggle against the French before independence, and against apathy and internecine feuding afterwards, had tempered him, bringing him to a degree of glory reached by only a few notable personalities in a few countries.

As Si Sabir said, "Politics is like commerce in a free country: it chokes the children it has created." But I was always thinking of the feelings of those who had attained tremendous heights in their past and had fallen from them obscurely and suddenly. What was the true nature of their feelings? Did any of them dream of returning to the dais of true glory, untouched by troubles or falsity? With respect to Si l-Habib in particular,

I wondered, as I watched him pick another strawberry from the box, if his weak heart could bear the surprise of a happy moment.

He was confined to Mohammediya in compulsory residence. Had he been allowed to choose the place? I did not ask. All the coastal cities are surpassingly beautiful. Yet I knew he loved Mohammediya, preferring its old name of *Fadala*, the hidden pearl of the coast whose value had been discovered more than half a century earlier by people from all over the wide world. Still, even in his state of compulsory fixed residence and exclusion from politics, he was unable to keep from commenting sharply when he saw the lofty castles of the great side by side with the huts of the wretched.

In a time of trial he had endured when he was on top, he had been tempted by the idea of possessing a home in any area he might choose for himself, through the application of a law compensating the most important fighters in the struggle against the French. But he stood with Si Bayad Ben Bella and the councilor against it, so the law was buried alive, mourned by many honorable men who considered it a pension for their children in an uncertain world, and equally by a large number of time servers and opportunists.

Si l-Habib would say that he felt the whole city —Fadala —was his home, for the eternal green of this small spot refreshed the heart. It traced with a graceful hand dreamlike walkways that took the breath away, and small, gaudy asphalt passages that, between one stroll and the next, would break forth in cascades of flowers, crimson, violet, and yellow, making the city a checkerboard of unhedged gardens and small forests that embraced the paths at every turn.

At dawn the city was plunged in a fog that was soon scattered away by the rays of the sun, which turned it into a gentle mist.

It moistened everything, and on the leaves of the trees it left drops like shining tears.

Si Sabir's room was the school's library and business office. It was a large room, its shelves choked with thousands of books. The white windows to the west were open on a peaceful morning, perfumed by the aroma of climbing flowers that danced with each playful touch of air.

I looked searchingly at Si l-Habib. His dark, handsome face had a fine Arab-Roman contour of which he seemed completely unaware. His large black eyes shone with a sweet, childlike luster, unsullied by the disputes of political life, deceiving the onlooker with an endless simplicity. But I noticed, behind the thick black hair hanging down over his forehead, the traces of wounds that had healed over and were now barely apparent.

I spoke with Si Sabir for a few minutes about school matters, all the while aware of the presence of Si l-Habib, the first person I had ever encountered who had achieved such fame and universal respect. I suppressed my feelings—attraction to him and my growing affection—but I was like a closed pot that prevents hot steam from escaping, and finally they blazed up. I blurted out, "How I have longed to meet you!"

He laughed and took another strawberry. His childlike smile beamed again. This was the source of his attraction. No one estimating his age could give the true number! Forty? Thirty-eight? At twenty-five, I probably looked older than he did in his forties. What was the origin of this impression of youthfulness? Was it innocence?

"Really?" Uncertainty and disbelief appeared in his smile.

"Yes. That is how I felt. And more."

"More? Does that mean you were afraid to meet me?"

Si Sabir broke in heartily. "He? Fear? He's exactly like you."

7

I said quickly, "No, I'm not like you. I was a soldier, not a commander."

He shrugged his shoulders. "Soldier or commander…. There's no difference between them in an unequal battle." Then he looked at me searchingly. "Are you being attracted by defeat?"

I repeated, bewildered: "Attracted by defeat?"

"I'm afraid that what attracted you to me is your feeling that we are both in the same defeated camp."

"Does that matter?"

He nodded his head. "Yes. Feelings alone are not enough to build a relationship on a solid foundation."

Si Sabir interrupted, pointing to me: "Two things are never far from him: sex and politics." He followed his words with the wise nod of his head that he often used to underscore his statements, and added, "But in his country he only had politics. That's what confuses the picture."

Si l-Habib asked, "Then how can you look forward to the future there?"

"What does sex have to do with that?"

"A man doesn't walk with one leg."

Si Sabir burst out laughing, and added: "I've told you more than once, you can't work when you're hungry!"

Si l-Habib said, looking at me warningly, "They detained a lot of easterners last year."

Si Sabir added, "Yes—in the events of Casablanca, in '64."

I smiled. "But they released them within days—didn't they?"

Si l-Habib just laughed, but Si Sabir said: "Detention is easy. What's disastrous is kidnapping—and assassination."

We finished the strawberries. The fruit was sticky, and I went out to wash my hands. I had often talked with Si Sabir, who was a drinking companion, about the secrets of my empty life, and he must have told Si l-Habib something about me, for when I returned he was looking at me serenely with affection and understanding.

I have never in my life seen anything more beautiful, serene or understanding than his way of looking at one. His eyes drew a loving circle overflowing with truth and affection. I was in the middle of it. There was no need to speak; a strong bond had been created between us, an openness that removed all the chains that can shackle relationships between men. His way of looking radiated distinction in a way that raised me to his level, whence I looked down from the top of a wall on all the secrets of the past and present, becoming an equal partner in the destiny of peers.

I cannot describe how happy I was to meet him. He came into my life like a precise, modern, and comprehensive dictionary of everything relating to exploitation and colonialism, of the past of the Moroccan people, of their tribal and historical makeup and the aspirations that now began to be revealed to me.

Si l-Habib lived in one of the only two apartments on the ground floor of my building; I had seen him often, but he had avoided meeting my eyes, which killed the urge to give him the customary greeting. Nor was I tempted to look inside his store, which was located at the end of the shops on the same floor, though I had seen him sitting there, hidden by a window filled with a display of kitchenware.

Over our beers before lunch at the Maliki Hotel, my glance moved between the tired eyes of Si Sabir and the mature French barmaid, who at fifty refused to admit the defeat of her youth, retaining a wealth of attractiveness created by muted, sensitive adornment. Si Sabir told me more about Si l-Habib.

What most worried Si l-Habib, he said, was the family of Si Bayad Ben Bella, his friend who had been martyred, leaving a daughter, Zahra, in her third year of high school—a young woman who was characterized by intelligence and courtesy.

During the three months following our first meeting, a quiet, strong friendship grew between me and Si l-Habib, transforming a small seed into a towering tree, growing quietly but confidently. There were no longer any days when I didn't see him. That meeting of ours in the library became a defining date for me, leaving everything before it enveloped in fog, while light and music enfolded what followed it.

chapter 2

At the beginning of my vacation I woke up and realized I'd be spending it alone. All my friends had left town. I felt lazy, emptiness filling my spirit, and I was overcome by a sense of loss.

For three months in a row I would be isolated, without plans, and I knew I would lie awake most of the night, a stranger traveling over a broad sea without any companion or goal.

I could have gone to Al-Arish, to Tangiers, to Spain with al-Qadiri.

To Germany, with Si Rajih.

To northern Spain and France, picking apples and dancing on Sundays until morning, with al-Habashi.

To Tetuan with al-Khitabi, to Marrakesh with al-Mizwari...

But I did not go. When they were talking and planning I would hear them only half-consciously, as if they were planning projects for the far distant future. Suddenly, in the blink of an eye, I awoke to find myself alone in the apartment, whose beauty was no longer enough to keep me contented.

European tourists thronged into the city, as Mediterranean Europe bordered on Mohammediya, and I was enveloped by feelings of pain, and longing, and loneliness... longing for something unknown... creating delusions that made me believe I needed a real shock in order to achieve peace and stability.

The city had spit out all my acquaintances from teaching, and brought in other types, women and men from the shining white world, jabbering in dozens of languages, walking in the streets without officers or chains, smoking pipes, barefoot and nearly naked, adorning the yellow sands with their shining bodies, eating as they walked, each man embracing a woman, kissing her, dancing with her on the edge of the sea...

And I was a black mole on the shining face of Mohammediya, a slender stem without branches or roots or leaves, a true stranger, dreaming of happiness and love in unknown lands.

That morning at the beginning of July, I dragged myself to the shop of Si l-Habib. Somehow I had not expected my vacation to begin today like everyone else's. Summer had begun to stretch out, shedding harsh rays of sunshine on the buildings. Walking in the sun was tiring, the glare tormenting to the eyes as it refracted on the marble and glass of the shops.

It was ten o'clock when I stopped in front of the shop. Si l-Wakil was on the other side of the street in the companionable morning shade. A small European boy of about five and his shadow beside him were bouncing a small ball and chasing after it, and al-Wakil, despite his sixty years, began teasing him, blocking his way and dodging him. Si l-Wakil nearly tripped, righted himself, but his tarboush fell to the ground. He picked it up in one graceful move, his flowing white hair shining, and I could not help laughing, as did the butcher, al-Wakil, and Si Ibrahim. Al-Shalah called across the street: "Very cool," and the butcher applauded.

This simple laugh prepared me to find more fun inside the shop, even if it came in the form of surprises—a first step toward the heights I had perceived but forgotten in the bitterness of solitude.

The sun was beaming through the window, lighting one section while the rest was in deep shadow. Si l-Habib was sitting in the shaded half, ghostly in the deep shadow. In the dim light, I approached to take my accustomed place to the right of his table, but I jumped up immediately: I had sat on something human.

"Excuse me!"

I stared in confusion, ashamed. After a few seconds I could see a woman, plunged in a jellaba of cheap tricale, old, flowing, and striped, with a green veil rising to the middle of her eyes. It was impossible to make out their color. She was raising her head so her veil fell tautly stretched, forming an unavoidable declivity between the two hillocks that lifted her jellaba a bit, just between her breasts.

Did she see me? Yes, I had sat in her lap. But from the small expressive surface of her eyes—a few square inches—nothing appeared to indicate that she had seen me or felt my presence.

Si Qobb had been standing like a statue in the sun; he had greeted me and gone to bring tea, as usual. I had been staring at his elegant black cane, as usual, and I had wanted to sit in my place, as usual—and so it happened that I sat in her lap, because I was a prisoner of habit. I had felt her two plump thighs. The silence embodied my error, as if I had been soiled by mud. Si l-Habib cried, to remove the aftereffect, or perhaps the mud, "The lady is a relative of Si l-Jaza'iri. This is Si l-Sharqi. Please sit here."

A chair to his left. I sighed with satisfaction and extended my hand to shake hers; but she gave her head a small shake, coldly, and my hand hung twitching in the air, alone. She did not say a word. No doubt she suffered from some illness in her eyes if she wasn't blind, blinking her eyelids by force of habit only. But that was unlikely, and so her refusal to shake my hand was a pinprick in my dignity, confirming the shame and cowardice.

Qobb put down my tea, fragrant with mint, and I began to compare the color of her head covering with the color of the tea. There was a cup in front of her, which she had not drunk. Since there was no one else with Si l-Habib I imagined that she had been there for some time, because sipping tea takes more than half an hour with Si l-Habib.

Qobb was taking his place where he always was, in the corner of the shop facing Si l-Habib, leaning on the doorway, assuming a guard duty he imposed on himself. He was watching the street, brilliant in the sunlight; his magic cane seemed like something new and strange, as his hands toyed with it.

I said, chiding him, "Did you not warn me on purpose?"

The stiff features of Qobb's face began to move slowly. He just smiled. But his staid facial expression soon regained its place, in the dust of a cloud of diffidence. It seemed to move him internally as well as setting his huge body in motion. He disappeared.

"He's going to go to France."

"France?" I asked, disbelieving.

"His papers are complete. He's going to work there."

"You didn't tell me!"

"Before I was certain…?"

"Will he succeed there?"

"Do you know what Si Sabir says about him?"

I nodded, "Yes."

Si Sabir's words flowed into my head: "That giant is the stupidest man I've ever seen in my long life, Si l-Sharqi. I don't know what the relationship is between stupidity and strength! It should be the opposite, as Darwin says. Shouldn't it?"

When I defended him, saying, "But he's loyal," Si Sabir nodded in agreement: "Loyalty is stupidity." At the time we were sitting in the café and Qobb was passing in front of us. "Look at him—he can break the neck of any man with one squeeze, like a mouse. Crack, and everything ends." Qobb was solidly built, with the broad chest of an athlete and massive muscles. His clothes would swell when he moved, giving a true indication of his fearful strength. It was all the more fearful for his perpetual silence, which was broken at times by a voice he was careful to keep low, in order to hide a violent rattle in his vocal cords; but his effort would always fail, and he would retreat to the safety of silence.

"Will he succeed, even so?"

Si Sabir was open in his opinion, and everyone must have heard it. Perhaps that came to Si l-Habib's mind as we were talking about Qobb, and he wanted to dispel all those doubts about his stupidity. He added,

"He is intelligent. Anyone associated with him realizes that."

The image of Qobb's eyes appeared to me, brown and shining with a penetrating gleam like the eyes of a cat in the dark. But his eyes were always moving, lost and seeking permanent stability in the midst of chaotic, tumultuous movement.

"Are you helping him leave?"

He did not like to talk about himself. He shrugged: "Friends…" Then he added musingly, as I was still thinking about Qobb's intelligence: "Can you discover a forest the first time you walk through it?"

I finished my tea, and Si l-Habib sighed as if finishing a delicate task. He extended his hand to the woman, with the key to al-Jaza'iri's apartment. "Dear lady, please go with Si l-Sharqi."

"Dear lady": this phrase made me imagine the woman as an elderly or mature relative who had come to Mohammediya. It would be strange for a woman alone to take a summer holiday, so I expected that her family must be going to follow her later. I looked at her as she looked at the key. She was still sitting, perhaps wondering how safe it was to go with someone who sat in women's laps before meeting them!

I looked, and when I took what was in his hand I said, "These are two keys!"

"She may need something from my apartment."

I arose but she was still sitting. I thought it unlikely that she felt unsafe with me. Perhaps it was fatigue after a long journey.... Ah! Might she not be blind and waiting for someone to come forward and touch her hand?

I would have committed another blunder, had she not saved me in time by getting up with a sudden movement and picking up her small suitcase. I bent down. "Let me help you."

"No." She said it without shaking her head.

"Please go ahead." I pointed with my hand. The sun enfolded us, the shade of the shop sinking into a sea of light that made me feel as if my whole body was dissolving, becoming dispersed in the light. The mind alone remained to deal with this strange chaotic force. Qobb saw us while making us think he had not seen us, as he stood at a distance, on the other sidewalk.

In that moment it seemed to me that Si l-Habib's great caution suited the depth of his thinking, for at a time when his heart could not bear climbing stairs, he had not sent her with Qobb. Why? She was walking less than half a yard ahead of me, and I was trying to gauge my height and hers in the mirror of the shops on the right. She was erect, a little taller than I. I distanced myself and looked at her feet. If she took off her high heels she would be my height.

I entered the door of the building ahead of her. There were rapid footsteps on the stairs, and it seemed to me that I knew them.

"Where have you been, Si l-Sharqi?"

"Al-Baqqali? You haven't gone away?"

He embraced me, and I hugged him with real affection.

"Didn't I tell you?"

I complained, sighing, "Loneliness was about to kill me."

I wondered at myself—how could I complain when this was the first day of vacation? Yesterday we had stayed up until midnight bidding them farewell. Was it the fear of fate before its time? But al-Baqqali did not notice my complaint.

"Have you ever been to Casablanca?" He pulled me forcefully away from the middle of the narrow entryway to where we were facing the apartment of Si l-Habib. I thought from the secrecy of his tone that there must be some great good news making him speak at this amazing speed, his eyes shining. No, rather there was good hunting.

He shook my shoulder, as if he were waking me from sleep. "Listen."

I laughed. What else was I doing?

"It's not the time for jokes. I'm not going away as I had planned. Three girls are coming today from Casablanca. Don't be late!"

"At this hour of the morning?"

He cried in a loud voice: "Vacation, my friend!"

The impatient posture of the woman near the stairs doubtless made him realize that she was with me. He was silent, guessing that she must have heard everything. He moved his eyes between her and me. It seemed as if he was predicting an unknown fate, while I wished I could allay his misgivings by a sign or look. At the same time she turned her face to the wall of shining gray marble, drawing herself up in great hauteur. Al-Baqqali blushed, and I noticed real alarm in his eyes. Did he think he had made some mistake? I smiled encouragingly and whispered, "I'll see you later."

He grinned, like someone finding himself after being lost, and looked at her back. He signaled with his eyes, moving his nose and upper lip, dismissing her like an inconsequential insect. He tried to speak through a tumult of feelings which crowded together in his eyes, then gave way to one that allowed him to relax. But I extended my fingers to his lips and signaled to him to leave, so he moved quickly to the second door, leading to the garage.

She sensed his departure and looked at me. I said, as if hiding something shameful that had happened in spite of me, "This is Si l-Habib's apartment. Would you like to look at it?"

"Later."

That was the first sound she emitted, and it was an entire melody. Dozens of musical instruments in complete harmony sending melodies that echoed from a distance. I couldn't believe my ears—her jellaba was somewhat old, large and flowing loosely—and she was a relative of al-Jaza'iri?

I went into my apartment and she entered behind me. I looked at her and smiled. I tried to hear that voice again, grasping at any idea even if it was silly.

"This is my apartment."

The green veil did not allow me to see her eyes clearly. Her face was opposite the window, and the pale reflected light touched the small spot between her eyes with a delicate shine.

"And the apartment of Si l-Jaza'iri?"

There was more than a little blame in her question. But I closed my eyes as I rose and fell in a sea of melodies to which I was led by her mellow voice.

"This one. Permit me…"

I crossed the space between her body and the door, and she cautiously came behind. I opened al-Jaza'iri's apartment. "Please…"

She remained motionless as brilliant light streamed from her relative's apartment. Had her eyes been unveiled I would have been able to probe the secret of her great hesitation. But doubtless it concerned her embarking on a great risk by placing her confidence in a man who had opened his apartment to her when she wanted another. That very point confused me—why had I done that? Did it follow from having opened the door of Si l-Habib's apartment? Since I wanted to show my good intentions, my confusion made me fall into a second mistake: I rushed into al-Jaza'iri's apartment, though I soon drew back. This must have given her another bad impression, after my successive failures. I was alarmed, so I began to move my hands meaninglessly. My embarrassment remained, inscribing shame on my face, nipping at my cheeks. As she entered her relative's apartment, she was careful to keep away from me as far as possible, as if I had the mange; and I was careful to comply with that, as if I had experienced it from birth. But I followed her, stepping cautiously, for the floor of the apartment and all the rich old man's simple furniture was covered in a thick layer of dust—a soft, distasteful chalky powder that invaded the lungs without permission. In the glaring sunlight it portrayed a miserable human vacancy: a small table on which there was a small night light, whose green color had been turned to gray by the dust; an old, iron single bed; disordered, flimsy covers; a pillow dented in the middle, giving evidence of a rough, greasy complexion; a dirty, wrinkled sheet—that was all, and it emitted a penetrating rancid odor.

She sighed; she must have been very disappointed. In spite of myself, I cried, "What filth! How will you clean everything?"

"What's that odor?"

"Maybe it's from something rotten."

Without noticing I had come to the window over the beautiful street, and I took a deep breath. A new car with a foreign license passed, and Si l-Wakil raised his head. For a moment I thought he was looking at me, but he was following the trail of a jet high above; no doubt the sun blinding my eyes prevented me from following it. Still, I cried, "The view from here is wonderful!"

She was facing the light, and I was able to make out her eyes and lips beneath the veil. The dirty, depressing atmosphere of the room had given me the sense that I had done my duty and that I should escape, so I hurried out unconsciously; but a hesitant step or half step from her stopped me.

I had regained my composure. I half turned, and said, "I'll be in my apartment. If you need hot water, or towels, or sheets or anything else, let me know."

I stretched out on the bed in my clothes. I decided I would wait a few seconds only and then go to al-Baqqali. The door of my apartment opened, however, and she entered, filling the doorway with a green dress figured with trees stretched over a plump body; her swelling chest showed in a wide opening from which the dress receded. I was overcome with confusion, which she noticed with interest. Where was the mature woman of the jellaba? Before me was a young woman, not a "dear lady." God forgive you, Si l-Habib, you must not know her. I remained stretched out where I was, disbelieving, comparing her two appearances. Had I not seen the change with my own eyes I would have sworn it was impossible. I had often been deceived by a veil, especially when it rose to the level of the lower eyelids; but this was the first time it made me seem like an idiot. I thought that if I had been standing I would have seen the attractive valley between her two shining breasts; but I resisted the attraction, especially as I felt that she wanted to reassure herself. Her stance combined command and execution. Her eyes were the power from which flared a provocative flame, exasperated with existence: they shone, while her closed mouth gave a wan smile, barely bending that dark red streak.

"When will the water be hot?"

She put down the suitcase. Once again the melodies began to set me adrift on a dark path. It seemed to me that I would become drunk, as had happened before. The inflections of her voice seemed to bring together lines that coiled around the resistance of any man, pulling him toward the power flaring from the burning eyes so that he melted in the flames.

I couldn't help myself, I stood and stared at her. Her face contained enough beauty for half the girls in the world. I nearly cried, "From what sky have you descended, O enchantress?"

"It seems I'll be spending my day here. After I rest, I'll clean the apartment."

I rejoiced—no, I nearly flew from joy. But I trembled, and sweat began to drip from my fingers.

"Where is the bathroom?"

"Discover it yourself, my apartment isn't Buckingham Palace."

"You know how to joke, coming from the East!" She said the last word with great scorn and disdain.

She took off her shoes near the door and put on my sandals, taking everything without asking my opinion. I stretched out again and closed my eyes, as she hummed a popular tune without words. The rustling of her silken dress enveloped the room in an air of domesticity which I had been deprived of for a long time in my life. Sounds of interrupted lovemaking. It reminded me of a *muwashshah* poem in which birds chirped and nightingales warbled and sang as the soul leaves the body, swimming in endless depths of pleasure. There I would meet in it diaphanous colored bodies, beloved, on a bed of cottony clouds, in a happy childhood world which disappeared only with the end of the notes of that *muwashshah*.

Since I knew from long observation that I become embarrassingly confused in any situation that requires me to harmonize, spontaneously, a state of rapturous love with appropriate external behavior, I withdrew to the balcony and began to wipe the abundant sweat from my hands on the thick hair of my forearms. The pretty Jewess whom the Ethiopian claimed to own was on the roof hanging clothes. Her tall house overlooked the little low roofs spread out to the distant west.

"Your apartment is prettier. It's not bad."

She stood near me at the window, her figured dress touching my trousers.

"But al-Jaza'iri's apartment is cleaner."

The joke was silly, but her laugh was contagious, so I laughed not only out of courtesy but with all my heart. There was something else: I had begun to disintegrate emotionally, collapsing in a way I never had before, and which I could not stop. Why?

"Do you clean it?"

"I have a maid." My voice came out broken and weak, with nothing manly about it, so I was worried. But I kept my smile, even though I guessed it was inane.

"Pretty?"

"Who?"

"The maid."

"She's about forty."

"I didn't ask you about her age!"

Often in a situation like this provocation would arouse me, and I would welcome it because it would restore my self-confidence. But I was not aroused. I shrugged. "Maybe, but I..."

What did I want to say? The words escaped me. Any word would seem stereotyped, especially to someone doubtful.

She rescued me. She put her tender fingers on my lips in an accustomed movement, as if she had known me for a long time, setting in motion many wishes. I envied others their ability to deal with situations like this and get what they wanted in a mirthful manner. I could have kissed the beautiful finger, on which shone a beautiful large stone. I could have bitten it. But I did not. I condemned myself; it was insipid, sensible behavior.

"And Si l-Jaza'iri, does he have a maid?"

"Not that I've noticed."

I had begun to get used to my elation over her sweet, musical timbre. She nodded, gesturing toward his room. "A miserly old man doesn't care."

"How are you related?"

She smiled and shrugged. "He's just a relative."

Her words were empty of any feeling of love, or hate, or pride. It was scientific language, as if she had said, "my dress."

"Then you're Algerian."

"No."

She stretched out on my bed as I leaned on the window, her exuberant chest rising and falling. She closed her eyes, and her long eyelashes against her white cheeks formed the symmetrical rays of a black sun.

"How so?"

She put one foot on the toe of the other foot. She was balancing something hidden. The green dress fell away from her shining white leg and its plump calf, and she began to move her feet like the pendulum of a clock. She said musically, "Does it matter to you to know?" She lowered her legs, sat up, and moved her head, so her long hair fell to her shoulders.

"No. I like interrogations." I withdrew; my hesitancy returned to me and I was silent.

"Is the bath water hot?"

"Yes."

"Where will I take a siesta?"

"Don't you like the place?"

She wrinkled her nose as her eyes moved over my modest furniture. "Not bad."

Then she leaned on her arms as if she were about to get up. "At least there's no rancid odor in your place." She stared at me with her bold eyes, and inclined her head to the left. "Tell me, are you a thief?"

I laughed. "I don't have anything valuable."

"Where did you get this good television? What do you have for lunch? Or do you eat in a restaurant? Can I use your towels? And first, do you have a clean towel?"

I believed she wanted to arouse me, for she poured out continuous questions not for their own sake but just to talk— dozens of questions that interested her about her relative and his wealth, which she said she despised, and the neighbors. When I answered her she didn't pay any attention.

The lunch left by the maid that morning was simple: cooked vegetables, some tomatoes and dried mint, lemons, sardines. Before we ate she darted to the kitchen where I kept several bottles of drinks; without asking permission she opened a bottle of old wine, set out two glasses and filled them, simply.

A sudden happiness came over me, and I wished wholeheart-edly to extend the lunch hour for the longest possible time.

"Talk to me about Si l-Habib."

She clinked her glass and mine, and I realized what was jarring about our conversation: she was the one who always took the initiative and I remained withdrawn. Why? Her sleeves were knotted behind her back in preparation for eating, revealing her desirable forearms, which lit a blazing fire in me. I nearly choked on the wine. "Si l-Habib?"

She nodded her head, and said in chiding tones mixed with joking to lighten the sharpness, "Do I have to ask the question more than once?"

"What do you want, the past or the present?"

"The past is in the newspapers; we know more about it than foreigners. Talk about the present."

The word "foreigners" stung me but it did not offend me. If I had heard this dry answer from anyone else I would have been annoyed, but her manner, her voice, her enchantment all made me pleased with myself for ignoring the affront. "Tell me exactly what you want to know."

"What does he drink?"

I laughed heartily, saying mockingly, "Martini vermouth."

"Only?"

"Champagne... gin."

"And the food he prefers?"

"*Bastilla*, couscous... grilled lamb... chicken with olives."

"Fruit?"

"Strawberries... cherries."

"Does he have a servant?"

I unintentionally bowed my head, as I always did when words escaped me. "Not a servant exactly, because he doesn't consider him one. You could say he's a friend, or a companion, or a brother." I was silent, but the word flashed before me, and I said, "An assistant—yes, an assistant. But he's going to France."

She smiled with satisfaction. Before eating she had tied back her coal-black hair in a striking fashion, which made my eyes ache whenever they strayed from her. She spoke spontaneously, and her good table manners seemed automatic.

"The statue?"

I began to laugh. "Yes, the statue."

"He's a dumb lamb."

I cut her off. "He hasn't harmed you."

"I don't like him. But tell me more about Si l-Habib."

Her cheeks were flushed after several glasses of the wine, and her lips had begun to shine. Cigarette smoke formed magic pictures as it circled her face.

I had the sense that I was falling passionately in love with her. Nonetheless, I repressed a flare of lustful tension: I felt clearly that she was safely on the other bank of the river separating us.

"Why?"

She smiled. "I love him."

I began to laugh. "That fast?"

She laughed too. "I swear to God." She set down the glass and raised her right hand as if taking an oath in court.

The sun occupied a few inches of the window sill as a light that wasn't strong began to pour into the room and reflect on her face. I laughed for no reason. "Is he the first?"

"No."

Her shining eyes were fixed on the remains of the wine in the glass. Her voice had the ring of truth that drink causes in some people. It occurred to me that her attractiveness, which I cannot begin to describe adequately, came not so much from her unique, glaring beauty as from something else. Perhaps it was her candor, her amazing capacity for delicate behavior. Maybe that's what pushed me to make a big mistake, for I cried unconsciously, "And will he be…?"

The word "the last" was written clearly in my mind, but my courage failed me before I spoke it. She smiled, leaving me certain that she realized what I had wanted to say, but that my silence after this little outburst pleased her. Then I enlisted under the banner of a long daydream, which made me a partner in a silent conspiracy that seemed absolutely immoral. Finally she looked at me with her bold eyes, and wondered, "And women?"

I got up and went to the window to hide the signs of my tension. "What of them?"

"What kind does he like?"

"All women."

"Dreamer!"

"Who?"

"You."

I smiled again. "He loves all women but he will never have a relationship."

"He hasn't found the right one." Then she looked grave, as if she were taking the first step in a plot: "He has found me now."

She got up, so I said, "You cannot."

She made a sign with her eyes. "We'll see. Do you want to bet?"

I stood like a statue, staring at her. I had never dreamed that any woman in the world could combine desire and candor. At that moment I doubted my manhood: she had not categorized me as a rival for her; rather she made me into a being with no value sexually. Since I felt I loved her and wanted to possess her, she had brought me into a struggle of severe torment where I had no desire to be, a struggle whose outcome was foreordained.

"Where will you have your siesta?"

I came to, and said in confusion, "I'm going to Casablanca, and I'll be back in two hours."

"To Casablanca, or are you going to bring Casablanca to your friend's house?" She burst out laughing, a symphony of rippling pleasure.

"What's his name?"

She began to think, smiling, the alcohol making her glow. "Hmm…Al-Baqqali."

"You're a devil!"

"Know then that I am going to sleep now and that I won't open the door before four."

chapter 3

Someone leaving the heart of Mohammediya and passing the Ibn Yasin High School comes to a new brown wall in the old Moroccan style, which rises to enclose the Casbah on its eastern side. The eye is beguiled by its massive white arches and hidden doorway, with their carefully studied harmonies that speak of a calm, mythic greatness. It ends in a square surrounded by a group of modest concrete apartment buildings, which the sun heats with lashes of flame from noon until sunset, leaving them like a pimple appearing on the beautiful features of a young face.

Since this was the only area devoid of beauty on the secondary road to Rabat, the regular traveler would turn his eyes unthinkingly to the wall, preferring to read from a book of secrets going back to a time just before the dawn of the present. But someone leaving for Rabat could not help but forget this a few seconds later, as his spirit took its perpetual pleasure in the embrace of the sea and the dewy forest alongside a road reflected in its waves, swelling in tearful longing for the anxious shore. Since I remember the place through my senses, I was prepared to probe its depths closely.

After the marvelous afternoon I had spent drinking with al-Baqqali and a group of fascinating young maidens, Si l-Habib was waiting for me. Qobb told me so in front of the building by a single word, possibly regretting that he had not been able to replace it with a sign.

Si l-Habib smiled. "Where is the key?"

I remembered that he had given it to me that morning, when I escorted al-Jaza'iri's relative. I began to search in my pocket among several keys for the three apartments, which I had mistakenly copied in a drunken state.

"I want you to come with me."

"But I'm drunk."

"You don't look it. Come on."

At his gentle touch, I moved opposite him. The intensity of the sun had abated. I was full of wine that was working calmly and effectively inside me; that made me fear going up to my room, where the most beautiful devil a man could dream of slumbered on my bed. Since there was nothing else to talk about, Si l-Habib asked me how I had spent my time since leaving him in the morning. Had I been in any other state, I would have thought about what he was getting at. The sun was filling the tall trees with its extract, foaming yellow.

I did not tell him that I had been forced to go to Casablanca to copy the key, which I had lost. Leaving that afternoon I had been distracted by two intertwined matters: the first was that Si l-Habib avoid the trap into which the devil had announced she would take him, and the second was my strong desire for her, the wish that occupied my whole vision, to have her under any conditions. I had wanted to be alone with my thoughts as I walked. But with a sense of defeat dictated by constant failure in long struggles on many fronts, I found myself at Si l-Baqqali's place, with his three young

Casablancan girls, when I should have been at the repair shop whose address the Chinaman had given me, after issuing a strong warning that this was the last time he would lend me the master key.

I had not found any girls, just a dark young man from Marrakesh; he had a large mustache and good features, and he had reached a state of extreme emotional disintegration. I asked al-Baqqali about the girls with a motion of my eyes, and he pointed to the shower where they were all washing off the salt after their return from the sea, in a small bathroom. The Marrakeshi clinked my glass twice in succession, contrary to custom. Since I was afraid the repair shop would close, I finished my first glass and got up, promising to return. But the Marrakeshi, whose intimate friend I had become after those two immortal drinks of wine, became extremely alarmed at my attempt to leave. He was afraid I would get away after this meeting, which for some reason seemed historic to him; so he insisted on taking me on his motorcycle to a workshop which, he asserted confidently, was no more than five minutes away at most. Since his eyes were blazing with an alcoholic fire, and it wouldn't have surprised me to hear he had been battling it for several successive nights, I thought he might use force against me if I refused the generous offer of a very dignified young man. I tried in vain to enlist the help of my friend al-Baqqali against this unjustified persecution, but at that point he had given way to his passion for the oldest of the three girls, who had just emerged from the bathroom. They filled the little house with their sweet laughter, dispersing it with drops of water that fell from their hair, and with their exciting flirtation.

I realized as I went out that the lash of the sun would fall directly on my head; I hated to combine the sun and wine on summer afternoons. A large number of snails had retreated to the shadow under the leaves of the linden trees which shaded the walkway of the narrow street in front of the house.

"Hold onto me."

I clasped my hands over his belly and the motorcycle took off. Fear paralyzed me as I attached my life to a motorcycle racing the wind, driven by a drunkard lost in alcohol and love.

To my great surprise everything the Marrakeshi had said was true. The large repair shop, deafening with the work of innumerable great machines and workers absorbed in their tasks, was a monster that swallowed up tranquility and assaulted the mind, making alcoholic transports a heavy burden on civilization.

We were greeted by a lively young man, short and dark-complexioned, covered in grease and iron filings. He hesitated to shake the Marrakeshi's hand, but the latter attacked him with an embrace. When he learned why we had come he made light of the matter, and I gave him the two other keys (the ones for Si l-Habib's apartment and for al-Jaza'iri's), as a precaution.

During the short time it took to copy them I went to smell the flowers in the courtyard of the workshop. They were varied, planted with skill and care, and they had a penetrating aroma; I resorted to them as a natural reaction, to cure me of the headache of the huge machines. For some reason the picture of the playful devil danced before me, as I was enraptured by the beauty of a red rose aflame in the sunlight.

"Here you are, Si l-Sharqi."

We returned to the Casablanca girls in less than a quarter of an hour. They were drying their hair flirtatiously, virgins who were proud because they had something on which depended the fate of many residents of the world, in one way or another.

As we surrounded the round table, the Marrakeshi cried,

"We are three and you are three!"

The oldest one, who had enchanted al-Baqqali, was not more than seventeen, slender, dark complexioned, and glowing. The sea had enhanced her charm with a bronze, wine-dark color; water dripped from her face, which made me think she had returned to the shower for a second time, and she had wrapped her black hair in a blue towel. Her black eyes were shining with additional temptation, and her eyebrows terminated in precise points, which at first I thought she has drawn. In the kitchen under the gaze of al-Baqqali, she had behaved with the freedom of one who owned the place because of her possession of its owner. Her eyes and her expressive movements were full of coquetry and pride. The two others were younger by a year or two. One of them was fair, firm, and pretty; the other was without any attraction except for her ample breasts, in a body which otherwise resembled that of an adolescent boy. They were vying with each other in preparing a light meal of eggs, sardines, dried meat, and vegetables. Their carefree bursts of laughter and suggestive whisperings were mixed with bewildering secret commentaries that made a man wish he could be honored by listening to just one of those secrets, perfumed with their excitement.

Before they finished preparing the meal, the fair, firm girl had walked to the corner of the window and faced the small garden. It was divided by a concrete walkway about a yard wide, and its flowers and grass sprang up untrimmed. The rays of the sun penetrated the tree leaves washed by dew, showing their networks of veins, lightening the dark green color of the leaves to a fascinating mix of herbaceous yellows. The girl put her hand on her forehead and leaned against the wall, as if she suffered from a slight headache. The moist sea breeze provided from time to time, as it touched my hot forehead, a pleasant coolness that I loved, and that would help me overcome the heat of the day, which was only intensified by the alcohol.

The chairs Si l-Baqqali had were not enough, so we brought the table over to the bed where the Marrakeshi sat. The four chairs encircled it. Since it was necessary to drink a toast before the meal, as we began the drinking party again, we drank to Casablancan love. The dark girl sat on al-Baqqali's knees with a natural flirtatiousness, twining her right arm around his neck and lifting his drink to him in her hand, despite his insistence that she drink first. Instead she leaned over him longingly and finished the drink in the glass, while the other two drank only a few deceptive drops. During the meal, as the talk flowed amid sharp sexual tension, laughter, and sly winks, we drank more of the famous red wine.

The words began to come out of al-Marrakeshi's mouth somewhat thickly, the *r* becoming a *ghain* like the Parisian *r*. In fact his mouth, protected by his huge mustache, involuntarily began to shell us with many words of *français* in a wave of such irresistible charm that the girls, who thought they were in a school competition, all at once abandoned their mother tongue and plunged into a noisy dispute in French. When Si l-Baqqali tried to join in with the one foreign language he spoke well (Spanish, as was usual among the northerners, who had been forced to learn it in school), he found a negligible response. He must have thought hard before he raised his glass to his mouth and finished making himself drunk. Then he began to kiss his girl on her neck. She tried to slip away at first, then closed her eyes for a while, melting in pleasure; the two others kept stealing glances at her, laughing in shy desire.

Since we could not avoid watching the live show, the Marrakeshi cut it off by bringing up an important topic: that it was preferable that the girls keep their virginity. I believed that this blunt change of subject in front of three virgins would lead us all into a maze of sticky, contradictory feelings, so I decided to leave; but the two men opposed me strongly, and that made my adolescent companion, who had taken it upon herself to fill our little glasses, finish the fourth round with an elegant, skilled movement. At that I surmised that I was falling into a trap of pleasure, especially since they would not let me leave in any circumstance without taking another glass, although the preceding one had disappeared inside me only a moment earlier, and despite the fact that I felt no pleasure in electric subjects like this.

"There are a lot of wolves among guys today."

I nearly laughed at the comment made by al-Baqqali, because like me he was over twenty-five and under the law all three of us there would be considered wolves, since none of our companions was over eighteen. The coal-black hair of his fiery girl crowned her head; her teeth nibbled on his ear with avid pleasure from time to time while her right hand touched his neck, searching for sensitive spots in familiar moist corners. The youngest, the fair one, cried, "You haven't heard what happened to Malika."

The Marrakeshi's eyes widened and his mustache was raised in disgust. "I assure you, lady—they were not sons of good families…"

Al-Baqqali cut him off: "Enjoyment comes from companionship and caresses, so why the entanglements?"

The other girls exploded in laughter, their cheeks red with embarrassment, as the Marrakeshi smiled in victory. He added, confidingly, "The criminal is the one who abandons innocent pleasure for…"

His tongue stopped, as if under the influence of the alcohol it was becoming too heavy for speech. Al-Baqqali rushed to rescue him: "For illicit pleasure."

35

I deliberately tangled the conversation: "Then the relationship between a married couple is illicit?"

The girls looked at me doubtfully and anxiously, so the Marrakeshi clarified: "Certainly not! Otherwise people would not get married."

Al-Baqqali cut him off, imploring me with his eyes not to uncover the plot, especially as it was about to bear fruit: "I have a big surprise in this heat. I put some Pepsi on ice. Come to the kitchen and get a bottle."

The Marrakeshi began to dance drunkenly and clap while al-Baqqali drew his girl by the hand and opened the bottles with a swift, graceful movement so they made a loud noise. They began to give each other drinks as they embraced, and the liquid spilled on their chins and their clothes. They kept on laughing for a while, then darted into the bedroom, closing the door behind them. The Marrakeshi was in the middle of the kitchen, whispering intimately in the ears of the youngest girl, leaning on the edge of the basin with his arm on her shoulder. He was surrounded by an aura of mental dissolution mixed with the smell of wine, desire, and temptation, so that all that remained of him were his passionate glances and his trembling, whispering voice.

The thin girl was sitting on her chair in front of the table, happily sucking little mouthfuls from the icy bottle. When I emerged from the kitchen, belching, she stared at me with a lost look before which all the contradictions were equal. The unplanned events of the moment imposed her company on me; each of us was free, waiting for company on an exciting journey. But under the effects of the wine I decided that I had suffered a loss of respect by not being given the right to choose: they had left me the last of the girls, and the least attractive. I decided to leave quietly, without any fuss. I went to the door of the room, leaning against it and looking at her closely; she did not withdraw her gaze, and I sensed that she was warm enough for a cold winter's night. She continued dripping the icy liquid on her tongue, coolly and calmly, and I realized then that, whether from muteness or cleverness, she had not joined us with a single word, all afternoon. She must have seen a great deal in my eyes, and I discovered as I scrutinized her that she was as beautiful, if not more beautiful, than her friends. Her pale eyes were wide, a fascinating ash-gray light shining from their center. In her face, which seemed to have nearly reached maturity, her warm cheeks stood out with great elegance, harmonizing in captivating beauty with her small mouth. Despite all of that, however, in comparison with al-Jaza'iri's relative she seemed like a faint shadow.

I read in her eyes an enticing submission, like ash concealing a tempestuous rebellion in the fevered timidity of those two rosy cheeks. Her chest was rising and falling, in a movement that hid a test of nerves and pulsed with deep understanding. When I drew near she moved the bottle away from her mouth after one quick sip and closed her eyes, to allow me to act as I should. I kissed her quickly on the mouth and whispered, "Goodbye."

When I lifted my face a small, tender, scolding smile appeared on her face as my eyes swept her neck, which was carved with astonishing voluptuousness. Nonetheless I continued toward the main door, hearing the door of the bedroom open as Si l-Baqqali cried: "Where are you going? We're just starting!"

I motioned with my hand: "But I'm just finishing."

He ran barefoot and reached me in a few steps, then laughed: "You're crazy. At least put out your fire."

"I'm preoccupied."

He thought a few moments. "Ah—the woman in the jellaba, the old lady. Can someone like her preoccupy any sane person?"

I laughed. "Every sane man has moments of madness.'"

"Okay, I won't bother you. But remember that they will come every day at seven-thirty, so don't pass up the opportunity."

"No... No, I won't forget."

He still seemed unconvinced, and touched my shoulder. "I don't understand you sometimes. Your girlfriend is the most beautiful of the three, so why...?"

The word "girlfriend" struck me as strange and funny, coming from man's eternal wish for savage possession, so I laughed.

chapter 4

All along the short distance to where I met Qobb, as the street embraced me with its refreshing breeze, I kept thinking about how my eyes had deceived me. The first glance at the three girls had made me believe that "my girlfriend" was the least beautiful and fascinating of the three, but after a little examination she seemed to be the crowning beauty. Can the eyes deceive like this? Might I also be mistaken with respect to the one occupying my apartment with her bold and commanding behavior?

"Where did you wander off to?" Al-Habib's voice was calm and deep. He continued, "There's no harm in your having secrets. If you don't want to come, then turn back."

I came to suddenly and assured him, "No, I want to come."

"That's the house." He pointed to a wide door that stood open, and when we went into the little courtyard we were struck by a strong glare. It was the only spot I had seen empty, without a garden, outside of the Casbah. The white cement façade was divided by four doors, which deceptively led you to think they were the doors of gloomy bachelor rooms.

We stopped a moment; Si l-Habib must have wanted to make certain before knocking on the door. The glaring rays from the white façade increased and for a moment I thought that the breeze had died down in the whole city; were it not for the television aerials taking their pleasure by calmly bending on the rooftop, I would have believed that we were being held in a spot taken from the desert. But we entered the house, whose rooms extended lengthwise, divided by precise engineering to take advantage of every inch of ground, and found a tall French window open. The afternoon shade reflected on its gleaming white wood, and the breeze invaded the room softly, lightly teasing the curtains and releasing the air trapped in the room.

After we had sat for a moment I felt that we were alone, so I went to the window, where delicious little waves of moist breeze refreshed my face. The grass outside was amazingly fresh. The light had divided its blades with a magic sword into two parts, the color lightening to pistachio under the sun but a deep green in the greater part, overtaken by the shade, which swallowed the distance to the artificial forest that divided the city from the shore. I felt like someone discovering a new secret. I took a deep breath and closed my eyes, becoming filled with the songs of the sea and the whispers of untrodden grass, filled with fertility. I cried: "How exquisite this place is!"

I was answered by a feminine voice whose presence I had not felt before: "The view from the upper room is more beautiful."

After I entered I had noticed a staircase twisting to the left, but I had thought it led to the rooftop. The middle-aged woman added, affectionately, "Please come, Si…."

"Al-Sharqi." Si l-Habib introduced us.

I declined, as it was not necessary to see something more beautiful, once I had expressed my admiration for one pretty view. Si l-Habib encouraged me: "Go ahead." There must be something… but it would be some sort of secret.

I went up. Zahra was standing with her back to me, embarrassment burning her cheeks and paralyzing her tongue to the point that she did not return my greeting. The truth was that the view from above was astonishingly more beautiful, but I barely glanced at it, struggling with a feeling of ugliness that came over me as I enjoyed a poetic view while a young adolescent stood near me, dying of embarrassment. I quickly went down and took my place on the bench near Si l-Habib, beside the door. The breeze had become a strong current of delicious cool air, so I set a pillow against the wall and leaned back.

The mother, the wife of Bayad Ben Bella, was a stranger to me but Zahra was my pupil and so I knew a great deal about her. I admired her, in motion and at rest. She was no more than fifteen and had a degree of shyness I had never before witnessed, so I was careful not to agitate her. She concealed her beauty completely by keeping her head down, hiding behind her two thick braids; but her beauty shone like the sun in every direction, despite her efforts. What concerned me about her, in a fatherly way, were her two opposite characteristics: great intelligence and great timidity. Her blazing intelligence was hidden under the shackles of her timidity, for she would never raise her hand or volunteer what she knew. She would answer precisely and completely when asked, leaving the teacher no choice but to respect her, allowing her the freedom to sit down after answering, because her shyness and embarrassment increased when she stood.

Part of what really fascinated me was her unique ability to write miraculous compositions, which were beyond comparison with any composition that could be written by a person of her age or even older by any number of academic years.

Therefore I had adopted a plan at a late point in the academic year in an attempt to overcome this terrible shyness of hers. As a result she had been able to read her marvelous writing to the other students, something I couldn't have dreamed of at the beginning of the year; but the vacation caught up to me before I had gotten past this one lone step.

The wife of Bayad Ben Bella sat before us. Her position gave her an advantage, as her back was to the window, her face sunk in shade. The modest room with its thin cushions showed obvious want, concealed by a skilled hand and a mature mind that had created something out of nothing. She smiled, continuing to welcome us. "How is your health, Si l-Habib?"

I gave a short, foolish laugh, in an attempt to overcome the awkwardness of a first meeting and said, "I have been wondering, since I first saw Zahra, who inspires her in her beautiful writing. Now I see that her room is wonderfully poetic."

Her mother had passed forty, with a severity in her look that was accentuated by a strange calm. When she smiled I noticed that her unadorned face showed the remains of beauty, arising from regular features which her only daughter had inherited from her.

"She admires you very much."

I laughed in surprise and said, "She doesn't show it. I didn't think any of my students admired me so much!"

"She mentions your name all the time, and especially after the issue of the gold."

One of the French female teachers had demanded strict enforcement of the ban on gold jewelry, after a student had been caught wearing dangling gold earrings and had been punished. But the issue had also been raised in the staff meeting that preceded the final exam, so I supported the suggestion, as did others, on the condition that it include the teachers also.

That stirred up all the female French teachers against me.

"I regretted my rashness," I said.

"Why?"

"One person alone cannot change the way things are."

The subject was new to Si l-Habib and a surprise to him, so he seemed to be using the time to collect his thoughts, preparing to talk to Sayyida Ben Bella about a long-term solution to a problem that was confronting her.

"This house…" She gestured to the floor with a nervousness that she cloaked in deep courtesy, though she did not succeed in hiding its bitterness. "This house is the property of the municipality, and they are taking it over."

As the steam rose aromatically from the tea she had served, diffusing the scent of fresh mint, I realized that I was still feeling the influence of the wine. It muddled my view and increased by enthusiasm for the rights of a widow arrogantly trampled underfoot by a stupid law.

Speaking with great emotion, she presented more details about the installments paid while her husband was alive. She had tried to explain her plight to officials, and had delayed payments on the property for several months, on the advice of a lawyer. But all of this only made the problem worse, as the sum had now reached 4500 dirhems, and all would be lost if she did not pay it immediately. There would have been no problem if her husband, the revolutionary hero, had been alive—or if she were willing to dishonor his memory by allying herself with the new government and becoming like others who now lived in comfort.

I nearly added: Or if Si l-Habib possessed that sum, because I knew many things about both Si l-Habib's financial situation and his medical treatment; but I refrained, in order to allow him to act. His mustache was well shaved, showing the dark roots of the hairs surrounded by a thin band free of hair around his mouth. His steady smile and his attention to the woman showed no concern, except for the pressure of his hand on the glass of tea. The pressure made him lean forward with his right side, as if he were getting ready to have a picture taken in which he was required to look like a statue. What took my thoughts beyond the present moment was purely observing how he would solve the problem, despite his own straightened circumstances. As the effects of the wine made an orderly withdrawal from my veins due to concentrated, serious thought about the problem, I felt that I was witnessing a difficult situation demanding rare nerve. For dishonorable withdrawal from the battle was not among Si l-Habib's characteristics, nor were lying promises.

"Permit me first to work on a delay," he said. "Three or four months. In that time we will have arranged for the money."

But this was not the only problem to torment her. She was in a constant state of watchfulness and hope. Her conversation was a mirror conveying with deep feeling the intricacies of her thoughts. "What do you think will happen, Si l-Habib?"

Her question was a decisive announcement of a move from the private to the public.

He rubbed his hands and fixed his eyes on the floor. "No change in the short term."

Her face darkened. For a moment it seemed as if the emotion had taken her back ten years. "Is the political situation hopeless?"

"Where there's life, there's hope."

"So?"

"Change won't come about at our hands or in our time."

She was falling into the depth of despair. Tears came to her eyes and her voice quavered: "And the sacrifices?"

44

I went over to the window. I was not in a state to follow the conversation, which began delicately, disconnected and filled with allusions. I knew Si l-Habib's viewpoint in detail, and I was aware of public opinion, and perhaps my being with them was hampering a free spontaneity that would pull me into a life like that of the quiet countryside. In spite of that, bits of the speeches of "Al-Za'bul" and "Al-Sukkar" forced themselves on my ears, along with the everlasting struggle between the strong and the weak, revolutionary thinking, labor unions threatening to split with the National Union, and the necessity of arming the workers with revolutionary thought.

Some of the words were spoken in whispers, which made me imagine a secret operation distributing arms to the partisans.

On the way back Si l-Habib seemed grave. I waited until two men who were hurrying toward us had passed and we were free to talk. Then I cried in earnest, "I heard everything."

I stared into his eyes and saw no effect. He answered coldly, "Those weren't secrets."

"You know, for some time I've started to feel as if I don't know the ABCs of politics. If I were to start over I would choose another path."

The pressure of dazzling light which wounded the eyes had begun to lessen, but it kindled the heat of the alcohol. What amazed me was the woman's clinging to the memory of her husband and her repetition of the word "hero," with the pride familiar to those who are wronged and who deify their dead. But Si l-Habib, who in the great uprising had lost his companion, famous for his skill in propaganda, insisted that the word "hero" was a dwarf-like description for a giant of unplumbed depths. For some reason this hero appeared before me as a statue of cast iron, his flaming eyes radiating fire.

chapter 5

Because of the fear that was always with me during my multiple meetings with Si l-Habib, I stayed within limits and did not exhaust him with anything that might tire his weak heart. Thus, when we met Si l-Sabir and al-Miludi after this tiring interview, I considered it a rock cast by chance to stem the rushing tide of debilitating memories. Events had failed to sever his life, but the memories would not fail to sever his heartbeat.

The two drove up in al-Miludi's big taxi with the black meter, which he drove only outside the city. They greeted me with, "How are you, Si l-Lubnani?" and prevailed on us to get in, and despite the objections of Si l-Habib we drove through the enchanting city on the afternoon of an amazing day. I shared laughter and exuberance with Si Sabir, but I began to think fearfully—as I had at various periods during the day, ever since I had left al-Jaza'iri's relative lying in my bedroom—of what surprises awaited me on my return. I believed that delay, however long it might be, was perhaps the best course. But after a little while I realized that it was as if we had fallen into a spider web.

It was not pure chance that had led us to meet al-Miludi and Si Sabir now, nor had it been chance a month previously. At that time we had been coming out of a bar on the afternoon of a gray day. The clouds floating above had seemed like a canopy for our drunkenness, which was at its height and which we would do anything to maintain.

We had stumbled upon a lovely tradition in a bar run by a pretty Frenchwoman, not yet thirty, under the watchful eyes of her husband, who always had a wan smile fixed on his plump features. This was our third or fourth visit to the peaceful bar, with its quiet western music and dim lights, and the pretty young Frenchwoman served us some warm mussels with an outstanding flavor, refusing to let us pay. It was the free day of the week for regular customers, although Si Sabir, who insisted on treating others in a civilized way, whispered to me that we should not exploit the situation.

We were in an excellent state created by his sympathetic frame of mind that would never allow him to spoil a day like this by drinking too much. As we left we showered the owners with expressions of gratitude, and Si Sabir assured me that this tradition was a custom of modern business in developed countries. This small custom gave me a welcome feeling of my own importance as a resident of the city, not differing in any way from the people who lived there.

Just at that moment, at the height of that exquisite moment of sweetness and security, Si l-Miludi had pounced on Si Sabir, overflowing with welcome and genuine expressions of praise which we could not doubt were sincere, especially coming from the tired mouth of a middle-aged man. His work as a taxi driver gave him a knowledge of every inch of the environs of city and their hidden places, and he had learned where to track us down. Every tree had a thousand eyes in its branches, and he knew where he would find us. A teacher was watched by everyone, out of either good or bad intentions. He called me "the Lebanese" and recalled Zahle, *mezze, tabbouleh, hamam* and all the other words which had sunk into his memory since the Second World War, when he had been taken to the east as an enlisted man in the French army. In a few hours of merriment he must have encountered some small moments of joy that remained in his memory until now, coupled with the famous enchantment of the Lebanese mountains.

In no way could I convince him that I came from far beyond Lebanon. That was because he grouped together Algerians, Moroccans, and Tunisians, all of whom ate couscous, wore the *burnous*, and drank green tea with mint. He could not imagine another group.

He was over fifty, and his only son was going to take the elementary baccalaureate examination in two days at our school. I did not believe that I, as the supervisor of a group of proctors and graders, was able to help any student in any fashion whatsoever; but I promised him verbally, on the initiative of Si Sabir, that I'd try. I still don't know how he managed that.

I succumbed under the influence of disgusting egotism, in order not to spoil the passing moment of happiness, not knowing how I would keep the promise when the time came. It happened that Si Sabir reminded me of it on the morning of the exam, to my great distress. Concerned, I had met the little boy; he had intelligent eyes and a shaven head, which gave his face a terrified, persecuted look. I reassured him and patted his head, ignoring the prickliness of his hair like a porcupine's; he smiled innocently, making me think that for the first time he felt an enviable distinction. According to my information the boy did not need any external help of the sort that I was anyway incapable of providing. But his father didn't properly appreciate the good score he got, doubting the abilities and capacity of a little boy who cried when he was denied a sweet and whom his mother helped to dress. He was saying now, "If it weren't for you—don't defend him—if it weren't for you, that boy no higher than a hand span could not have succeeded."

His language made us roar with laughter, and Si l-Habib responded willingly and began to joke. That cheered me, so I asked him now, as he drove us toward the entrance of Wadi l-Nufaifekh, if he had ever seen a more beautiful view. His eyes wandered and he mumbled a single word: *Ifran*. Here we saw two mountains bearded by great forests above a sweet little river so hidden by tree branches that no trace of the water was visible from the road. Our black car must have looked like a little crawling insect as we descended the valley, plunging into an ocean of green, replete with cool, heavy air, where only the twittering of the birds and murmur of the waters could be heard.

Si Sabir wished for a drink as we were walking along, the dry tree leaves crackling underfoot. Si l-Miludi showed he was ready, because the trunk of his car was filled with every sort of drink one could wish for. But that put Si l-Habib in an awkward position, as it had gotten late and the sun was about to set; so I refused for us all, and we turned back.

I thought our driver had forgotten the matter of the exam, but he returned to it. I could not remain silent before such great praise for something I had not done, so I tried to evade it; but I sensed after a while that my attempts were being interpreted only as great modesty dictated by "elevated manners and taste which I had inherited from my original environment, since I was a pure Lebanese," so I gave up and let the matter pass.

The sun began to plunge into a horizon awash in color. We returned by way of the road that bordered the sea, where the high tide was crashing on the shore, breaking into showers of shining white foam in the light of the velvety dusk. I would have liked to sit on one of the rocks and let the pounding waves get me wet, as I had dreamed of doing since I saw the beach for the first time.

When night fell, since it was impossible for Si l-Habib to abandon his chosen principle of abstaining from alcohol, we dropped him at his apartment. We ended up in the hotel La Caravelle, where our host had reserved a room for us with the manager, Si Ibrahim, a man of medium height, compactly built, with a dark countenance and pale eyes. The room had a large bed, four chairs, a table, and a low window; when we opened it we found we were overlooking a tree-lined side street. Al-Miludi brought us a full "case," as he said, filled with "good beer, gin, whiskey, champagne, aged wine, etc." He began to set out the bottles in rows on the table before us, explaining how he had given up alcohol and returned to the fold of godliness and piety long before; thus he excused himself from joining in our drinking.

Disappointed that he wanted to treat us without partaking, Si Sabir and I exchanged looks of embarrassment, which al-Miludi noticed. His left eye seemed noticeably smaller than the other, creating a clear impression that it had not functioned for some time. He closed it and his face wrinkled up. I thought he was going to cry, but he was just thinking. He opened his eye and suggested to us warmly that he could take us to any bar or nightclub in Casablanca or Rabat, and wait for us until any hour we chose.

But we sensed a desolate emptiness in a project for our pleasure that we had not planned ourselves, first, and secondly, in which our host would not share; so Si Sabir refused the idea from first to last. Once more our host's left eye wandered, and he scowled. Then he made a new suggestion: that he bring us any two girls we knew, or that we leave the choice up to him and he would bring two girls of unsurpassed beauty (for he believed in the popular proverb that "one who pimps for his brother is not a pimp"). If it weren't for our profound sense that he sincerely cared about our feelings with his crude suggestions we would have laughed openly. We met his offer with excuses that did not fully convince him. Then we left the hotel after handing him the case of alcohol through the window to avoid carrying it through the crowded bar.

No sooner had al-Miludi begun to drive than he swore that he would not leave us until we had had a wonderful time on this night, which he was determined to make the most beautiful night of our lives, even if that required him to violate his religious obligations. He was confident that God would forgive a person's sin, but he would not forgive himself the crime of ruining a night on which he was determined to make us happy.

He stopped at the intersection of the road from Rabat to Casablanca, in front of the zoo. There was a bar there, hidden by a hedge of climbing plants and surrounded by white flowers suspended like stars in a green sky. The bar began as a passageway to a small, pretty hotel, and it seemed that the owner was a close friend of al-Miludi.

Si Sabir suggested that we begin with strong drink, since it would be a long evening. But after we smelled the aroma of grilling in the hotel we chose to delight our bellies with several skewers of grilled meat, accompanied by extremely good aged wine, rather than eat at al-Miludi's house, where many good things waited for us, prepared with care for this happy occasion. After we ate, we left for Rabat, stopping at another bar where we had a lone drink, al-Miludi joining us with orange juice.

The barmaid was an Arab, which Si Sabir declared was unusual. She was thirty-five and somewhat plump, and Si Sabir began to flirt with her persistently, despite the decay that showed in her teeth on either side of a wide gold cap above her lower lip. We hadn't drunk much, but Si Sabir rushed things, contrary to his habit: first he took her hand and introduced himself, and I sensed he was squeezing her fingers tightly. She concealed her laughter under an unexpectedly kind smile, which nonetheless suggested ample experience that had given her a sophisticated resistance in situations like this. There was a band of French men and women nearby, absorbed in having a good time. In an attempt to distract Si Sabir, the waitress pointed to a small body in the middle of the group, raised her voice, and asked, "Do you know who that is?"

Si Sabir nodded his head, resentfully; I thought he was going to say something bitter, but he smiled. We looked where she pointed: "Monsieur Kazi, the French champion marathoner."

"Screw it." We laughed, and Si Sabir added, "Al-Ghazi left him in the dust."

She joined wholeheartedly in our laughter, giving an amazing display of the map of her decayed teeth, upper and lower.

The marathon was unique in that it was covered on television from beginning to end. For a reason which could only have been pure chance, the rivalry became intense between the Moroccan champion, al-Ghazi, and the French one, Kazi. But the Moroccan had outrun him by a long distance, and his win had aroused unprecedented enthusiasm.

We began to look toward Kazi unthinkingly, as one might play with a painful pimple in a sensitive spot. Si Sabir looked at him in disgust as he left the place, after the barmaid had withdrawn and left the shift to a large man whose eyes were already sleepy.

In Rabat we went to a western club at Si Sabir's suggestion. He was attracted by the smoke-filled air, the dim, colored lights, and the small open space where several couples danced to the music. Si Sabir, choosing a table to the right of the dance floor, cried, "This is the atmosphere I want!"

His voice was loud, but no one paid any attention to him. With an embarrassing impudence, he inspected more than five girls, whom I am certain he would have rejected were it not for the influence of the alcohol. He invited one of them over, a woman with a slight body like his own and whose face showed both grace and calm. She had no sooner settled into her seat near him than he cried: "You must come from an old family."

We laughed, which annoyed him. He directed his words to me: "There's no reason to laugh."

Our host cut him off unexpectedly: "We are all from old families."

He called for a drink for her and she began to sip it calmly, as if she were in a backyard swing enjoying a peaceable afternoon. That made Si Sabir cry, "Pour it on the ground or in my glass, if you can't drink it."

She laughed and poured the contents of her glass into his, agreeing: "That's a good idea. I hate whiskey."

He touched her tender forearm and said, "Didn't I tell you she's from an old family?" I didn't laugh, and he continued, asking, "From Rabat?"

She chose not to lie and denied it with a shake of her head. "From Wadi Zam."

Si Sabir's face showed displeasure and disappointment. He was from Rabat, and I would have dearly loved to see how happy he would have been had she not disappointed him.

I wanted to clear the air and say, "There's no difference between cities," but I noticed Si Sabir's sharp look, so I refrained. I expected one of the violent outbursts that appear suddenly when he drinks, but abruptly the music changed to the kind he likes, and he began humming along with it. It was soft and light, like the whisper of a breeze, and the murmurs of a tall black man dancing with a blond Frenchwoman rose with the dreamy song, amidst smoke that massed like a fog.

"You're beautiful," said Si Sabir, squeezing the girl's delicate arm. "But let's get to the point frankly: will you…" He signaled with his eyes and unmistakable hand gestures. The girl understood his intention and laughed, so we laughed too. She seemed to be slipping away, making studied excuses and with disjointed words about being forced to remain until two-thirty, about how her lonely mother was waiting for her, about her quiet habits and…

Si Sabir got up like someone deeply offended. His personality took its unique, full form under the influence of the drink, and he began moving away with readily apparent indignation. "We aren't dupes. We have to get what we pay for. We won't throw our money into the sea. Let's go."

That was an order addressed to us: he walked out, and we followed him. It seemed as if his slight body was becoming inflated until it nearly filled the dance floor, leading me to wonder whether the car would be big enough for him.

I expected we would go to an eastern club, especially since he had been trained in playing the *oud* when he was young, but I was surprised by his cry to Si l-Miludi: "To Casablanca!"

I was starting to feel the effect of the alcohol just when I couldn't do anything about it, so I looked on with complete neutrality and felt no annoyance. On the road Si Sabir urged al-Miludi to go faster, and the car rushed along at the highest speed the nerves of its aged driver could take. When Si Sabir realized that, in returning from Rabat towards Casablanca, we had passed the halfway point and the bar with the woman of the gold-capped teeth, he let fly an expletive that made al-Miludi laugh and suggest turning back; but some famous old song of Ahmad al-Baidawi diverted his attention and brought him back to his untroubled expansiveness. He began to hum along with the songs without any more whims, not even noticing when we finally arrived. The car began to weave through side streets in a poor neighborhood made up of new, small houses, all of the same design. The car stopped at the beginning of a street numbered 34, and Si l-Miludi knocked on the door of a house there. Si Sabir laughed and said, "We haven't finished drinking yet."

Si l-Miludi winked his small eye in a way that promised secrets and very cautiously opened the door. We entered, our exuberance curbed by the pale, wan light, and the door was closed behind us by a thin, severe-looking woman in her fifties. She welcomed us and led the way across a small hallway. Behind her we entered a room empty of everything but an old round table and low chairs; the wretched look of the room and its simple, faded atmosphere suggested secret agreements and sexual arousal. The room was rocked by popular songs from a well known *shaikhas*. Si l-Miludi nodded his head to the tunes, welcoming us along with the aged woman, and we anticipated surprises.

It wasn't long before a girl in her twenties appeared, carrying glasses and several bottles of red wine. She arranged them on the table, and she and the older woman brought up the chairs. Young women's voices rang out and we moved aside; two other girls of about the same age sat down among us at random. They began to drink with us, their eagerness mixed with desire. As the game began to take shape, I found myself— as had happened that afternoon—comparing the three girls with the relative of al-Jaza'iri who had so fascinated me: while each of the girls had a specific trait of beauty, that most fascinating one combined traits equal to those of innumerable girls. I liked one of these girls. She was very dark and plump, with thick, coarse hair and a penetrating perfume, but I didn't find enough inducements to carry me, in spite of myself, to the top of the waves as had happened in the past. An important part of my feelings was back in my room, far away from the body sitting with Si Sabir and al-Miludi.

"Drink up, Si l-Sharqi. You're not yourself today—drink."

After the first glass the conversation took off, and I became accustomed to the atmosphere. Even the unpleasant sallow light now seemed natural. The laughter of the professional girls and their professional, exciting touches began to scatter bright colors wrapped in clear hints. But in spite of everything I remained so detached that my dark companion began to think her efforts were in vain. She whispered to me that she was ready to satisfy all my whims, especially since the two I was with were older than I was. At that their two girls got up, one after the other, and went to neighboring rooms, and my friends followed them.

When they returned, their girls were glowing. All my friends' urging made the girls look at me doubtfully, so at last I got up too, troubled, and went to the room from which they had come. The atmosphere was heavy from their sweat and with their smell, almost a shadow presence in the room, which ate into my soul for a few brief moments and turned me into a wild animal like them, seeking satisfaction.

chapter 6

We had our supper in al-Miludi's house as dawn made its way through the treetops, immersing the wisps of buildings and the wide streets in its gray essence, mixed with dew and the breath of the sea. When I went up to my room and reached into my pocket, I found several keys, originals and copies, and I had a hard time finding the one that belonged to me. Once I had it I was astonished to find the door open; I closed it behind me and turned on the light. I had been waiting for this moment since the morning. A snowy forearm shone, emerging from the light cover on my bed. The beauty of her face, her closed eyes, her black hair covering the pillow—all of that stunned me, and I stood frozen in place.

The strong light surprised her, and her fascinating face wrinkled in resentment. She did not open her eyes, but rather turned her face to the wall in an instinctive movement, pulling the covers over her body so that the appetizing white arm disappeared.

It looked as though she had improvised a place to sleep on the floor from numerous blankets, used it for a while, then decided I wasn't going to return and abandoned it for the bed.

I was intoxicated and tired, my head weighed down by severe dizziness and my hands by something else. The first day of the vacation had passed in the best way I could have hoped. I had drunk an enormous quantity, which I had never imagined I could absorb; and what happened to me after my arrival from Casablanca and on the morning of the next day passed as if it were a faint figment of the imagination.

I plunged into a deep slumber, during which there were echoes of delicate feminine voices, touches, and serious attempts to wake me, after which I would open my eyes and see the image of a beloved woman, amazingly beautiful, wrapped in blue, plunging with me in vast dreams. I followed her form above the clouds, touching her hand emerging from an airplane window, grabbing her fingers for fear of falling. But she withdrew her hand, laughing and filling the world with happiness. I fell and saw her falling under me, as music welled from her laughter, dissolving me. Then she landed on the ground, a distant spot of sky blue, and my alarm abated; but I remained suspended between the sky and the earth as she rolled on the grass below me.

How many times did the events of the same dream recur? I don't know. When I awoke the room was plunged in shadow but was not dusky, as a sharp shaft of light struck the bed from the kitchen. The door had closed just at the moment when I was savoring the touch of the blue silken garments above the clouds. I closed my eyes for a while in pursuit of the delightful dream, but the light in the room was turned on, and feminine laughter rang out.

I tried to get up but I discovered that I was nearly naked, and fumbled with the sheet over my middle.

She laughed again, went into the kitchen and brought back a cup of concentrated lemon juice. She sat on the edge of the bed. "Get up—drink first, then get up."

Despite the concentration it was delicious, biting the tongue.

"Drink it—the effects of the alcohol will disappear right away, and you'll be able to drink again. Drink. Do you like al-Jaza'iri that much?"

I was still drowsy. "What?"

"You repeated 'Al-Jaza'iri' more than twenty times in your sleep."

"But I don't talk in my sleep."

She laughed, and I returned to the surface of the clouds that had carried me all night. I closed my eyes, remembering two other eyes in whose enchantment I had wandered through the heavens.

"Are you going to sleep again?"

"No."

She was close to me, and my chest was uncovered and bare. She hit me playfully. "That was colossal drunkenness!"

The inflections of her voice rose and fell as if in a great hall, then broke into echoes before reaching me.

"How were you able to carry that case when you were in such a state?" She stretched her hand toward a case filled with bottles of alcohol.

"Al-Miludi must have carried it."

"Where did you get it? Don't you feel better now?"

"Yes." I looked down at my naked body and said to her, "I don't sleep like this!"

She laughed again. "The maid helped me strip you and carry you here. What a funny situation! You kept pushing us away, and one of your socks is still on your foot."

I could feel the sock now. I pushed it off, and worriedly made sure that I had on my underwear.

"Do you always sleep in your clothes?"

I laughed, attacked by hunger. "It's the first time."

She repeated once more: "What drunkenness!" She got up and went to the kitchen, and brought me a sandwich of grilled meat and began nibbling another herself, after diluting the lemon juice.

"There was only the word 'Al-Jaza'iri.' Was your relationship with him strong?"

I said, "He's not the kind to have a strong relationship with others."

I began to eat ravenously, and she confirmed what I had said: "His only strong relationship is with money." Then she wondered, looking at me closely, "Why, then?"

I lied to her as I devoured the sandwich. "I don't know. An inner feeling, maybe."

She looked at me doubtfully. "Are you...?" She didn't finish. She sat on the edge of the bed. I became tense, not knowing what she intended. She changed the question. "Is he queer?"

I cried, "That's pure nonsense! You're way off."

Her doubtful looks were still shooting arrows at me, throwing me into confusion and making it extremely difficult to confess what had been bothering me since I first saw her. This was especially so because she was behaving with a naturalness that made me think she would never leave my apartment, and that made me very happy, placing under my tongue the pleasure of savoring something new for the first time. For some reason I believed that confessing how she tormented me would spoil this beginning of pleasure. But keeping her mind locked in doubt was too horrid and bitter. "What's your name?" I asked.

She laughed, and stared at me. "Aren't you rushing things? You've spent all this time with me and don't know my name!"

I smiled. "You are only 'al-Jaza'iri's relative.'"

She stood up in surprise, knitting her brows. Then she came back and sat on the bed again. "You poor thing." She understood that it was she whom I was talking about in the dream. She laughed and added, not allowing me to speak: "A new victim."

I was aroused and didn't know how to control it. She looked gloomy, and frowned a little, but lost none of her charm. "I cannot love you," she said, "so don't even think about it."

I touched her hand and whispered, my voice quivering and coming from my heart as I lost myself in the enchantment of her eyes, "God, you're beautiful! Is this a dream, or am I awake?"

She laughed and kissed me lightly on the forehead. "Is that enough?"

In fact I did feel as if it was enough to plunge me into happiness, to make me lose touch with my senses again. But I was torn by a feeling of rebellion over her indulging me like a child.

She rubbed my shoulder. "You are handsome, and I like your hairy chest. But I want to be frank and tell you that it's not possible for me to love you. Don't torment yourself."

She said the last words with compassion, staring at me intently. Her face was radiant, compelling, in one of those rare moments when one's effect on others becomes preordained fate. In her features there was a magnetism that attracted the light, which seemed to embrace her with tenderness and humility, as if deep in prayer, begging her to confer immortality.

She confessed, "I also fell in love, the moment I first saw Si l-Habib."

Mockery escaped me in the form of a laugh. But her eyes were radiant with happiness, which overflowed the room and seemed to spill out the window to fill the universe. I repeated, "Was that the first time?"

"No, and it won't be the last."

"You amaze me. Who are you?"

She didn't listen to me, for her spirit was far from the apartment. Then she took my hand and pulled me to my feet. "Come and see what I've prepared!" She was speaking as if she had inherited a great joy unexpectedly, her voice trembling with hope and love.

"Throw me something to put on, first."

"No need for that, you're not completely naked."

She pulled me behind her, holding my hand in a loose grip, but I slipped away. Her sitting near me had made me tense in spite of myself. I pulled on my pants and followed her slowly into the kitchen. She was waiting, a lock of black hair falling on her shining forehead. "Look!"

"What's this?"

The small area of the kitchen was full: couscous, *bastilla*, strawberries, cherries, grilled meat, stuffed vegetables, Martini vermouth, good champagne.

She whispered, "All the things that Si l-Habib likes. Your maid and I prepared them. I worked the poor thing all day, especially when she was cleaning Si l-Jaza'iri's apartment and preparing the food."

"Who told you that he likes them?"

"You, yesterday at lunch."

I burst out laughing. Then I shook my head, changing the subject. "For the first time in history my apartment has things to drink in such quantity and quality."

She too laughed happily and extended her hands as if she were dancing. "When do we start?"

"Making love?"

She laughed, and struck me again on the chest. "Don't joke."

"What are we starting?"

"The celebration!"

"Of what?"

"Of our meeting."

"Haven't we already met?"

"No."

"How's that?"

She laughed. "Do you know my name?" She turned around playfully, again as if she were dancing.

"No."

"So, do you see? I'm going to make it a secret."

She stared at me but she certainly did not see me, for her eyes penetrated the walls into the unknown. I went into the bathroom, closed the door, and plunged into a warm shower.

When I came out, my hair wet, buttoning my shirt, she was wearing a white dress, which rippled gracefully with her dancing movements, tight at the waist but loosened over her bosom. It ended at the shoulders where her soft arms emerged, nearly melting in their delicacy, her coal-black hair left to flow over her shoulders. She stood looking at the table, adorned with flowers and candlelight, and trilled warmly, "Now I'll turn out the lights."

I was drying my hair when the pale candlelight took over the room, thin, pallid and undeveloped, pouring out the romanticism of bygone centuries with a deceptive frivolity. She realized that she had failed to create the poetic atmosphere she sought, and cried, "Oh—I forgot the colored lights."

The bathroom door had remained half open, so she pushed through it. I saw her face in the mirror, sometimes hidden by her hand as she combed her hair.

"Now, Si l-Sharqi," she said. "Hurry and finish dressing."

"Then what?"

"Then go down and invite him."

"I'm not the one giving the invitation."

"You are the messenger, and you must convey the message."

Her gay movements, her twittering melodies, her glances, her tones—all of it was a brilliant flash reflecting the warmth of the anticipated meeting.

"Remove this 'must'."

She came close to me and toyed with my ear. "Do what I ask of you."

"Have you thought about the effect of that on him in the future?"

"Are you thinking of him or are you jealous?"

"Thinking of him."

"You're wasting your time."

I sat on the bed, saying, "Rest a little."

She never ceased circling the table with her astonishing grace, her dress rustling in angelic music. She adjusted the placement of a bottle, pulled down the table cloth to even it, changed the placement of the flowers, and looked at the table from several angles. Finally she went out and came in again. She stopped at the door and trilled, with her sweet, human song, "The first view will be from here!"

I laughed. "Listen—think!" But my voice was lost in the ocean of her graceful movements, so I got up and stopped her, my fingers digging into her arm. Trying hard to keep the emotion out of my voice, I said, "His heart is weak and could stop at any shock."

She closed her eyes and trilled, "Are there shocks in love?" Then she laughed loudly. "Love is life."

"Promise me you won't harm him."

It seemed as if my words were lost in the short distance

between us, like the sighs of a sick man on a crowded a street. Since I was staring intently at her face, I held on to the rays of charm emitted by the pale candlelight and refracted on her shining complexion.

"Don't be jealous."

"You and I are worlds apart."

She stared at me. "Don't you love me?"

I thought, troubled. "I want you… I'm fascinated by you… I'm prepared to do anything in order to win you, but…"

"Hush, then—you're jealous."

"Of everyone except him."

"What a contradiction! I don't understand you."

chapter 7

I had been out of cigarettes since the day before, and I went out as if defeated, unable to express what stirred in my breast. She was convinced that I loved her and that therefore I was jealous, and nothing could make her understand that what I cared about more than anything was Si l-Habib. Joy and anticipation filled her spirit with radiance.

The street had begun to greet the clear summer night. The moon was a crescent in the far west and a cool breeze sprang up, refreshing me. When I went into Si l-Habib's apartment he had just finished shaving. Qobb was looking at the Jew's apartment in the adjacent building; its pale light, with the shadows of two girls preparing something, filled the courtyard. His black cane with the head carved like Cleopatra was in his hand. "Let me see your cane," I said.

He stretched it out to me and ordered, "Pull hard on it."

The handle was in his hand and when I pulled on it his hand held a shining knife blade, thin, silvery, and sharp, about a foot and a half in length. He stood looking at me proudly without speaking.

"Let me see it. How did you come by that?"

"Be careful, it's sharp. You won't tell anyone?"

I laughed. "Where did you get it?"

He turned his head, and my question was lost in his pale, motionless eyes. He had spoken more words than I had ever heard him say, then returned to his silence, staring out of the opposite window as if he regretted his outburst. One of the girls passed through the pale light, carrying in her hand something that looked like a tray.

Si l-Habib set out to break the silence. "A friend who was a medicine salesman gave it to him." Then he stopped. "Is someone calling you?"

Her voice echoed from the top of the hall as if it were in another world.

"I just remembered—please come to my place."

"Why?"

"You'll see."

He laughed. "I'm not used to sudden whims from you."

"It's not me."

"Who then?"

"A surprise."

"For me?"

"Yes. Come on."

I pulled him away, the scent he wore penetrating my nostrils, and he began to climb the stairs calmly and unresisting. She must have gone back inside when she sensed us coming, as I heard the sound of steps moving rapidly above us, though I did not hear the door close. When I opened the door and invited him to enter I saw the total astonishment in his eyes: it was the first time we had been together under one roof with a young woman. His eyes moved between me, the glow of the sun in the apartment, and the table with the candles.

"What have you prepared?"

"I'm not the one who prepared it."

She was standing near the table, the candlelight reflected on her face. She chided, musically, "Aren't you going to begin by introducing us?"

She extended her arms as if to embrace us, in a wide movement, and I laughed. "The lady related to al-Jaza'iri, Si l-Habib."

Surprise knotting his tongue, he cried, "You?"

The word emerged from his depths. He was not expecting this vast difference between the lady in the jellaba and this alluring woman—exactly as had happened to me.

"You were with me yesterday?"

I laughed. "I was deceived also."

She said, with a firmness that did not lessen the enchanting effect of her voice, "I'm tired of 'al-Jaza'iri, al-Jaza'iri'—don't I have a name? My name is Ruqayya."

The meeting had excited me, making me go after laughs, however foolish. "What a weighty name!"

Si l-Habib cut me off, however, as he moved toward the table. "I don't think so."

She clapped her hands like a little girl. "I win."

Still standing, Si l-Habib inquired, "Is there a winner and a loser?"

She stared at me stubbornly, so I answered, "In the long term."

"It's a puzzle."

She trilled, musically, "Time can solve all puzzles."

I turned on the light, dwarfing the wretched candlelight. She asked merrily, her inflections melting me, "Why do you hate the magic of candles?"

"All I hate is their pale light—it reminds me of prison."

"Then I'll put them out."

"Leave them, as long as there is strong light."

"Electricity and candles. Light is like the heart, there's only room for one."

She began putting out the candles with a puff, as if she were kissing a hovering spirit, her eyes overflowing with a happiness that held her fast. She said, in her refined voice, "Please sit down, Si l-Habib."

He remained standing. "Not before I know the secret of all this!"

I stared at her. She was looking at him with obvious passion, so I said, "A get-acquainted party."

Si l-Habib smiled. "What an unexpected party!"

She interrupted, altering her delicious tones, "Tell the truth."

My eyes widened. "What, then?"

Si l-Habib joined me in my question. "What?"

She said, "A celebration of love."

Si l-Habib laughed heartily. "Have you fallen that fast, Si l-Sharqi?" I did not answer. Her enchanting eyes shone. He added, "I hope it turns out well."

I laughed. "Dream on."

She sat opposite him, her eyes on his face, refusing to leave it. Within seconds of his arrival she had become a part of him, like his pungent scent. She asked, "What's your opinion of love, Si l-Habib?"

I shivered, and watched him with compassion and fear, like someone watching a child crossing a busy street. But he remained unchanged, apparently considering the matter as an onlooker only. Still, I was afraid the situation would change suddenly. I began to cast about in my mind for some quick action that would soften the onrush of her attack, but without success. More than once my mouth opened, my lips parted slightly, without producing a sound. I looked at her imploringly, but she was paying no attention to me. She was a shower of light spilling out in a sea of darkness, a river of happiness overflowing its banks.

"Yes, Si l-Habib—what's your opinion of love?"

"I don't understand what you mean."

"Don't you know the meaning of love?"

"Certainly, I love the people."

It seemed as if love was reflected on her lips. "And am I among these people?"

Si l-Habib nodded. "Yes."

She interrupted firmly, but with enough gentleness to avoid arousing a negative reaction: "I don't accept being one among everyone; I want your love purely for me."

I could no longer bear it. "You're selfish."

Despite my provocation, she showed no evidence of having heard me. She was dreaming, swimming in a delightful, fragrant ocean, depending on the inexhaustible strength of youth.

A silence descended on the room. I was afraid that any movement of mine would be foolish; at that moment I even despised the smile fixed on my face.

Then Si l-Habib leaned his right elbow on the table and cried, "Let's begin the party! Sit down, Si l-Sharqi."

She opened the bottle of Cinzano, poured a glass, and held it out gracefully to Si l-Habib. "Please have some."

He took a sip, which did not wet his lips, and she protested loudly, "What's this?"

"It's what I can manage."

"You're joking."

He asked me to confirm what he said, while she urged me, "Tell him…"

I laughed, and Si l-Habib asserted, "I don't drink, and Si l-Sharqi knows that."

She stared at me reprovingly. "You deceived me." Then she laughed, smiling and filling my glass. She explained, "He told me that you drink all these things."

Si l-Habib chuckled in surprise. "It's the first time I've seen Si l-Sharqi play a joke." Addressing me, he said, "I haven't known you to act like that."

"She created the whole thing herself with no intervention on my part."

We clinked our glasses with Si l-Habib's empty glass, and she sipped daintily, licking her lips. Looking at Si l-Habib she repeated, as if talking to herself, "But why don't you drink?" She asked as if she were faced with an obscure mystery, her enchanting voice rippling over the table.

"He's ill," I said.

Si l-Habib interrupted: "Even if I weren't ill…. It takes a long time to explain."

She wanted to express something but she held back and shrugged. The words burned in her mouth, but she spoke only a single sentence. "I never imagined…" and then was silent. Suddenly she cried, "I am alive, and I will drink!"

It was the counterpart of her first sentence, and it fell into the flood of feelings that raged within, expressed in her second sentence. Then her face became grave, overcome by a light wave of sadness. Si l-Habib realized that he had made a crack on the surface of our evening by his refusal to join us in drinking, so he smiled and cried, "Don't be sad—here, I'll join you in the food."

He tasted the couscous, its steam still rising. "It's delicious." Then he ate a little of the grilled meat and arose, just as she seemed absorbed in preparing something important to say, for which she was marshalling all her strength. But his movement banished everything else from her mind and alarmed her. She cried out, her voice drawing me down to the depths of her sadness, "What's this?"

"It's time for me to go."

"But you haven't eaten."

"Thanks be to God, I've had enough."

She followed him to the door, disbelieving, then looked to me to make him stay. I disappointed her, shaking my head.

"You aren't joking?"

"Never."

I added, "He's that way. He doesn't eat much."

She regained control of herself and began to laugh, looking at me: "You've gotten me into a fix." Then she blocked his way, leaning on the door in a graceful, alluring movement. "I won't allow you to leave. Spend the evening with us without drinking."

"I cannot."

"Then let us spend the evening with you."

He parried, "I go to sleep early."

Her eyes shone with an enchanting challenge. "Are you afraid of me?"

He reached for the doorknob and she placed her hand on his. He fixed her with a stare that was at once anxious, expectant, and beseeching. He said, "There's no longer anything in the world that I fear."

"But I will subdue you, you will submit to me."

"I don't understand you."

"Yes, you do."

"You won't be able to."

"Will you bet?"

"Yes—though I cannot withstand shocks."

Then she looked at me, making me a partner: "Will you bet along with him?"

I shook my head in refusal. "I have lost all my bets in the past, so I won't bet on the future."

He extended his hand, patted her head with fatherly affection, and left.

Several long moments passed while she remained frozen, not moving from her place. A jolt was needed to bring her back to me, to being alone with me. I clapped my hands several times and she looked at me hesitantly, adrift in a distant world. Then she asked urgently, seeking to illuminate something intricate and obscure, as if it were divine destiny: "Why? Why? Do you know the reason?"

"No."

She poured another glass and laughed, as if to dispel the dejection left in the room in the wake of Si l-Habib. "What a strange man he is! He doesn't drink! He doesn't stay up in the evening! He doesn't eat!" Then she laughed, hoping that laughter would lead her to the correct solution. When she got no results, she asked, "What will we do with all this food?"

"Qobb—he'll take it to his family."

"That statue."

"He's a man, not a statue."

She reached over to open another bottle, but then stopped. "How do you spend your time here, your evenings?"

I shrugged without answering.

"Is there a dance hall?"

"Just one. It's only for the French."

"Haven't you seen it?"

I shook my head no.

"And the casino?"

"For non-Moroccans. I always go there."

"I'll go to it another night." She stopped, sighing deeply. "How do you while away the time, then?"

The same difficult question had returned. She got up with greater energy, the wine giving her eyes a strange glow, and moved about the room like a butterfly dancing. At that moment I thought she was determined to escape boredom by any means, so I told myself that I would keep watching her, however long the night. She stopped suddenly and cried, "We'll spend the evening in Casablanca!"

"Who with?"

"With you."

"I'm not going."

She laughed, her rebellious voice once again filling the room: "You'll come, you know that."

"How?"

"You'll see."

She went to the closet and brought out a chiffon dress, in which a light violet color embraced dark gray against a fresh white background. At the hem it would have been wide enough to shelter three men from the rain, and with her graceful movements the dress rippled calmly into a small sea in the open space of the room. This was the third dress she had worn during the day, and like the others it revealed the beauty of her full, alluring breasts. Her possessions filled my apartment, even though when she came she had been carrying only a medium-sized piece of hand luggage!

The new dress seemed to have the same angelic air with which the white dress had surrounded her. I realized then that she chose her dresses with care, to go with various occasions, wishing to create specific effects.

She went into the bathroom for a while and emerged with the jellaba and face veil obscuring her attractiveness. Laughing, I cried, "The dawn has become a moonless night."

"Say that the whale has swallowed the sun."

She leaned over and brought me upright, submerging me in her fragrance, and I forgot my hesitation. I felt pride as I stood next to her and then drew her to me by the shoulders. Her eyes showed alarm, as if she believed for a moment that I was going to kiss her, but I laughed to dispel her fear. "How are we going to go to Casablanca when the last bus left hours ago?"

She said mockingly, "Don't worry, leave it to me."

The Bab al-Tarikh road was empty up to where it met the Casablanca road. The moon had disappeared early and the stars were shining in deep black space. If it had not been for the pale street lights, the night would have submerged everything in its black enchantment. I wished that she were my lover so I could surfeit her with embraces and kisses beneath the stars. I said to her, "I wish I could walk with you here, in an atmosphere like this, after our relationship is established."

She trilled, "Our relationship is established."

I laughed. "But it's not the kind I want."

"That day won't come."

"Yes it will. Will you bet?"

She pinched my cheek, and it hurt. She said, "You haven't seen anything yet."

We had drawn near to the Buhaira Park on our left, and she said to me, "Let's go in here."

"People will think we're lovers."

"Let them think what they want. They say there are marvelous fish here that jump into the air to catch bread-crumbs from the onlookers."

"My intelligent friend, fish sleep in the darkness!"

"I didn't know you were such a genius." Then she took my arm and asked, "Are you afraid of anything?"

"Why?"

She laughed, pushing me toward the trees in the garden. Her nearness began to warm my blood and kindle my desire for her, so I pulled her closer. She said, "I had a friend dating a teacher who was afraid to walk in the street with her. Do you know why?"

"No."

"Guess."

My desire was keeping me from thinking clearly. "Her family?"

"No."

"What then?"

"Because of his students." She burst out laughing then stopped still, so I pulled her forward. She began to chide me. "What hypocrites you are!"

"Who?"

"Teachers."

I laughed. "Why?"

"You take on the role of the Prophet in class, but outside…" She stopped, and I laughed again. "Go on—what, outside?"

"You seduce girls."

"Did a teacher seduce you?"

She laughed. "I would have broken his neck!" She stood still, gasping with laughter, her hand under my elbow. I suddenly felt lonely and distant from her. "That friend of mine—he got her pregnant and ran off to France."

Her voice had been like an *oud* solo, and when she fell silent I imagined I heard it echoing on every side. The silence between us allowed the creatures of the street to occupy the emptiness—frogs, crickets, distant dogs, the screeching of cars on the Casablanca road.

The quiet was torn by a merry voice that startled me—someone smelling strongly of drink was near us under the trees.

"Is that you, Si l-Sharqi? Why didn't you come today? Who's with you? It must be a real prize. Bring her with you to my place, the house is full."

I had not noticed that I was walking near al-Baqqali's house. He was talking while shaking my hand, and making an obvious effort to steady steps badly affected by drink. "Who's this who's stolen your reason?"

She laughed and put her arm around my neck. I felt a sudden, overwhelming happiness. I introduced them: "Si l-Baqqali… Ruqayya."

"How do you do, Si l-Baqqali?"

They shook hands. Her voice must have astonished him, rendering him mute. He kept staring at us in the darkness, as the pale light reflected on his narrow forehead. I asked him, "Who's there?"

He answered in a broken voice, with none of the pride that had been there, "The girls from Casablanca."

"All three?"

"Yes."

He must have been comparing her voice to the voices of the others. He said, "What devils they are! A thousand lies on the phone—the neighbors' phone."

"Why?"

"Don't you know? To get rid of their families. I'm looking for something to eat and drink before the bars close. I saw you from a distance and said, let's invite them. Come with me, let's finish off the evening."

Ruqayya interrupted him: "But we want to extend it, not finish it off."

Her decisive answer astonished him. I said, "We're going to balance the equation."

"What equation is that?"

"We're going to take Mohammediya to Casablanca."

He laughed, and she said, her voice dripping with sarcasm, "*Bon appétit* for your 'blanca."

"What devils you women are!"

He turned, saying goodbye, and I grabbed his wrist: "Here's my key—there's a lot of food and drink at my place. Take what you like before Qobb sweeps it up."

He shook his head in refusal. "I won't take leftovers."

"We didn't touch a thing. The food is just as it was, not left over."

Ruqayya broke in, "Is there anything more beautiful in all of Morocco than 'Fadala'?"

She meant al-Mohammediya, making a pun on its old name of *Fadala* ("God's grace") and *fadla* or "leftover." But al-Baqqali didn't understand her and turned up his nose: "Leftovers are not for me, and that's the last word."

His vanity nearly swept him away, driving ahead of him a whole herd of wonderful dreams for an enchanting night. There was a passionate light in his eyes, looking everywhere for pleasure.

"Haven't you ever seen him with a woman?" Her voice sounded like the modulations at the end of a loud piece of music, diffused in successive calm, short breaths.

"Al-Baqqali? He has more than—"

She cut me off. "What Baqqali? Would I ask you about that boy?"

"Who, then?"

She signed impatiently. "Si l-Habib."

"No."

"Is he queer?"

The question did not provoke me! Perhaps her genius lay in this, she could say the most awful things in a friendly way that destroyed a man's ability to react, that blunted his defense and took him in the net of an enchanting captivity that he accepted willingly. I answered: "No, but why would you think so?"

"A man can't live without a woman."

"He's ill."

"What does love have to do with his heart?"

"It weakens it."

"Nonsense, it's the opposite."

"Are you an expert in these matters?"

"There must be another reason."

"I don't know of anything else."

Her elbow dug into my side, and my left arm enclosed her shoulders; at the touch of her soft body I felt an irresistible intoxication, and I began to float in the sky above the darkness, endlessly, like a balloon.

"Woman was only made for love, for happiness. All other acts and activities are only preliminaries, preparing the way for the delicious nighttime meal."

She was speaking quickly, and I wished she meant me with these rapid words. They seemed like the introduction required of an *oud* player before beginning a piece, so that the rush of its melodies would stir nostalgia in the heart and rekindle memories. She went on, "Tell me the truth."

"I hate lying."

"Then what are you waiting for? Are you waiting to get me?"

Once again I felt no anger. Even though she was reading me from the inside and her question was a punch landed by an experienced fighter, where was the pain and the provocation?

"I desire you," I confessed. My confusion seemed like a discordant note in a harmonious piece.

"And then what?"

"But if Si l-Habib desires you I will try to tear you from my breast."

"What did he do—cast a spell over you?"

"He's an ordinary man, not a magician."

It was a little after eight o'clock and the lights of al-Mohammediya were grouped together like the eyes of wolves at the foot of barren mountains, protecting themselves in their pack from the icy cold. The breeze was stirring the huge banana leaves, which would briefly veil the fading light coming from the garden, then return to their place, once again allowing the light to breathe. A silence reigned, peaceful, like a sea whose waves had died away. Were it not for the cars passing from time to time we would have had the honor of exploring the area alone, enjoying the quiet of the night.

"We'll get to Casablanca at dawn."

She laughed. "In a quarter of an hour."

"How?"

"Let's bet."

"Why do you insist on betting?"

"Ignoramus! Retarded! All of life is one big gamble."

She distanced herself from me when we got to the street. She stood on the sidewalk and adjusted her jellaba like an employee preparing to greet an important superior; then she signaled to the next car that came along, and it stopped. She cried, "Casa?"

The young Frenchman looked at her with tired eyes, puffy under his glasses. His hair was thinning, giving signs of baldness to come; he had lowered the part to a little above his left ear. He called out in French, inviting us to get in, so she sat next to him in front and I sat behind her.

In his new role of host, the Frenchman acquitted himself of his duties as well as one could wish. He began with a question about the weather, expressing his admiration for the hot sun and beautiful sea and sand. She jabbered with him for a while, causing me (since I didn't speak French) to withdraw from the light into the shadow, like an actor who loses his leading role, takes on an insignificant one, and will be listed among the extras.

They began to laugh together in the intimacy she habitually created with anyone she conversed with. I touched her shoulder, and she looked around at me, wiping her mouth on a tissue under the veil. I said, in annoyance, "Now I'm starting to get jealous."

She reached out and patted my head, then pinched me hard on the ear, making me groan aloud again. She laughed. "You poor thing!"

The Frenchman smiled and they were soon plunging into laughter again. She turned and asked me whether I had understood what he had said. When I told her that I didn't care, she said that he was giving her the choice to sit next to me if she liked, adding, "He's a polite young man."

I reached for her hand. "It's a good suggestion—come next to me."

She burst out laughing. "Before I sit next to you I'm going to make him fall in love with me."

Her frivolity was remorseless, but I was not provoked then, either. I was like someone watching a pretty child pretending she was good at many dangerous games. I said calmly, "I don't care. But if you do that he will look down on me, not you."

She chuckled, and the contagious laughter spread to me, so I joined in. The driver smiled, but without opening his mouth. Rather he pressed a button and peaceful melodies began to spread happiness in the car, as the trees on either side danced gracefully. Ruqayya said, "I'm afraid to look at trees in the dark—they're like ghosts."

But she had barely gotten the words out when we came to the edge of the city. Our host insisted on taking us all the way to where we were going despite our objections, so we gave in to his wishes. We parted like old friends.

chapter 8

As his car roared away, Ruqayya headed for a four-story building. The small, ill-made windows made it look as if it had been designed for families of limited income. It was solid and soulless, like a large cement block dropped carelessly on the ground. Inside it had been splashed with whitewash, without any color or trim. It was impossible to miss the traces of numerous children on the miserable walls, where they immortalized scenes and names, hearts pierced by blood-red Cupid's arrows, math problems, ads for sex, and exaggerated insults. The area between one building and the next was no more than a hundred yards, but in the dark it seemed large and gloomy. Here and there small, young bushes were planted in circles, with a tall palm tree in the middle of each; in the heart of the enervating dark they looked like guards undefeated by the wind. The ground was paved with black brick, adding a human touch in the form of a vestige from the past that disdained modern asphalt.

Ruqayya's knock was answered by a boy of ten, who gave a striking impression of severe malnourishment. The pale light that suffocated the building's entry turned him into a statue of misery; Ruqayya must have teased him, for he began to laugh, and I was amazed that such an emaciated boy could laugh. Then she gave him something, perhaps some money, and he was overwhelmed with joy. He tried to kiss her hand, but she slipped away gracefully, pulling me by the hand and dancing in childish elation. I looked back at the boy, who stood saying goodbye: his eyes soared wildly to intricate, complex secrets in dark forests and forbidden places lustrous with enchantment.

"Where to?" I asked.

"Never mind."

She put her left hand on my arm, but the jellaba screened her from direct contact, and I wished it weren't there. We began to walk, and I wished that the walk would continue endlessly. When we reached the street she let go of my arm, put two fingers in her mouth, and surprised me with a sharp, piercing whistle. A little taxi stopped; it took us to Muhammad Khamis Square, where bright lights shone, cars of all kinds passed, and endless noise rent the peace of the night.

"I want to eat *glace*."

I did not object. The warmth of two glasses of wine inflamed my head. I took her arm again as we headed for the shop and whispered in her ear, "You are full of surprises."

The shop was not crowded, and I wanted to go in, but she preferred to stand on the sidewalk while we ate our ice cream. I watched as she lowered her taut veil from her mouth in a movement that displayed her unnaturally rounded cheeks. I said, "Get rid of the veil, it deforms your face."

She laughed. "Where's the jealousy then?"

Our laughter attracted another couple, and we made a circle of ice cream eaters; it enlarged again, after three young men emerged from a nearby bar, becoming an obstruction on the sidewalk, crowned by the colored lights of the shop and permeated by soft eastern melodies from an old radio. One of the drunks stared at her, attracted by her eyes.

She ate the ice cream with her teeth as if she were eating fruit, while I would melt a small piece under my tongue. She smiled and said, "Is it true that he doesn't eat much?"

"Who?"

"Si l-Habib."

I was truly annoyed. "Are you still thinking about him?"

"He eats like a bird."

"Excess is bad for the heart."

She asked me gaily, "Do you want a bird?"

"I?"

"Yes—a sparrow…a nightingale…"

"No."

"I had one when I was little. It would always fly over my head, and it would land on my hand and share my food."

"I envy him."

"You're joking."

"I wish I could change into a nightingale now, so I could keep you company always."

She chuckled, and the drunkard began to hang on her words. She said, leaning on me, "I'm going to buy one now."

I looked at her doubtfully. "At this hour?"

"Yes!"

I just laughed, and she changed the subject: "Give me a taste of your green ice cream and I'll give you a taste of mine."

I scooped a little with my spoon and fed it to her. The drunk burst out laughing, watching us, and called to his friends, "I'll feed you, dear."

He began to feed a plump, pock-marked face, both of them overcome with vulgar laughter. I felt that it was aimed at me and I resented it, but she took it in stride, even joining in their laughter, though without looking in their direction. The other couple quickly finished what they had and left, and I began to watch the situation until she had eaten her ice cream. I drew her away, and we strolled to the avenue; tensing for a fight had spoiled my relaxed mood. She noticed and stopped, chiding me: "It's a bad beginning. Take me as I am…"

She didn't finish, but I understood what she wanted to say, and I had to choose, as she stood staring soberly into my eyes. Then she offered me her arm with an affectionate movement that forced me to give her mine in return, and we walked a little. But she stopped in front of a large coffee house and cried, "I'm going to buy a nightingale!"

"You won't find one now."

"I'm going to try."

"Where?"

"Come with me—the place is nearby."

The shops had closed, and the elegant side streets had turned into desolate, cold, deserted alleys. We strolled to the right, where the cold air was imprisoned and laden with moisture. I don't know how she could know that someone was still sitting there, at this hour, but that is what happened; if I had been alone I wouldn't have been able to make out the barely lit shop. The hardware salesman was an old man whose oil-stained blue apron had faded to a dust-covered gray, the oily skin of his shoulders showing through its folds. He stared at us tiredly, with little interest in the world beyond his hardware. Long ago, he had hung up a dirty white piece of paper bearing a number in blue and the word "hardware," barely legible, in old-fashioned Moroccan calligraphy.

She asked, "Is a nightingale a kind of hardware?"

Her rosy laughter pealed out, substituting for the song of

a nightingale that had never existed. The aged man stared disbelieving from behind his clear glasses, and she began to chatter with him in a mix of French, Berber Chilha, and colloquial Arabic. All I understood of it was, "Tomorrow, God willing... God willing."

We left the shop with an appointment that one party believed was definite and the other was sure would never happen.

I was a captive of tyrannical fate, on board a ship guided by a capricious captain. Were it not for my fear of loneliness, first, and secondly, the beginning of hope that I was going to win her, I would have rebelled. But I was lonely during the vacation, so I loosened the reins, giving them to a beautiful, alluring, immature guide, to take me where she willed.

She stopped in front of a large display case in front of the Arab Bank. Absorbed in the varieties of sweets and gum, she said, "Give me some change."

I extended my hand and she took some coins, using them for two sweets with a few drops of whiskey at the center.

"Taste one."

"I've tasted them before," I said, but I took it.

"Do you want a Pepsi?"

"No."

She began to sing with the candy under her tongue, so her voice came out deformed, with many extra r's: "Hold on... hold on to those girls... we've got factories..."

I began to laugh. "Isn't there a better song?"

"They're all better. Listen to this: 'O crystal cup...'"

I didn't like that song either, but the peace of the street and Ruqayya's exquisite inflections made me lose myself in her. She was humming in a soft, mellow voice. Then she suddenly crushed the piece of candy between her teeth, letting out a laugh that filled the empty street. I felt a sudden great intoxication; I wrapped my arm around her and nearly kissed her, but she put her hand on my lips. My left hand was on the firm mound on her chest, and she whispered, sweetly and without fear, "We are friends."

"And so?"

"Do you like that?" Then, candidly and somewhat threateningly, "You will not cross the line."

My hand fell, and I was frozen in place. But she smiled with the same sweetness as before, and said, "Give me your hand."

She took my dead hand, then pulled me with it, and we walked as before, while she hummed sweet tunes. At a distance in front of us appeared the arms of the cranes in the port, a forest of tangled iron branches under a faint, unsteady light. When the light was blocked they seemed like a black fence, like a belt of night atop distant buildings.

We went up to the second floor of a building crowded into a barren back street. She lifted the veil from her eyes and leaned on me as we climbed, whispering, "I'll kill myself if I don't find her." But when she saw the little point of light in the keyhole, she cried, "She's home. Luck is smiling on us."

She bounded up two steps at once and knocked hard on the door, leaving me on the landing, my mouth watering with the last few drops of the whiskey candy. The light in the stairwell was very faint, and misery had eaten away the paint on the walls. Had it not been for the feeling of normality created by the noise of the cars, I could have imagined I was a burglar waiting for quiet in the hallway so I could break in.

Stronger light spilled from the sudden opening of the door, and the plump, smiling face of a girl appeared. As soon as she saw Ruqayya she beamed with delight and moved aside to let us in.

Why did I feel, when we entered, that I was a piece of clean clothing, floating on soap bubbles that had washed away all the dirt? As the door closed, it seemed to cut off all contact between us and the outside world.

A wave of kisses and embraces swept over the two girls as I stood watching, a smile on my face, preparing instinctively to make the smile my passport to a new world. The girl was short and plump, verging on fat; she had long hair teased in high puffs, which added several inches to her head. Her eyes were wide, honey-colored, with a network of brown lines radiating in her pupils, promising to probe the depths. As she was kissing Ruqayya she threw me a searching look from time to time. Her broad smile urged Ruqayya to end the embrace and begin the introductions.

"Lalla Zina… Si l-Sharqi."

Her short fingers, plump and soft, barely touched my hand, as if she were afraid of being polluted. I felt a shiver as I stared at her: she was wearing a single garment of yellow gauze, beginning at the shoulders and ending at the knees, which showed every inch of her dark flesh in a pleasantly alluring fashion.

For a long moment I kept the stupid smile frozen on my face. I expected she would move away from me and run down the narrow corridor to the room that appeared in shadow, to cover what she could of her body, but she did not. She pushed Ruqayya gently toward the room and turned on the light.

"Take off the jellaba."

Since I was left alone leaning on the door I noticed how her body's contours danced as she walked, how her armpit pushed some little hairs toward her back, how her buttocks were compressed under a small green triangle. Without noticing, I had become aroused, as had happened several times with Ruqayya on the way here; then the darkness had concealed my arousal, but here I had to control myself forcibly by remembering sad or distant things.

Ruqayya went ahead of me. With her slender, draped stature she looked like an original painting on a level that could never be reached by the millions of misshapen copies that surrounded it.

"Come, Si…"

She pulled me by the hand. Zina darted off to the right where a strong light was burning and announced theatrically, "There's a surprise today, a dear guest. Ruqayya, ladies and gentlemen!"

"Ladies and gentlemen"—I recoiled. Was it fear that I would be neglected because of the presence of others? It was an instinctive sense whose true nature I did not know, dominated by a strong fear of ignorance. I moved ahead slowly, as another wave of embraces and enthusiastic welcome arose.

The young man was thin and dark, with thick hair that seemed like a halo around his head. With his arm he tenderly embraced an *oud*, as if he were afraid its melodies would be lost if he left it. He wore short khaki pants, his chest bare and hairless. On his right was a girl of middling beauty, with a small, weak body; her nose was very thin and too long for her face, and her eyes were black. Her dress was of blue taffeta, open in the middle all the way down, so that her bare chest appeared, as well as the folds of her abdomen and what was between her thighs.

The dress seemed like a jellaba except that when she sat the wide, embroidered Moroccan collar bent gracefully to either side. This revealed a wider area that showed the rounding of her breasts, her maroon nipples gleaming with amazing luster. The gold buttons on the right side of the dress shone. I was aroused anew, and sat down immediately to hide it, still staring at her. There was a round table with three cups of red wine, three small plates of sliced carrots on a bed of vinegar and olive oil, and a large dish of cherries and limes.

The small room was bare of everything except two low Moroccan seats and three new black chairs. The wall was covered with pieces of colored cardboard; in the middle of each was an elegant shape made of colored paper, bearing writing in French that looked like poetry. If it were not for a small window high on the wall, the smoke would have blinded us.

We sat opposite the two, who seemed to have been expecting other visitors. After the flood of urgent, repeated questions about health and family, Zina began to move with quick, flirtatious steps, like a waitress who loves her work. She brought two more cups and more wine, as well as spoons which she put before us on the edge of two plates of sliced carrots. After the first sip of the red wine the musician with the puffy hair began to ask me a succession of sharp questions about my country, politics, and the way of life in other Arab regions. I became so absorbed in the discussion that before I had finished my cup I felt as if I had known them for a long time, even though I couldn't stop looking at the way the dress opened over the body of his companion. Her large white navel attracted me like a magnet, throwing me into confusion.

When Zina sat down on my left, I said to Ruqayya, "We've been introduced to our lovely hostess, but we have not yet met the gentleman and the lady."

I got up and extended my hand, so he raised his torso a little while his companion just extended her hand.

"Shuaib Belaid."

"Al-Shahba Fatima."

It seemed to me that the names were familiar to me, as if I had seen them or seen their pictures. Where? My memory betrayed me.

Ruqayya apologized in joking, half mocking tones, "Forgive us, we must have interrupted your music."

Belaid looked at Ruqayya affectionately and embraced her, patting her slender arm and said, with seriousness, "Melodies continue as long as there are flowers."

It seemed that he was referring to al-Shahba with this remark, though it included both girls in its generality. Zina smiled and Belaid took the *oud*, after finishing his wine with a large gulp. He began to hum, as if he were putting his fingers on the strings for the first time. Zina stretched her hand to Ruqayya behind me, so I leaned forward and felt their breath and hair tickling my back. I leaned to the right to make room for her, and my eye fell on Ruqayya's knee, while Zina's legs were a little open because of the way she had to sit in the narrow space, revealing the undergarment that kept her from being completely naked.

"Why did you leave Si l-Salih?" asked Zina.

"Why would I leave him?"

"He was dying for you."

"He still is."

"Did he ask you to marry him?"

"Yes."

"And…?"

"Don't you know my opinion?"

I pressed on Ruqayya's knee. "Sit next to each other so you can talk more comfortably."

"Don't bother about us, we're fine like this," she answered.

"We must do what we must," Zina remarked.

"I'm not old."

"It's not only age." They both laughed.

Ruqayya said, "There's pleasure in something new. I'm going to direct the Paris office."

"When?"

"After a while."

"Take me with you."

Ruqayya laughed. "I'll write to you when it's time."

"Is this a new face?" I thought she was referring to me.

"Just a friend. But the one who has infatuated me is another important person."

I trembled, and once again the conversation heated my back with the fragrant breath of the two girls.

"Who?"

"It's a secret."

"What a whore you are!"

Zina flung the ugly word with a laugh that diminished its extravagance, then straightened up. I was seized by overwhelming anger, for which I didn't know the reason; I wished I had a strong enough will to make me leave and end my relationship with Ruqayya at this stage, before it developed, but I was paralyzed. There was pleasure in the present that outweighed the loneliness in which I lived without a steady girlfriend, and the drink acted on my weak points, providing ample justification for ignoring the red light.

The singing began to flood the air in the room, blocking all the exits. Al-Shuhba melted into the melody, her hair on Si Belaid's elbow. She had leaned against him gently, without putting her weight on the hand that was playing, her eyes half closed and wandering with the sad tones in distant climes. The melodies ascended in fragments from a wide, peaceful ground, speaking of oppressed groups, powerless, sad, ill and afraid, killed by ignorance and killing each other—groups without number, from the lowest social strata, dreaming of change, health, hunger satisfied, and smiles. For a few moments opposites embraced in the air of the room: sadness and joy, sweet childhood moments whose simple desires die within the limits of the possible, singular personal and public pain, passionate first love snatched away by the oscillations of reckless fate.

"O my husband working far away…"

Al-Shahba's voice was deep and strong, flooded with warmth and sadness. I marveled at its greatness, at the combination of sorrow and strength and promise and hundreds of other inexpressible things that came together to make this piercing magic, compared to her deceptively frail appearance. Was it possible that this sorrow and strength and promise and the hundreds of other inexpressible things that combined to make this piercing magic—was it possible that they were coming from this thin, small body? I closed my eyes as I sipped my wine; the melody continued to rise, delicate, leading. It spoke of a woman left by her husband who worked far away, year after year, while she cherished the hope of his return and of the wealth he would bring. She waits, there is only waiting and letters coming from beyond the sea, but she always remembers:

"Our last embrace,

The tears upon our face…"

The voice was filled with delicacy, the melody was quiet and sorrowful, and the performance was excellent: all that fused in a moment of fellowship. But when I asked about the poet, Si Belaid laughed:

"Why do you care about poetry?"

"Isn't it what's essential?"

"There's always good poetry, but you can't find anyone who chooses well."

"This kind of song is completely new, it's extraordinary."

"It's the true face of the suffering of the people."

"Can you broadcast it?"

He laughed, and hugged al-Shahba to his chest tightly: "What do you think of the question?"

She answered in a trembling voice that did not correspond to her performance in the song: "It has no answer."

Belaid concluded: "They don't accept anything except clichés."

Ruqayya asked, "Do you expect them to accept insults to themselves and their systems?"

Si Belaid looked at Ruqayya: "Let her sing for you. She knows a lot of songs of both kinds."

Ruqayya parried, playfully, "Why are you teasing me?"

I interrupted: "Ruqayya doesn't need to sing, her speech alone is a constant melody."

Belaid cried, "That's exactly what I've been telling her ever since I met her." Then, addressing her: "Let me give you the melody for a song in which you just speak, ordinary words inspired by the melody. Listen... the *oud* only... just talk without singing."

She made light of it, leaning against the wall. "What would I do with the songs?"

"They would be a surprise, the event of the season."

Al-Shahba begged her earnestly: "You'll outdo all of us. You'll leave us in the dust."

I looked for jealousy in al-Shahba's voice, but without success. I decided that the subject had been discussed more than once, and that talking with Ruqayya about it had become boring and repetitious.

"Do you want an ordinary song, Ruqayya? I have a good poem of Ibn Zaidun's. Everyone will love it."

I interrupted him: "A few moments ago you made me think that you believe in what you compose."

He shrugged. "Only in our private gatherings. What's sung publicly is foolishness."

"Don't you regret that?"

He spread his hands in front of him. "Only at first. Then we accepted the dichotomy as fate decreed by heaven. We have no other way of earning a living. The same issue affects all the artists of the underdeveloped world. The exact same thing happens in your country, doesn't it?"

The room wasn't hot but the wine had produced its effect. I opened two buttons of my shirt, and al-Shahba pointed to me and exclaimed, as if she had discovered something exciting, "Look at the thick hair on his chest!"

Belaid shrugged mockingly and squeezed her. "Is it worth all that attention?"

Ruqayya laughed and said, "You see? I told you that you have a handsome chest."

I overflowed with happiness, and wished I could kiss her cheeks, glowing with the wine. Then I forgot the matter completely, losing myself in her eyes. She turned away, as Si Belaid addressed me: "Women are women. Look how they've changed the subject!"

I asked, "So you believe that struggle for the sake of change is worthwhile?"

He agreed with a confident nod of his head, and muttered, "We can't avoid it."

"And the means?"

"There's nothing but revolution!"

"Revolution? Artistic, you mean?"

"In every area."

"Including society, and tradition?"

He shook his head, as if showing his complete lack of interest, and said, "A traditional movement will not succeed in changing our society. We have to destroy every type of old feudal behavior, we have to tear out all the roots of feudalism."

I agreed with a nod of my head, and he concluded, "There's more than one way, and the most devastating is sex."

I smiled, and he said: "I'm serious."

"And I seriously want to understand."

Ruqayya reached out and clinked glasses with us. He cried, "A toast to the destruction of feudalism!"

She burst out laughing, and he winked at her, saying, "She's drinking a toast to the destruction of her class. Traitor!"

Laughter reigned in the room, and we drank the wine, whose note of acidity was no longer noticeable enough to give me an aversion to it. I looked toward Belaid, urging him to continue. He said, "Having sex in any place—the street, for example—is a weapon against feudalism in this time. We're in the twentieth century, we must destroy all feudalistic complexes, the psychological and the lived. Have you heard of the songs of the *shaikhas*?"

"Yes, but I didn't like them." The remoteness of the dialect, some strangeness in pronunciation, the group participation in the singing, the strong clapping—all that was behind my aversion.

"But if you understood them you would change your mind. I'll sing you one, but in a dialect you can understand."

Al-Shahba warned, "You won't be able to change the words."

"Just listen."

He began with familiar tones like a drumbeat. Then he signaled to the women. They began the sort of group clapping that most people can do well. He signaled me with his eyes to pay attention.

"Divorce me, set me free!
Hunger's killing me,
My God, he cheats on me,
Let everyone listen to me."

The words were a guide I followed with eyes newly opened to the waves of people who were struggling in the mud for a decent life.

These songs were the beginning; after that and for as long as I stayed in Morocco I would wait for the songs of the *shaikha*s, which I had always dismissed, with the same longing as a fan of chess or crossword puzzles who waits for them to appear in the next issue of his favorite magazine. I tried to decipher their allusions with great patience and perseverance. I began to feel that I had acquired a distinct advantage by my direct access to the underclass, which creates life and then is crushed underfoot by it. At that point I realized why the songs of the *shaikha*s are collective: everyone suffers, hungers, and feels pain, and the songs reveal all. There are no secrets and no fear, and nothing is sacred.

Belaid paused, then asked, "Have you known a feeling like this before? What do you expect from a girl who has been selling her body since she was ten, under the lash of Oufkir?"

Al-Shahba leaned against his bare chest and embraced him, and he looked at me, wanting my opinion. I said, "I believed that organization was enough to change everything."

He guffawed. "Let's use every means; having sex in public destroys the dignity and psyche of feudalism. Let organization work to destroy its existence."

Then he went off into a long kiss with al-Shahba, after which they both seemed refreshed and glowing with overpowering happiness. Zina suggested, "Let Ruqayya sing for us."

Al-Shahba clapped her hands and Belaid urged her on. She asked me for two coins. I objected jokingly, "You won't find anyone to sell you a nightingale here."

She began to beat the table with the coins, to the tones of the *oud* and the clapping of al-Shahba. Zina tied a yellow shawl around her hips as we swallowed the wine without reckoning how much we drank. We cleared the table, and it was easily transformed into a small stage, which Zina mounted. Ruqayya began,

"Friends, it's been three days since I've seen my gazelle…"

Belaid addressed me from between Zina's plump calves, "She owns the one she loves, like any of her feudal ancestors!"

As long as I had lived I had yearned to become completely drunk, and this was the first time in my life it had happened! I don't know how much I drank, but I know I reached a state of intoxication I had not experienced since I was created. After that I would weigh all my failures against what happened to me that night and still think that I had come out ahead. Those few hours, however, which passed in the blink of an eye, had the opposite effect afterwards, for they deprived me of the gift of being able to take pleasure in any kind of evening party or concert, private or public. That modest concert was the acme of stimulation and intoxication, and all the songs I heard after that and all the concerts I attended were no more than jumbled, discordant echoes coming from a plain and simple world.

That night Belaid let loose melodies that tore away the veils from spirits plunged in delusions; were it not for the drink we would certainly not have been able to understand the targets at which he aimed his arrows. His white pick not only touched the strings of the *oud* but also tore down the walls which until that moment had blocked the light from the seeds of extreme purity, and his tones were enough to stimulate their growth.

A collective creativity that I could not explain poured out of us, and we continued singing even when one of us would absent himself and then return.

It must have been after three o'clock when the party ended spontaneously. Belaid had carried al-Shahba to the darkened room, kissing her between her breasts, and Ruqayya pressed some money into Zina's hand and looked at me:

"Don't you like Zina?"

"Of course," I answered, since she was surprised by my desire to leave. I understood what she meant only after a while, and then I felt a pain in my chest. I looked at her reproachfully, and she wrapped her right arm around me and gave me a quick kiss, fragrant with wine, to make up. Her moist lips left a rosy circle on my cheek, and I would touch that place for a long time as if it were a holy relic. When Belaid and al-Shahba emerged from the room, absorbed in each other, Zina's eyes suddenly lit up. She crossed over to me with lightning speed; I thought she was going to hit me, or that she had seen something wrong happen behind me, so I looked. But she wrapped her arms around me and planted her mouth on mine. Everyone burst out laughing loudly, embarrassing me and making me try to push her away, even though her warm body had begun to dissolve my resistance. No sooner did I succeed than Ruqayya took my hand, and we went downstairs, Zina waving to us, her cheeks glowing with lust.

We got into a small car going to al-Mohammediya, its exterior in need of a lot of repair. I took advantage of Ruqayya's nearness to lean on her shoulder, making a pillow of the fresh softness of her body and imagining its contours as if she were not wearing the jellaba. I lifted her hand to my mouth and began kissing it; she did not resist and at the same time did not encourage me to do anything more. That made it hard for me to take my mind off her, and I fell into a very deep sleep, with no knowledge of what happened later.

chapter 9

"Dear Si l-Sharqi:

Here are fifty dirhems for your honor. I borrowed them from your honor yesterday and gave them to Zina.

[Signed] Ruqayya. Merci."

I spent a few minutes thinking about the style of the letter and its mistakes, and then I pocketed the money. I stood in front of the door of my building; it was a little after eleven-thirty. I was still under the influence of yesterday's wine, and the dazzling sunlight was sticking sharp pins into my eyes.

I crossed the street, greeting the owners of the shops, and then I entered a shop that sold lightweight clothing. I had a passing acquaintance with its owner, and I'm still grateful to him for having brought me an elegant, lightweight Moroccan raincoat, suitable for the climate of al-Mohammediya. He kept it for me all during the term break, giving me the pleasure of walking in the warm rain.

I began looking at perfumes, women's underwear, skirts, and

costume jewelry. I was in a state of complete confusion when a familiar feminine voice called out, "Those things aren't for you."

A jellaba and a veil, a dark complexion, two shining eyes…. Who? I smiled and the girl laughed. There were several girls with her in the shop, chattering noisily, laughing, and turning over the things on display. The jellaba and the veil confused me—I had not acquired the Moroccan skill of recognizing any girl at a glance. Why did they cling to these masks, which kill the warmth of an encounter?

"How are you?"

She was large, her eyes honey-colored like Zina's, but she was taller.

"Don't you know me?"

I smiled foolishly.

"I'm al-Shaqra."

She was not blond like her name. Rather, she was dark, her features not at all harmonious, her nose unexpectedly wide. Her eyebrows needed constant attention in order to look like a modern girl's eyebrows, and the hair on her legs was as thick as a man's. She did not attract me, although her well-developed body stood out from the bodies of the other female students and caught my attention. But her pretty, playful friend Zainab, who was skilled at flirting with her eyes, had succeeded in making Si l-Qadiri fall into a transitory relationship at the end of the term; and since Si l-Qadiri and I were inseparable friends, al-Shaqra, perhaps with the motive of keeping Zainab company, considered me one of her victims. In class, she sat with Zainab in the seat directly in front of me, and began uncovering a pleasant area above her knees, deliberately and constantly. She kept trying, and at the end of the year I discovered a strange, unique beauty in her face, as well as sexual power and great maturity.

She laughed, and I shook her hand. It seemed as if I had parted from her a long time ago.

She said, "What are you looking for?"

"I don't know."

"Is it a gift?"

I smiled. "Maybe."

She laughed. "It's a gift for sure, otherwise you wouldn't be so confused."

"Let's assume it is."

She whispered sweetly, "Who's it for? There's something strange in your eyes."

I unconsciously turned my face to the street, where the sun was heating the black asphalt with its fiery lashes. I felt her eyes and those of her companions boring into my back. "You wouldn't know her," I said.

"Is she the new resident—the owner of the airlines?"

"Airlines?"

"Don't you know? Or are you pretending?"

I was astonished. "You wouldn't believe it if I told you that you know more than I do."

"Poor professor." Then she added, as if warning me, "Don't you know that she's rich, that she could buy all of Fadala?"

Al-Shaqra's father owned the building where the shop was located, which faced the Chinaman's building. I had thought that the residents of one building were above keeping the residents of the other under surveillance.

"Why do you care about me?" I asked.

"Why wouldn't I? In the end you'll have to come to me."

"What do you mean?"

She winked. "Don't you know?"

I had thought the simple relationship between Zainab and al-Qadiri had ended completely, but now I saw I was mistaken.

"How much are you going to spend?" she asked.

"Fifty dirhems."

"Isn't that a lot?"

"Are you joking?"

She laughed, intentionally raising her voice, and one of the girls looked at her and smiled, addressing her friend in a muffled voice.

"Give me your money and I'll save you from your confusion. I'll buy a present suitable for a passing love, and I'll keep the rest to buy myself something to remember you by."

I gave her the money, and she returned in a few minutes with an elegant small package.

"What did you buy?"

"I won't tell you, but don't open it."

"Is it a bomb?"

"Yes, but of a different kind."

She was pretending in front of the others that I was one of the captives she kept in reserve, while I looked on her attempts only as an observer. Once the gift was in my hand, I imagined the encounter was over. But she hung onto the conversation, blaming me emphatically for having wasted opportunities rich in possibilities for pleasure and companionship, spoiled by my strictness, for which there was no excuse. I left her after great effort, and after she had dragged me into a discussion of various topics, among them the fact that she had suddenly become engaged. She thought it would cause me pain; and that led me to think deeply, trying vainly to remember any small example of bad behavior that had given her the impression that I found her charming or loved her.

I hurried to the shade provided by the Chinaman's building, under the pressure of many feelings crowding my imagination, about airlines, Ruqayya, surveillance, and lost opportunities.

When I got to my apartment, the sight of the numerous keys I had made for the three apartments, in a state of complete drunkenness, made me feel like someone who spies on others' moments of pleasure, giving me also a sense of unparalleled privilege because I had a secret unknown to others.

What a secret adventure, fraught with danger and excited by curiosity, lay in entering Ruqayya's apartment while she was gone! The change in al-Jaza'iri's place was tremendous: it had been turned into a royal room, with embroidered pink silk curtains; lacy pink sheets; extremely beautiful figurines portraying horses, cats, and dogs; a vase of colored crystal filled with flowers that perfumed the room in a pleasant country fragrance; elegant nylon chaises of a kind I had not seen before; a green table lamp in the shape of a fish; and a Formica table, also in pink. Even the neglected little bathroom had become extremely clean and shiny, welcoming its guest with an azure flower pot embracing a green plant with small buds that were preparing to climb still higher.

I put the elegant box on the table and picked up a pen.

What should I write?

All of the words seemed foolish, and I felt tired. I sat on the soft bed. How and when had she moved in, and changed everything in the apartment for the better? There was no doubt that she was extremely rich; everything spoke of aristocratic luxury.

In my confusion I realized how superior she was to me. Despite her fragmentary expressions, she had found something to write to me; my thoughts were scattered. I stretched out on the bed. I felt like a true pioneer, the first stranger to enter the apartment and sleep on the bed: what a distinction!

The feminine touches that create life in a desert were clear in everything, and perhaps they were the secret of the peace that descended on me, a familial peace permeated with child-hood. I took a deep breath and smelled the flowers in the vase, and a wave of dreams mixed with their fragrance. I realized that I was like a traveler hesitating to board a train, distracted by watching the huge black wheels turn as they gathered speed. I put my signature on the blank paper without writing any words, and then I went out.

Mental stiffness paralyzed my thinking, even about something trifling—why? I wanted a small drink to clarify my thinking, but instead I found myself leaning against the door of the building, a statue of stone.

I stared at the shop I had entered a while before. What had al-Shaqra put in the box? Who can plumb the thinking of an adolescent? I felt my heart beat faster. It was the utmost in stupidity to give something without knowing what it was. Maybe it was nothing. But I could not make myself go up again to find out. I was a man without a will, who had easily given away something that had been very important to him.

chapter 10

The voice was strong and familiar: "What are you thinking about?"

"Si l-Arabi."

Standing at the door of the building, or in any part of the street between the two facing buildings, means being completely open to conversation, noise, and chatter, exactly like the coffee shop. He had just crossed the street, leaving his brother, the butcher.

I spoke first: "What do your colleagues in Parliament think of al-Za'lul's speech?"

He swallowed a laugh. "Have you taken to discussing details? It's no more than a prelude."

"Are you satisfied with that?"

"Let's not talk about that now."

It annoyed him to discuss anything that pertained to the leader, so I was deliberately teasing him about his weak point. He asked, attacking, "Do you feel special because your country is a republic? A military republic is no better than feudal rule."

The topics of monarchy, republics, feudalism, and sex were

like sores on my body, and I felt better when I scratched them. I said, "That's my opinion exactly."

His gaze turned aside, and he said in a near whisper, "When his majesty wants to strike or act he will choose the appropriate time and pretext. Other than that it doesn't matter whether Za'lul is exporting Indian figs or changing the educational system or opening a new sugar factory."

"Will he take power himself?"

"That's what we think. He took advantage of the situation to confront the people. But it's only a prelude. But tell me, how is your friend?" He meant Si l-Habib.

I laughed. Si l-Arabi was always asking me about him, and I wished they would meet once in my presence so I could learn the true reasons for the difference between the schismatics and those who had remained in the party.

"He was your friend before I ever saw him."

"That was in the past. Then he split with us."

"It's not too late."

"Yes, it is."

"What do you want to know? About his health?"

He made a gestured that said I was free to talk about anything relating to Si l-Habib.

"His health is fairly good, but—" I mentioned what had been keeping Si l-Habib awake at night since our meeting with Si Bayad's family. I asked, "How was your relationship with Si Bayad?"

His face wrinkled in distress. "Besides the leader of the party, it was the three of us who were closest to the Counselor. Then differences crept in, and the terrible split happened."

He was obviously in pain, as if the split in the party had happened only days before. I watched as his dark face creased.

"Then the two of them sided with the Counselor and I stayed with the party. The price was enormous for everyone. The ministry didn't last. It was a gift, and the beginning of his intervention."

"I think they regretted it, despite being justified in their position."

He shook his head. "What's the use of regret? The one force that wrested independence for the country and that could have done something split into different divisions: the army of independence became governmental, the young people sided with the Counselor. His majesty will begin to turn the unions against them with a new game, and we're left with the old men. We've become four separate factions, and separately we can't act decisively."

"You could have changed your thinking to make sure the young people stayed with you."

"It's too late to change, and the government alone has control of everything—in spite of us and in spite of the young."

I laughed. "Anyone hearing you would think you're an old man."

Si l-Arabi was, in fact, a fairly young man, just past thirty-eight, with penetrating eyes and black hair invaded by a little early gray over the temples. His youth, his enthusiasm, and his elegance, which seemed natural, without any artificiality—all that had made me doubt the accuracy of what Si Sabir had said one day when we were sipping coffee on the sidewalk at the beginning of the school year: "That young fellow is the representative of al-Mohammediya in Parliament."

A number of questions had risen in my mind, but they were suppressed by the arrival of al-Khitabi, al-Qadiri, and al-Mazwari. We were compelled to change the conversation, and then we divided into two teams to play checkers.

It was pure chance that I had met Si l-Arabi. I had been buying meat from his brother, the butcher, who was talking about the shrewdness of Ahardan following a particularly intelligent remark he had made in a press interview. That had surprised me, because at that time he was far removed from power. Si l-Arabi was there, and he introduced himself to me with great modesty just as his brother opened his mouth to do the same thing. His unpretentious behavior and candid verve had seemed to dissolve much of the obscurity I found in this strife-filled country, and for that reason I had opened up to him.

Once again I explained to him the problem facing Si l-Bayad's widow, and the possibility of discussing a solution for it with his fellow representatives. He said he'd be willing to help her personally, but hinted that any other solution would be impossible. He added that they were racing against time to wrest a few concessions that would benefit everyone, so they could not dissipate their forces and lose the few good opportunities available to solve any one person's problems.

It was clear to me that he was depending on my honesty and candor when he asked, "Did Si l-Habib ask you to bring up the subject?"

I denied that convincingly and he dropped the topic. He asked me to walk with him for a few minutes if I wasn't busy. We walked in the shade behind the Chinaman's building, then headed for the bus stop of the Rabat-Casablanca route where a little car squatted, locally assembled and old, on a side street. He opened the door and invited me in. I thought he was going to ask me to lunch, following a generous custom that had blossomed in this society in an unknown era, which was to take the first person one saw to share one's food when it was time to eat. Therefore I hesitated to get in and made excuses, but he insisted, making it clear that he was going to show me something and bring me back, eliminating lunch from the agenda, however regretfully.

The car crossed the Casablanca road and climbed toward the train station. After a few moments we were in al-Aliya, where I went every Sunday to a local festival featuring a rural market where everything was on display. Now, the place seemed unpleasantly empty and poverty-stricken. The car advanced slowly to the left, where after a few seconds we suddenly found ourselves before three tenements. Between the buildings were modest lawns turning a miserable pale yellow, killed by the play of many children, surrounded by wretched borders of dried, neglected flowers. Had it not been for some small willow trees that rustled from time to time, we would have been plunged into the silence of a hot, dry midday.

He asked, "Have you ever been inside one of these buildings?"

"Yes."

His eyes opened in surprise, and he smiled. "You really get around." Then he laughed, and without giving me time to think of an answer, asked sadly, "Is it a girl? These poor girls are often very pretty."

"No."

"Politics?"

I burst out laughing. "I left politics in my country."

"What were you doing here?"

"What am I doing with you?"

"They are buildings for workers."

"I know that. The rooms are small and unfit to live in. My first week in al-Mohammediya I met a guy in a bar, and he invited me here."

The young man's name was Si Ibrahim, and he had insisted on my coming to lunch. We had arrived at eleven on a beautiful spring Sunday, and as we climbed the stairs I could smell various simple dishes that were being cooked, and hear the shouts of children playing. We didn't see any of them in the narrow hallway; their existence crept out to us from behind closed doors, but their play was clearly inscribed on every inch of the walls.

The apartment was cramped, and turned topsy-turvy. The only woman there, who he said was his brother's wife, seemed surprised to see us. She made us wait in the entryway, which was only big enough for two people standing close together, and hurried into the room ahead of us to tidy it up. She came out after a time that seemed long to us, stammering in shyness, her ample, long, rose-colored dress blessing the floor with musical touches, sweeping everything in its wake. When we sat down, she asked us, in a trembling, mellow voice, to hand her a pile of clothes she had forgotten in her confusion when we dropped in on her.

Si Ibrahim's hospitality did not succeed in dispelling my discomfort. I insisted on leaving, but he stopped me with a pleading motion, the smell of the wine on his breath enclosing our faces like the halos surrounding the faces of saints in the Middle Ages. In order to place before me a fait accompli, he went out and returned, seconds later, with the good news that she was going to start preparing lunch immediately. Nonetheless I succeeded in convincing him that my cleaning lady would have finished preparing lunch by now; and even though we had already had plenty to drink at the bar, I had a bottle of good wine that we could finish off with the meal. As we were leaving, he urged the woman not to stop coming to them; and when I reminded him that she was his brother's wife he laughed and said they had not gotten married yet, whistling unconcernedly and ignoring my doubtful expression.

Si Ibrahim was a mixture of all life's contradictions: courage and weakness, lying and truthfulness, generosity and insolvency. The day I ran into him in the bar, he caught my attention because he was searching his pockets for money that wasn't there, so I paid his bill—but cautiously, because I was still a stranger. But when he left he showed me gratitude beyond description, promising me as he shook my hand that he would never forget what I had done. In fact he flooded me with gifts from the large paper plant where he worked, which I don't know how he came by: tape of various sizes, excellent varieties of elegant writing paper, datebooks, colored pictures, albums, cards for various occasions, and much more.

But despite all these gifts, the appearance of Si Ibrahim before me always meant implicitly that he needed a drink, and also that he needed to liquidate the stock he had collected of news about society, which combined seriousness and jesting, rationality and folly.

He was the kind of person you have to accept as he is, with all his contradictions, or not. I had accepted him in spite of his little irritations, which sometimes caused me some small amount of worry and anxiety. Nor was I one to be greatly upset by what happened that one night, or to see in it a reason to break off my friendship with him. That night I had returned replete with drink and in the company of a thin, pious girl whom I had picked up on an afternoon in Ramadan, and who had promised to meet me after breaking the fast with the evening *iftar*. We had gone to an out-of-the-way bar near the fish market, where we drank, bound by the condition she insisted on imposing that we put off our pleasure until the pre-fasting meal before dawn.

When we got back to my apartment we were surprised by Si Ibrahim, who was full of agitation and embarrassment. With him was Aisha, a small, charming young woman with a lovable speech habit: when she pronounced the letter *k*, it sounded as if she were cracking a hard nut. On her wrists jingled several gold bracelets, which I learned were her entire fortune. Her fear was apparent in her face: she had been arrested several days before on suspicion of prostitution, for she lived alone with a female relative in a doubtful lane inside the Casbah. She had been set free that afternoon without any restrictions or conditions, but when she was heading home she had seen a police patrol taking up positions in the area. Since she did not want to become entangled in anything dubious, she had accepted Si Ibrahim's suggestion that she spend the night at the home of his noble friend. He told me all this with great naturalness, requiring me to simply accept it as a fait accompli.

As for the rest of the problems, such as the existence of only one bed in the room, they solved them by spreading a blanket on the floor after moving the table and chairs near the door to the kitchen. This made room for them on the other side of the bed, and they rolled up another blanket for a pillow.

We laughed all that night, as Aisha told us about the women's prison, the prisoners' need for men, and what they resorted to.

In the morning Si Ibrahim repaid me with unparalleled sweetness. He criticized my extremely thin girl, who had said goodbye to us and left for her job in the central post office. He then placed Aisha completely at my disposal: her full body, her jokes, and her endearing speech habit.

With effort, but firmly, I refused his offer, trying not to hurt his feelings. With all the cunning he possessed he set out to remove from my mind any link between Aisha and prostitution. It wasn't an important issue for me; I wanted to live without any fetters imposed from the outside, whereas he only wanted to be useful to me. If he had been talking to any other man, spewing that furious wave of assurances, it would have developed into a sort of battle; but I had managed to bring the topic to an end by pretending to believe him and telling him I was soon going out of town.

Throughout my tour of the building with Si l-Arabi, Si Ibrahim invaded my memory, and with him Aisha and the alleged wife of his brother. I was overcome by something that excited me, something between laughter, satisfaction, and pain.

Si l-Arabi's voice claimed my attention again: "The workers' buildings have few amenities, but the meager monthly rent is hardly worth mentioning. Now come with me."

We advanced down the wide, dusty street, filled with trash, with tin shacks ranging on either side. Si l-Arabi slowed the car so as not to stir up the dust where some children had stolen the shade under the rows of rusty shacks. Some of them were playing with bones, bits of dirt, stones, and small sticks, creating their own little deprived world. But their hungry eyes fastened on the car, observing it with interest, and they called out the names of girls with a wickedness that was probably sexual.

It seemed that this long street, and another of the same width that crossed it, depended for water on a single faucet at the crossroads. Near the faucet stretched a long line of girls and boys carrying containers.

The slow movement of the car meant that we were entering hell. The heat burned down; July roamed here like a Berber horseman, taking pleasure in his terrible strength. Everyone was suffering from the fierce, wretched midday sun. The car had to move so slowly that no air stirred, and we were sweating from every pore. Small beads the color of his skin shone on Si l-Arabi's lips; strung together they would have formed a charm for a unique magician. We looked out at the dirty yellow faces of children with thin legs and inflated bellies. The shacks were made of sheets of tin taken from open containers, and they threw the heat back and forth across the street, like mirrors in the hands of children amusing themselves by burning one another. The heat of the equatorial July seemed to double with every change in the angle of the sun.

"Have you ever been inside one of these shacks?" He asked it as if he were looking for a point he had lost in the unexpected stream of the heat.

"No."

I looked out of my window and sensed terror: a few children fled, leaving a girl not more than two years old who began to scream loudly, frozen in fear.

"You won't find any worse than these."

A middle-aged woman hurried out of one of the shacks, her old, torn dress soaked in sweat, her face painted with a thick, shiny golden substance. She looked at us with deep-seated hostility, picked up the child, and shot us a curse we didn't hear.

I continued, "I've seen worse than these."

"In your country?"

"In my country but also here, in Settat."

"Settat?"

"Yes—shacks of straw. When I saw them for the first time I thought I was in central Africa."

He nodded, his eyes wandering far away. "Misery is the same the world over. But straw is more comfortable in the summer; tin is torture and slow death."

The doors of the shacks were pulled open, so that nothing was concealed. Two children slept near one, in the shade, bathed in sweat, and naked except for the layer of dirt. An emaciated young woman, her eyes hollow, fanned them with a small piece of cardboard. Her pale cheeks were tight over a hidden pain.

"Straw is acceptable winter and summer, but tin is unbearable. If you stayed in one for ten minutes you would be soaked in sweat. Look at that."

He pointed out of the car window; there was a shack crowned with several new tin sheets, shining brightly enough to burn the eye. It seemed to swagger in its shininess before the others, which were covered with many stages of rust.

"You could fry an egg on it now, and if you touched it, you would be burned."

My senses were dulled, and I yearned with all my heart for a cool breeze. Si l-Arabi's eyes were still wandering. "I spent my childhood in a shack like these."

This confession surprised me, and I did not know what to say in response except to joke, to lessen the oppressiveness of the memory: "That's where you get your tan."

He laughed shortly. "We're from the south." He waved his hand toward town, and I understood that by the word "we" he meant his family. He shook his head. "It's a miracle for a child growing up here to stay alive." After a silence, he turned the car around and said, "It's the most miserable stratum of society."

I added, "There's nothing harsher than this life."

His eyes glowed: "Should we be satisfied with charity alone?"

Fresh water was roaring from another tap, and here it had turned into hard currency. A boy of fifteen was filling a can and teasing a group of children whose feet were plunged in the mud, splashing them with the water before carrying off his can. He shoved his head under the spigot and shook the water from his hair like a wet bird. His shirt was soaked and stuck to his chest, its blue becoming more intense; he was doing it deliberately to delay two skinny little girls waiting their turn, cursing daringly in their impatience.

The heat was burning everything not covered by clothing, the blaze of it burning the eyes and distorting thought. We watched the children, who all rushed toward the pouring water and began to push each other, trying to stay under it the longest, yelling, laughing, and cursing. A little girl fell under their feet and began to cry; they snatched her away quickly and pushed harder, until the biggest took control and sat down directly under the spigot. He shielded his nose from the water in order to breathe, while a circle formed around him, a fence of little bodies snatching at the water, their threadbare clothes sticking to them, their bones protruding on every side.

"I used to do the same when I was little," he said, and his voice came from the depths of the past, which was still alive in him. He wanted to harden his feelings by means of personal suffering, as had happened the first time.

Once we had left the shacks behind, and the breeze began to moderate the air in the car, Si l-Arabi said, "We're going to try to erect three more miserable buildings like the ones you saw. We are struggling to keep the money that's been set aside for housing these poor wretches from going into the pockets of the fat cats and being lost."

I asked, "How would that happen?"

He sighed deeply. "It's an old game, and it happens in every country of the developing world. One of the opportunistic representatives demanded that we build a mosque with the funds, another demanded that we build a post office—imagine, a post office building in Fadala! Two huge buildings that will meet its needs for fifty years. They waste the money on anything luxurious that will serve for propaganda at the expense of these people."

I wondered inwardly, as I soaked up the bitterness his words were steeped in, whether he was plunging into a battle that would decide his fate rather than the fate of the people he was talking about.

He went on, his voice rising: "That's why I don't like to squander time on personal problems. We have built three apartment buildings in al-Mohammediya, and we will build three more this year. We will keep building as long as we draw breath. If someone says 'I am worried, therefore I exist,' or 'I feel, therefore I exist,' then I say, 'I build, therefore I exist.' When what I want is finished, death will be better for me than living." His tremendous determination lit sparks in his eyes, and I could see he was a man who was happy to engage in battles.

I remained silent when he brought up the problem of Si Bayad's widow. I realized that it was fruitless for an express train to turn aside to pick up someone helpless in the middle of the journey. But he did not forget to warn me that al-Habib should take precautions. Oufkir, the king's man, would not leave him alone.

I asked, "Assassination?"

He laughed. "No." Then, looking into the distance, he said, "There are a thousand new ways."

chapter 11

It was one-thirty in the afternoon, the time of Si l-Habib's siesta, and the miserable world of al-Aliya had settled into a distant corner of the mind where it made no trouble. I opened the door to al-Jaza'iri's apartment, walking softly, so as not to awaken Ruqayya from sleep, but no one was there. I would have liked to see her reaction to seeing me. When I saw my card empty just as I had left it, no desire to write anything materialized. It was as if not writing anything was a matter that had been settled and ended some time before, and need no longer concern me.

I heard footsteps in the corridor, so I hurried back to my own room. My heart began to beat like an adolescent's, but it was al-Baqqali who came in. He burst out reproachfully: "Where have you been? You're wasting the best days of the vacation!"

I laughed. "Nothing is being wasted."

"I'm hungry." We went into the kitchen, and I sensed his happiness when he saw the display of dozens of bottles of the finest drink.

"What do you want me to drink?"

"What do you want?"

He exclaimed like a child who couldn't contain his happiness: "The choice is mine?"

I smiled without answering, and he began to talk to himself: "Champagne, night is the time for it. Gin, whiskey, too strong for the middle of the day. I'll take this rosé."

"A good choice."

He brought the bottle to the modest table and licked his lips after the first sip, his eyes glowing. "Shall I pour you some?"

"Please."

"The girls are waiting for us on the beach."

"The whole group?"

"Yes—all alone."

The idea appealed to me. I was alone waiting for Ruqayya and a long, hopeless wait makes the heart despair. I quickly put my things in a small black bag, and we left for the beach, which was not far away.

Once we had passed the wall of huge trees that separated the sea from the city, the ocean rippled, displaying countless colors in small, random movements, while in the far west the waters were dark green, shading into azure.

The bathers were spread out over several miles, covering the sand of the beach with their bodies, forming a moving ribbon protecting the trees from the onrushing waters of the ocean. The breeze was cool and sweet, so most of them had stretched out and drifted into a pleasant siesta under the sun's rays.

The three Casablancans were doing the same, a small umbrella planted in the sand keeping the sun off their faces. I don't know why they seemed to lack something without al-Marrakeshi. When I asked about him al-Baqqali answered carelessly, as he cast amorous glances at the dark adolescent who had spent that short time with him, "You won't see him after today. He was only passing through al-Mohammediya. He has to travel for his job."

The girl with the honey-colored eyes made space for me. I lay close to her, because of the tight space, and the heat of her body spread to my forearm. The dark girl laughed over nothing, staring at me chidingly, and then smiling. I said, "Is there no way to avoid her being alone, without a companion?"

Al-Baqqali answered, "It doesn't matter."

He stretched out close to his dark girlfriend, leaving a patch of sand that was only large enough for my companion if she lay on her back. But she turned over on her right side and stretched out her arm, then patted the soft part of my shoulder with her fingers. I hesitated a long time before stretching out close to her. She hugged me and put her hand on my arm, hiding her pretty face in my chest.

I closed my eyes, and dreamed of Ruqayya in her place. Unconsciously I embraced her, the tender body lying in front of me, and she responded to the pressure, kissing me on the chest. I opened my eyes and froze in that state.

Close to me on the other side was an African with many pimples on his broad face, embracing a European woman whose hair was white as snow. It seemed as if they were in the purest moment of harmony that love could confect. His head was on the sand and his lips were nibbling her right ear, bringing her to a tremor of intoxication from time to time, which I felt when his sticky sweat moistened my arm, unknown to him. We were more than close, and we had to be careful of sticking to others before we slept; as for what happened when we dozed, that was something we didn't think about.

But I wasn't ready to sleep and there was something affecting me, perhaps the extreme crowding that turned the beach into one large band of sardines, too many for the can. The space at our heads was occupied by a Moroccan woman with captivating blue eyes. Her sturdy white body had crossed the line dividing the plump from the fat. It was very seductive, and as I unconsciously began to compare her with Ruqayya she shot me an indulgent, flirtatious look. I had a sudden burning desire to possess her. I had made love only to slender women, and I thought it would be a specific sort of pleasure to plunge into a mountain of soft flesh. The conversation of our eyes lasted only a few fleeting moments, swept away by a mistrustful look from her giant companion, which sent me back unconcernedly to the honey-colored eyes that were in my possession.

I lifted my head to speak to al-Baqqali and collided with the African's back, which seemed like a warm log. I said, "You didn't tell us the ladies' names."

It wasn't a significant matter for him. He drew close to his dark friend and said, in a voice that was nearly lost, as the stout Moroccan woman looked at us without interest, "Each one can introduce herself."

"Maryam."

"Rahima."

"Khadija."

I was afraid to collide with the black's back again, so I pulled Maryam to her feet, as she affected a flirtatious manner. As we stood on the cool beach I examined her. Despite her slenderness she had a well-proportioned body and a deep, provocative navel. Her bathing suit was blue with designs of red flowers, and when she moved a strip of brighter white skin appeared. I shivered—she had surprised me with cold water that filled her hands. I had a real fear of cold water, even though

I knew that it would not seem cold as soon as I plunged in. When she sensed that I had been surprised she came closer and began pouring cold water on my arm in a way that made me laugh uncontrollably. Then she drew me toward the water, and surprised me again with a splash of cold water. She began to run in front of me, and that meant the beginning of the game. I was less anxious for the game than I was to please her: I splashed her and then began to chase her. She threw herself into the water under my legs, and I stopped—I don't know why I thought of Ruqayya again! I don't know how long I was lost in the thought.

Maryam's hair fanned out in the water, a soft, spreading circle in a magic blue valley. She noticed my sudden coldness; how did I explain it? I don't know. She began to laugh. She liked the game and it seemed as if she was determined to succeed in it, to participate in it with all her limbs. She tripped me, and I fell on her, turning myself to the left for fear of hurting her.

Not far away al-Baqqali was lying with Khadija in the shallow water. I headed out to sea and swam, distancing myself from Maryam. But she had an amazing persistence: every time I thought she had become distant, no matter what direction I swam in, I found her near me. The water had lost its cold sting and had become inviting.

Suddenly I found myself in front of al-Baqqali, who was stretched out on his back in the shallow water, propped on his elbows, with Kahdija astride him. I stretched out on my back in an open space near the beach, with the water covering my middle and my chest when the waves came in; Maryam did the same and I sensed the heat of her body struggle with the cold of the water at my knee and my shoulder. Al-Baqqali and Khadija were sitting astride each other by turns in front of us, and we drew back a little toward the sea. I told her to watch the waves cover me and I had no sooner finished speaking than a wave did cover me, filling my mouth and nose and all the openings in my head with sand, salt and the smell of fish. I got up coughing, and she looked at me, disappointed; she had thought I was playing some game. Then she began to laugh, and her little skull with her hair sticking to it looked like the planet Earth without the seas. The water was dripping down over her swelling breasts and she moved her lips as if she wanted to say something; then the thought miscarried and the words were lost.

After al-Baqqali had been exhausted by what he called "riding horses in the sea," he borrowed a ball from a boy whose mother was about forty, pretty in an olive-colored bathing suit, with her hair in a huge braid. She smiled as she gave us the ball. Maryam hugged me and began biting my shoulder, which threw me into such confusion that I didn't know what to do. I began to pat her shoulder, as the woman said, "Ask for anything you want."

It was a kind of courtesy; what would one ask for in the sea but a ball? I said to al-Baqqali, "What do you think of her?"

He laughed. His eyes looked tired, deprived of sleep by passion, broadcasting frankly that he was a ladies' man who neither tired nor lost interest. He pointed to his arm muscle, smooth even when he bent it, and said, "I'm a man..." We moved away a little and he finished, "If it weren't for Khadija I would flirt with the mother." He began to laugh. "If Khadija stays here another week, I'll die!"

The two girls were walking a little behind us. I said, "But she's only spent three days with you!"

"Two and a half days." He looked at me. "I don't know which of us can't get enough!"

I laughed and hit him on his chest: "You!"

He was short in stature and thin, his deep-set eyes filled with desire. When he spoke he would pronounce his words emphatically and it would seem as if he were panting. For a long time I was at a loss to understand the secret of why girls liked him. When I couldn't figure it out I brought up the subject with him; the expression in his eyes deepened and he began to think seriously. To make things easier I wrote this equation, and asked him to fill in the blank with anything he could think of:

"5 percent good looks + short stature + ordinary thinking + _____ = a ladies' man."

He did not object to any of the parts of the equation. He began to laugh, took the paper and folded it with care and then put it behind a wretched picture he was proud of, a picture he had brought from Tetuan of a girl praying in the Christian way.

"I'll fill in the blank some day."

Now he said, as we were trying to avoid the many bodies stretched out on the sand, "Why are you neglecting Maryam?"

"I haven't neglected her."

"Are you preoccupied with that whore?"

"What whore is that?"

"The whole town knows! The new resident."

I laughed. "But I'm the only one who doesn't know anything."

"Are you sure?"

"Yes, except for one thing: she's not a whore."

"She buys men and spits them out after she's had her fill of them. I'm afraid for you."

Stopping near the sea, he looked at me with affection and begged, "Stay away from her, please. She's a sorceress. We know everything about her, and you're a stranger who doesn't know anything."

I put my hand on his shoulder affectionately: "A stranger when you're with me?"

"It's not the time to joke. You're neglecting Maryam, that alluring gazelle. It's not like you—why?"

"I don't seem to be aroused."

The two girls wrapped their arms around us. Al-Baqqali's words about Maryam made me discover aspects of her beauty moment by moment. The five of us began to play ball, each throwing it to the one facing. I was the weak link in the chain, since everyone had played sports on the beach since they were little, and that was an advantage I had not had in my miserable childhood. The circle grew by three young men attracted by the morsels we had hooked. I withdrew. Al-Baqqali noticed the presence of the strangers among us and their attempts to get close to the girls, and jealousy flared in his eyes. He took advantage of the ball falling into his hands and put it under his arm, running away with great speed, bounding over bodies and darting through groups. Khadija followed him, and I began to walk leisurely, while the three guys bombed us with ringing abuse. I reached him after a bit and found him panting among the girls. He spoke first: "They thought they would get the better of us!" I laughed, and he said, "Let's play soccer."

The place where we were standing was very crowded, so we withdrew to a small open space that obliged us to play with our nerves rather than our feet. I had no better luck with soccer than I'd had with volleyball; al-Baqqali was excellent at deception, and my backwardness was obvious from the first moments in front of the girls, so I was embarrassed. But the ball came to me one time and blessed my foot with a light touch. I was delighted by its approach and stopped it for a short moment, then I threw it hard toward the sea. The girls began laughing and al-Baqqali started to curse the beach and everyone on it, as he went down to the sea to get the ball. I went back to my place, which no longer existed. It was occupied by a dark young man whom I had often seen on the beach, stretched out and rubbing on suntan lotion for hours at a time, until his skin tanned and seemed half burned. He would lean on his elbows and smoke, and when he finished his cigarettes he would have recourse to me, in the way of someone who had known me since childhood: he would only point to the cigarette and extend his hands toward the package, without asking or thanking me, and then carelessly return to smoking and staring toward the open sea. I don't know why I imagined, when I saw him in his eternal pose, that he was waiting for a magic stroke of luck that would make one of the European women fall in love with him and extricate him from unemployment, ruin, and the killing wait for something that does not come. But what attracted me to him was his silence, which protected me from exposure to other people's affairs and from empty chatter, and his way of smoking: I sensed that he pulled the smoke into his deepest recesses, not allowing it to emerge until he had extracted every possible pleasure from it.

Now I found only a small patch no bigger than a square foot between him and the woman who had given us the ball. I sat down without asking permission and he moved over a little, so I was somewhat comfortable. The woman smiled again and made space for me under the umbrella. She said, "Stretch out and make yourself comfortable."

I stretched out under al-Baqqali's little umbrella, with my feet under hers. I closed my eyes. The sun had settled into the westernmost quarter of the sky, and its rays seemed too weak to combat the cool breeze: it made a wet body shiver and it inevitably also gave it goose bumps.

The lady opened a can of peppered tuna, put it on a crust of bread and then handed it to me. I refused because I did not feel hungry. She insisted, while her son looked at me with a big smile and asked, "Have you finished with the ball?"

His mother scolded him: "What will you do with it? You can't play with it alone, people will take it from you. Leave it with them."

Al-Baqqali was sitting on the ball with his face to the sea, giving a serious lecture to the three girls; from the gestures of his hands I sensed he was explaining a game they wanted to play. I called to him more than once. The Frenchwoman who was lying under the black man woke up, started at me angrily, and then returned to her warm dreams. When al-Baqqali turned and found me eating, he cried,

"Where did you get the food?"

I pointed to a stand near the beach.

"But I don't have any money."

"My clothes are in your bag—take some from my pocket."

The girls rushed toward us, beginning to protest: "And we won't eat?"

I laughed, and al-Baqqali called, "One of you come with me."

Khadija ran, and I said to him, "Bring seven bottles of lemonade."

I pointed with my eyes to the woman and her son so he wouldn't betray me with a question while she was watching me. I realized from her position that she didn't have any more than the bit she had given me. She had put a yellow striped towel over her thighs, and I was watching drops of sweat fall to the sand from under her arms, from time to time, despite the coolness of the breeze.

Rahima and Maryam sat near me, their mouths watering with hunger. The woman began to move her back between me and Maryam, who had made me feel that she was consecrated to me. I had wrapped my arms around my knees, so she wrapped her left arm around my knees and rested her head on my right shoulder, letting the breeze tickle my side with her hair, which had become woody with the sea and the sand, turning stiff and scratchy. She must have been looking at me from below; I did not try to discover it, but I saw the lady smiling widely, telling me of it. Maryam's right hand was playing with the hair of my thigh above the knee. The lady said, very proudly, "We are your neighbors."

She shook the sand from the towel, revealing her firm thighs, while her little boy hugged the ball and leaned on his mother. She must have realized my confusion as I mentally reviewed the residents of the few apartments neighboring mine.

"We rented the apartment of M. Boucher two weeks ago."

I smiled and said, "I didn't know that."

"He's going to spend two months in Lille and then return."

"I don't usually pay attention to who comes and goes."

"Do you remember the vinegar?"

"The vinegar?"

She laughed and her son laughed with her, sharing in something I didn't know. When she began to explain I remembered that the maid had turned away a boy who came asking for a little vinegar. When I asked her why she said that we only had half a bottle; at the time I had ordered her to take it to them, and when she returned I gave her money to buy a new bottle. She had protested at that, saying I didn't know how to deal with people and that they would take advantage of me. I laughed and accused her in turn of being lazy, annoyed at having to buy a new bottle of vinegar.

The boy's explanation was that he and his mother were alone, and that his father took all the money out of town.

When al-Baqqali came and saw me deep in conversation with them, he called, "Which of us needs to fill in the blank in the equation?"

I handed bottles of the drink to her and her son without paying attention to al-Baqqali, and she accepted them with a simplicity that nipped in the bud any heavy, affected courtesies. She began to talk to us about Khouribga, where her husband worked as an engineer in phosphates. The girls joined the conversation, and Khadija mentioned that her sister was married to a technician there. She did not manage to give a description that led the lady to the sister or her husband, and al-Baqqali whispered, "Your sister must be ugly."

"She's prettier than I am."

"Shall we go there and compare?"

She pinched him hard. "Damn you."

He said more loudly that he had been to that beautiful area but that he hated the taste of the water there. The lady did not argue, as it seemed she had adapted to the surroundings there. I said to her, "No one looking at you would believe you are from there!"

"Why?"

"Your teeth are not eaten away."

She laughed heartily, and slapped my hand in an innocent understanding that made Maryam jump; for a moment I thought I had said something I shouldn't.

She said, "You think about everything," and scrutinized me with a look that plumbed the depths. In a flirtatious manner she borrowed from the adolescents who surrounded her, she said, "My husband, Si Ahmad, has decided to invite you to lunch. His vacation begins Saturday morning, the day after tomorrow. It will please him to have the honor of meeting you; you are a kind man."

Al-Baqalli jumped in, pushing a huge bite into his cheek which assumed its shape: "We thank you."

Khadija burst out in a loud laugh, and everyone joined in. She said to him, "Why are you butting in?"

The lady looked at the ground without saying anything, the smile still filling her face. I felt the sting of a cold liquid: Maryam pouring her icy drink on my middle in front. I wanted to ask her why she chose that part of the body: out of desire or spite? But I did not; I made do with a laugh. It seemed she was trying to attract me by any means she could. She moved away, laughing. Al-Baqqali got up, chewing his last bite, and cried, "Follow me. I'm going to ask for a diving suit from a friend, and we can dive one after the other."

The girls followed him, and I ignored a seductive look from Maryam, closing my eyes. The cool breeze was pleasant, and its light gusts wiped away the fatigue and the headache that muddled my head whenever I stayed on the beach for a long time. The noise was loud, and the voices of the people playing in the large open space were contentious; but when my eyelids closed they let down a barrier shutting out the visible world and ending the world of daylight, preparing for the world of the depths to pour out its contents. Then Ruqayya comes to fill the world— her voice, her movements, her singing, her caprices…. At first everything seems like a small point, then it grows and grows until it becomes everything. Why do I feel this delicious numbness moving deep inside me and drawing me toward the unknown? Why am I disturbed, losing my reason and my feeling? Why am I not sorry for wasting these opportunities, which I never dreamed would be showered on me, since I saw Ruqayya?

I must have slept; I felt a gentle hand covering my chest with a yellow towel. How long did I doze? I don't know. The fatigue went away and the headache disappeared. I went back to my dreams, but with visions unaccompanied by numbness or intoxication. Sleep fled.

We returned at six, the sun then hitting the tops of the trees. But as we approached the casino it seemed strong again, chasing away the gentle, gray evening light. The Casablancans were talking with interest and pleasure about mosses and plants and colored rocks and extremely strange fish in the depths off the coast, though what excited them more than anything else was the large crabs. Al-Baqqali regretted that he had not caught any. Khadija said, consolingly, "Only the French eat them."

Rahima sighed. "Everyone eats them, but we pretend not to like them."

Maryam asked, "How can you catch them? They're frightening!"

"Yes, frightening! My God, their arms are longer than half a yard."

Al-Baqqali answered, "I learned from a Frenchman. You grab it on top near the head, hard, like this." He extended his fingers like pliers and caught one in the air. Then he added, "If I don't eat it I can sell it for thirty dirhems."

"How nice it would be for a man to become a fish," cried Khadija. She was extremely lively; her walk was like dancing. After she had emerged from the sea her rosy dark color had turned into the dark red of an apple. Returning in the evening by way of the casino lined by tall palms, by huge trees and by fragrant blossoms, was in and of itself an incomparable pleasure. It made Khadija walk as if she were lost in dreams, or swimming in a deep ocean.

Rahima answered, "They would hunt you and kill you!"

Khadija waved her hands as if she were executing a difficult, elegant dance movement. "Al-Baqqali caught me, and he's still eating me."

We laughed, and she gave us some of the white flowers, with their pleasant, penetrating scent, that she picked from hedges in front of the houses. "Here, smell these." She inhaled the scent with us. "They're wonderful!"

Al-Baqqali held the flower in his right hand and squeezed her waist. "You're the best catch in the sea or on land."

Then he kissed her, and she slipped away. She went up to a hedge to pick some flowers from near the door, but suddenly she fell to the ground. A dog, grandson of a wolf, had come from behind the hedge and attacked her. His rush and his bark were fierce and unexpected, making us shudder in astonishment—and had he not been attached by an iron chain which we heard rattling, we would not have been able to keep her from being torn to pieces.

We helped her up. Her face had darkened, and she was about to burst out crying as she brushed off what had stuck to her clothes. I don't know which of the other two girls started the laughter, but all of us soon followed her unconsciously and after a bit Khadija joined in also, embarrassed. She wiped her left elbow, which had been scratched, and extended her palm.

"There's blood."

Rahima said, "It doesn't matter, a little blood will clean the wound."

When we drew near to the Chinaman's building, al-Baqqali cried, "Are you going to come? It's the girls' last night."

Maryam was binding my steps with shining, silken threads.

"I don't know."

"You have to decide."

"It's not up to me."

The lady and her boy had drawn near, and al-Baqqali gave her a passing, doubtful look. She was watching the boy dribbling the ball in front of him with a quick motion, preceding her and then turning around her. Al-Baqqali said, "You're welcome at our house."

I answered, without interest, "I know that."

We stood for a few moments chatting about Khadija's wound and bandaging it. What scared Khadija, however, was the unforeseen consequences of the bad fall she had had. She said that everyone in her family had been affected by sudden illnesses after similar falls, so I smiled and winked at al-Baqqali. "Al-Baqqali has an effective treatment for falls."

She asked seriously, "What is it?"

Al-Baqqali laughed: "Never mind, he's joking."

I swore that I was not joking, so he insisted that I say what it was. So I said, smiling and mixing seriousness and joking, "Getting so drunk that you see…"

Rahima interrupted, finishing, "A monkey and think he's an ass."

We all laughed, then I finished, "Exactly. Then restful sleep."

Al-Baqqali took her hand and said goodbye to me. "We'll try that."

Khadija argued, "Why not? It's to your benefit too."

Maryam looked at me reproachfully. I was afraid to look at her, as I walked into the corridor of the building. The face of the boy peered down at me from above, eating a banana. He leaned on the banister, smiling winningly, proud of having arrived ahead of me.

chapter 12

I didn't see any light in al-Jaza'iri's room, so I was overcome by the dejection I felt at similar times when I was lonely. It was accentuated by the pale light of the corridor, which colored the small entryway with wretchedness.

I feared loneliness, and its worst times for me were between seven and nine. Before seven everyone was active, making dates and agreements, and if someone had the good fortune to get a date then he would spend the short time remaining preparing for it. If he failed, that meant he would amble alone, knocking on the doors of coffee shops, which closed around eight. That left only bars, movies, and wandering around, all of which ended around nine and did not satisfy. After that he'd be tired and would give himself to reading or listening to the news before plunging alone into a deep sleep.

My life proceeded in this fashion until I discovered the casino, which attracted me with its strange world contending over money—tens, hundreds, thousands of people rushing headlong to the green tables. Then luck emerged like a reckless giant striking irrationally, like blind fate choosing both the fortunate and the loser, at the roulette and baccarat tables. This game of money transformed the ennui of the long night.

I rushed immediately to the bathroom to wash the salt off my body under the shower. The air wasn't cold, but I still felt the pleasure of the hot water as if it had been winter.

"The impudent rascal has returned!"

My despair disappeared all at once, and the light returned to tear away the darkness; but I began to shiver under the hot shower. Why? I had lost my mind again. It was a good thing that she wasn't seeing me so disturbed in front of her. What's this, where's my manhood? I did not answer her; I had lost my voice.

She must have been hiding in the kitchen when I came in. Her sun and her music were reflected in shades and tones that flooded the room and overflowed to fill the calm with happiness. Even the light in the bathroom became stronger and brighter. I wanted to come out immediately, but I contained myself.

"Why don't you answer? Did you drown under the shower?"

I laughed loudly and happily. "What do you want?"

She opened the door, and I concealed my nakedness.

"Don't pull into your shell, I've seen everything."

"Aren't you ashamed?"

"There's nothing to be ashamed of."

"Isn't that odd?"

"I like to watch a man swimming naked."

"How many times have you watched?"

"A lot…"

"Aren't you afraid?"

"I'm not afraid of anything."

Why did I feel such happiness even when she was interfering in my affairs and invading my privacy? My God, how happy I was! Especially when I lost myself in following her voice, in its rising and falling volume!

Nonetheless I covered myself and cried, "Close the door!"

"And if I don't?"

"I'll stay here until Judgment Day."

She plunged into laughter, and my happiness increased. "Fine, I'll stay here till Judgment Day."

I pleaded with her, "I'll be out of hot water soon, it's a small tank."

She kept the door a little open and I heard her dragging a chair to sit near the door. She asked me, "How did you get into my room?"

My heart began to beat violently. She had seen the gift, then. "The door was open." I was lying. Why?

She cried, "How stupid of me!"

"And how did you get into my room?"

"The maid was here."

"When did you come?"

"I'm not required to answer your questions," she laughed.

In fact it was a silly question. I asked, "But aren't you afraid of staying in my apartment while I'm out? My friends might come over and try to seduce you."

"I'd throw them out. Now come out, you've been in there a long time. Are you a girl?"

I was even more anxious to see her than she was to see me, but I was wasting time on purpose. I had finished dressing and stood staring at her through the small opening, without getting enough of her. But she pushed the door open suddenly, so the steam from the hot water spilled out, and she drew back. It looked as if she was rising to heaven on the back of the clouds. Then she began to help me dry my short hair. I asked her, "Do you like family life?"

"No."

"But you seem to enjoy helping me."

"I like a little of it."

"Were you unhappy as a child?"

"Why? You're impudent. How can you ask such a question?"

"What's wrong with it?"

"And you, were you unhappy as a child?"

"Do you see unhappiness in my eyes?"

Her hands were on my shoulders. A moment before she had dried my ears, tickling me. Now she stopped still and I stared at her with mad joy.

She said, "I see only tremendous happiness, happiness with roots in the depths of the earth."

"Then how can you ask me that question?"

She began smoothing my hair with her hands, and I absorbed from her fingertips the greatest gift of pleasure given to me in my entire life by the sense of touch. It was a mixture of suppleness, abundance, delicacy, and tenderness, an elixir from the paradise of dreams in compassionate touches.

I took courage and took her face between my palms. Her hair was deepest black, a pirate dancing in the sunlight, a stream surrounding her with a crown undreamt of by the proudest queen. The blue color under her eyes had merged with the black of her eyelashes and the white of her creamy, radiant face. The red of her rosy lips called deeply to me to pluck the fruit, but I restrained myself, and hesitated.

"Looking at you is happiness always."

She laughed and moved away from me, her pistachio green dress a forest enclosing the sun.

"Were you pampered?"

"Very pampered!"

She approached again and touched my short hair, as if she

wanted to live through her senses. "Your hair is really ugly! Why did you cut it like that?"

"Because of the summer, the sea, and your relative's lack of skill."

"My relative?"

"Yes, the Algerian barber near Si l-Habib."

She laughed again, and I began to be intoxicated. She asked, "Are all Algerians relatives?"

"And all are your admirers."

She sat on the chair, her hair spread over her back. I felt indescribable happiness, like a thief who has made the theft of a lifetime and now is afraid of the extremity of his own happiness. She said, "And you?"

"My admiration borders on devotion."

She laughed. "I'm sure of that. But you haven't told me…"

"What should I say?"

"Whether you were pampered."

I laughed. "I used to find a crust of bread most of the time."

She laughed, and then was suddenly silent. With a serious expression, she asked,

"Do you mean that others didn't?"

"Certainly, just the way it is in your country."

She fled immediately from the pain, laughing loudly. She threw me a sharp glance and pursed her lips, and I dreamed of kissing them. She said, "I would like to see a woman more beautiful than me."

"Have you ever seen one in the past?"

She smiled, and her teeth shone. She took the question seriously and began to think. I said, "I don't think so. Maybe there is someone more perfectly formed, but she's not more lovely. And yet, the fingertips that sculpted you will continue to lose their way…"

She surprised me with a torrent of French, and I began to laugh. "What did you say?"

"I answered you with an expression as beautiful as yours, and I used French, because my Arabic isn't good."

I took her hand and kissed it, saying, "You poor thing. I'm not playing with words, I just say what I feel."

Her eyes filled all of existence for me, its past and its present, its good and its evil. I began to experience her as a transparent glass idol plunged deep into my soul. I was overcome by desire that burned my blood, but I despised myself for not being able to do any more than kiss her hand. I didn't dare continue. She asked, "What did you buy me, you impudent rascal?"

"Do you like it?"

"How did you choose it?"

I moved away and sat down in front of her, calling upon every bit of composure I possessed, as the whirlpool of her presence intoxicated me. "Would you believe that I don't know what I bought? I didn't see anything. One of my students came by, and she chose it for me."

"Are you in a relationship with her?"

"What gives you that idea?"

"The underwear that she bought."

I was devouring her, her body, her spirit, her laugh. I was burning! And there was no doubt that it was her spirit that was burning me. I said, "May I see it now?"

"I've put them on." Then she chuckled: "You're asking a lot."

"I'm not the first to enter Paradise."

She laughed again, and opened just two buttons of her outer dress. Between them I saw a brassiere and a chemise, each a light sky-blue.

"I've paid your price. Do you want to see the third piece?"

She began to fasten the buttons, smiling. I moaned and shook my head. "That's enough."

She laughed loudly. "You're lying, that's not enough for you."

"It's a first step. I have stamina."

"You're not going to get anything real."

She turned in the air, after adjusting her clothes, filling the air, and my nose, with her perfume.

"What did we want to buy yesterday?" she asked.

"What?"

"A nightingale. I got one today."

I brought out two bottles of beer. "Where is it?" I asked, hoping that the intoxication that enveloped me would never go away.

"I had lunch with him. I made him have lunch with me."

"The nightingale?"

"Yes," she laughed. "Si l-Habib."

"Si l-Habib? Where did you find him?"

"He was strolling near the fish market so I took him into custody. I pushed him into an out-of-the-way restaurant. My God, how little he eats! A real nightingale."

The intoxication dissipated, and I drank my beer without pleasure. She had begun to move away, to torture me. She said, "Why is he running away from me?"

I cried, in pain: "Why are you running away from me?"

She paid no attention to my pain, and the situation was delicate. I said, "What do you know about Si l-Habib?"

"Everything."

"How do you explain it?"

She said, "He's afraid of love. His heart is weak."

"Perhaps. But that's not important. Do you know how high he rose before he became ill?"

"Yes."

"And what he has now?"

"I don't know."

I said, "Nothing, except for a clean reputation, which embodies the reputation of the popular movement. He doesn't want to stain that reputation by any action his political enemies could exploit. That means you are asking for prodigious qualities that are rarely found together in a single man—a man who loves to drink but who does not drink, who can love but does not love…"

I had intended to speak with obvious sharpness; but when she began to drink her eyes started to shine, and I was afraid I would return to worshipping that fire that was burning me silently. It occurred to me that I was getting tired of my weakness and insignificance for her.

She answered coldly, "I have no objection to going down to him at night without anyone seeing me, or without anyone's knowledge."

I trembled, and was unable to speak. It was as if everything had lost its value. I felt that jealousy had begun to gnaw at my heart. "And yet here I am, knowing even before the fact."

She laughed. "You won't tell anyone. I have confidence in you."

I shuddered and cried, "Stop!"

"I love him. Do you know the meaning of love?"

My eyes flashed. "Yes. A few days ago I made its acquaintance by chance, at Si l-Habib's place."

She plunged into laughter, then stood up and put her arm around my shoulder, her sweet scent overwhelming me. She tickled my ear with her teeth, and I was submerged in wondrous pleasure. She said, "Help me."

She took my hand, but her tone was devoid of pleading, entreaty or any sign of weakness. I realized that she was profiting from my weakness and my love for her.

"How?" I asked.

"Stay away from him."

I laughed. "Are you joking?"

She too laughed. "No. No, I'm not joking." Her laughter continued. "Why won't you stay away from him?"

"Are you serious?"

"Yes."

"But you won't stop laughing!"

"I'm like that," she replied. "I achieve my goals by the most beautiful means."

"But where would I go?"

"It's a wide world." Her laugh, her smile, her manner, all were devoid of seriousness. She added, "Why do you stick to him—you and that statue, Si Qobb?"

She threw me into confusion. "I found this circle for myself," I said. "I feel happy in it. I don't intend to change the way things are."

I felt great pride that she was with me, coming into my room when she liked and behaving as if she were part of me. I wasn't able to express my desires with anything like her courage and spontaneity, and that's what lit the fire in my gut, torturing me and compelling me to worship her, to sanctify her, even if that fire moved into her hands and burned everything around her. All I could do was submit and wait; perhaps in the great fire there would be something that would cleanse my spirit and bring it peace.

She said, "All men love me and submit to me. But I never found the great love that would make me get down on my knees to keep it going or hold onto it, and I've found it in Si l-Habib."

"But he does not return your love."

"Perhaps not. But if he did love he would love with all he has, with his soul, for the sake of love. Don't you see that he sacrificed his health and his future and was nearly executed for the sake of a cause?"

"His country!"

"A country, a woman, they're the same thing. He's capable of sacrifice, and sacrifice creates great love… a great cause… great hope…"

Only then did a captivating seriousness blend with her smile.

I also smiled. "And me?"

She pursed her enchanting lips as if she were getting them ready for a kiss. "You aren't right for me: too young for sacrifice, poor, not attractive, average. You don't have a car or a political position, and you're not an artist."

All of that was true. I stayed silent. It was a severe, electric shock. Pain and anger and jealousy raged within me. But I did not let anything show, and tried to keep my features unchanged. As the twittering of the birds outside began to subside and disappear with the arrival of the dark, a killing despair began to grow inside me.

She finished, "But I don't dismiss your friendship. Let's remain friends."

I answered, as if the words were coming from another man, "I'm not prepared for that role. I value friendship, but I love you, and I feel pain when I see you with anyone else."

She cried, "That's jealousy!"

I nodded. "In spite of myself."

She laughed heartily, then got up, put her arm around me and kissed me on the forehead.

"My dear friend, come with me."

"Where to?"

"Casablanca."

I didn't move. Yesterday's trip had been delicious, and I had stuffed myself; I hadn't digested it yet. My spirit was still intoxicated by her radiance, which lit up my existence. I said, "I want to absorb the melodies into my being and my blood before I hear any others."

She poured the rest of the beer into her glass and drank it all. For a moment it seemed to me that I was seeing the drink flowing through her clear, glowing skin. She touched me. "We won't go to Zina's."

"Then where?"

"You'll see something new that you've never seen in your life. You'll feel pleasure exceeding anything you felt at Zina's, and you'll be sorry if you don't come."

I had closed my eyes, allowing the echoes of her voice to reverberate in my depths, amazing me, plunging me into rapture, taking me to the enchanting, happy air in which I had circled yesterday. It wouldn't hurt me to accompany her to her special worlds, for anything in al-Mohammediya was available to me every night, and the new always has its own pleasant, unexpected aroma.

"I'll show you things that will shake your concepts of manhood and marriage and happiness. What do you say?"

"Wait for me a moment while I go see Si l-Habib."

"I'll go down with you."

I insisted: "No, I won't let you this time. I don't want to seem to be a partner with you in this plot that I don't accept. Do what you like alone."

She laughed, making me drunk. "All right. Don't be long."

"A moment only."

I hurried down the stairs but I stepped on something slippery, a piece of soap, a melon rind, a banana... I rolled down the stairs and I fell on the edge of the middle stair. The world trembled and shook, and then in the flash of an eye I was at the bottom. At first I didn't feel any pain, but a sticky fluid covered my eyes and a strong light burned them. My left leg was paralyzed. I tried to get up; my head nearly exploded, my body was too heavy to bear, and I fell again, groaning in spite of myself. The pain disappeared, along with flashes of the pale light of the stairwell, and the noise of doors opening and cries for help. Afterwards there was deep darkness, and peace.

chapter 13

I saw Ruqayya's features in every face I saw, be it beautiful or ugly, as I searched for her beauty in different, specific proportions. Her beauty was exceptional, and perhaps she herself was an exceptional case. If people's facial features are connected, in that they are copies of an original, closer to it or more distant in terms of beauty and charm, that only meant that Ruqayya was human. Without that connection I would have thought she was a dream, no more and no less.

My imagination did not budge. I was completely prepared to do anything in order to remain with her, for life is too short to waste it in deprivation. Perhaps that was also what distinguished this contradictory human connection, in which weakness on my part and strength on hers changed into two inseparable things, each completing the other, forming a unit in which things were inverted to their opposites. Thus the unit would equalize the opposites, and would be a sufficient reason to continue the most miserable, filthy, and wretched human states. If it were not for gradations in beauty and ugliness, in strength and weakness, then the moral equation would be balanced in every instance, doing away with our relative concepts of nobility and filth, of honor and baseness.

Her voice, her singing, her whispers, her glances, everything in her.…Just seconds ago I had discovered the beauty of something new, her neck: a thousand sculptors working together would still fail to reproduce its polished beauty. I reserved in advance all I possessed of pride, manhood, and self for the sake of something that demanded sacrifice. I had learned that I must pay any price to be near her, that I must do away with anything that forced me to separate from her.

Yet I was forced to separate from her twice, and this was the first time. When I opened my eyes I sensed that the right one was dark, and I remembered the fall and the sticky liquid, and the pain in my leg; and I saw myself fastened to a leg in a cast, raised up, leaving me with dull pains in my back and my other leg.

The fall was tremendous, and had I not unconsciously put my hands on my head I would have been in another world.

There's nothing harder than the loneliness and calm of a hospital, and since my pain was minor, I begrudged it.

The light was coming from behind, from a window along the wall, which lit the small white room. It was extremely clean. On the right was a closed door which I assumed led to the facilities, and in the window near my bed stood a vase of red roses, pruned with care so that they would not take up too much space in the room. From under the roses bravely grew two stems of another climbing plant, of the cat's claw variety, which turned the right window pane and sill green, arranged to provide a fitting background for the red roses.

Since the bed nearly touched the wall on the left side, I kept exhausting myself in the effort to enjoy the view through the window. The first face I saw belonged to the head nurse, a

Frenchwoman of fifty. Her pale eyes were insistently searching for the quay in life like a ship that had not been anchored since it was first launched. Her blond hair was mixed with some scattered gray, but the care she expended on herself made her look at first glance as if she were at least ten years younger.

She smiled, and poured out a stream of French, and then Moroccan Arabic. She asked me if I felt pain or hunger. I answered that I wanted to smoke, and she just laughed. I tried in vain to find out how long I had been unconscious; then she left, smiling. I must still have been under the influence of the anesthesia; I plunged into a deep sleep in which the songs I had heard at Zina's recurred insistently, along with a throng of clashing tones and voices in chorus. Then they began to disappear, leaving only "*Friends, it's been three days since I've seen my gazelle*" leaping in the confines of my internal world. When I awoke the second time there was only a dispiriting, faint light over my head, making me feel a sharp depression, and dispersing the impression of the beautiful day. But fortunately my second wakening also did not last long, and I returned once again to my conflicting dreams.

The first thing I asked of Ruqayya when she visited me was that they place my bed facing the window. That required a lot of effort, and I saw many of the male and female nurses for the first time, as they helped turn the bed around. Although Ruqayya stayed with me for more than an hour, it passed as if it were a moment, for my longing for her was a desert that could not be irrigated. I learned that she and Si l-Habib had insisted on transporting me to Casablanca in the car of Si l-Miludi, who had just begun eating his supper. He had refused to accept payment, and she and Si l-Miludi had stayed with me until they were certain, from the X-rays, that my skull wasn't cracked. I learned I had stayed under the anesthesia for fourteen hours after the operation, and that the wound over the eye was not dangerous; it had taken only three stitches, and after three days the bandages would be removed and the stitches taken out. I also learned that Si l-Habib could visit me only with the agreement of the police, whose suspicions he must not arouse in any way whatsoever.

All these things, so interesting to her, seemed inconsequential compared to one thing. I asked her, "Where will you spend the night?"

"In Casablanca."

I felt pain. "I wish I could go with you." She laughed, without answering. I added, "If only you knew how jealousy is tearing me apart."

She patted my outstretched hand, and winked. "Jealousy is a weakness. Are you jealous of Si l-Habib?"

"No."

"You're lying."

"Are you going with Si l-Habib now?"

"No."

"Then why are you bringing him into this?"

"Because I love him."

"Now only?"

She laughed loudly. "Now."

Why was I torn to pieces when I heard she would spend the night in Casablanca? Even if she were alone…. She was like the rushing wind that stirred up storms and made victims wherever it went.

She said, "You're silent."

"Will you visit me?"

She nodded. "Every time I get to Casablanca."

"So I'm a secondary reason for coming?"

She laughed heartily. "Don't ask for more."

She kissed me lightly on the mouth. Then she presented me with a gold chain bearing a pendant on which was inscribed the initial *shin,* for Al-Sharqi, the name imposed on me here, in an attempt to make me feel that she had not forgotten a friend. She placed the small box under my pillow.

Her nearness had inundated me with her fragrance, which I had missed since we separated, and with her femininity, which now as then makes me feel that it overflows the universe. It filled the space she occupied when she bent over me, leaving traces there that remained as long as I stayed in the hospital.

It needed no more effort than closing my eyes briefly to feel her, her breasts, her scent, her kiss, the sound of the kiss, her soft, elegant fingertips with their charming movements, the rustle of her flowered silk dress before she once again put on the jellaba, the voice like the sound of birds.

She deceived me, for it's impossible that she only came to Casablanca that once, and it's impossible that she spent her evenings in al-Mohammediya that whole time.

On the average I received one or two visits daily. Si Sabir came a number of times, and al-Baqqali came regularly. Over the thirty-one days I spent there, during which I was forcibly separated from Ruqayya, I was visited by people whose relationship with me wasn't close: Si l-Arabi, for example; al-Miludi, the taxi driver, who visited me three times; the Chinaman who owned the apartment building; Si Ibrahim the grocer, and his gallant namesake, Si Ibrahim, who gave up the beautiful Aisha for me. Since the hospital was not far from the bus stop for al-Mohammediya, I realized that I was not the object of these visits, that it was no more than a pleasant diversion they preferred to loitering pointlessly until it was time for the bus. As soon as we began to approach four in the afternoon I would see them looking anxiously at their wristwatches.

I enjoyed it. At the same time, within my breast I fanned the flame of my terrible, disturbing watch for her. I would talk and laugh with my eyes on the door, perhaps unconsciously giving my visitors the impression that they were no more than the prelude to an enjoyable film that would be shown shortly.

Nonetheless the strangest visit was from "the lady of the vinegar," whom we had chanced to meet on the beach with her little boy, who owned the ball.

It was a pleasant evening, during the hour after my bandages were removed, and I was enjoying looking with both eyes at the garden blooming with flowers, predominantly purple ones. I was following a nightingale of the black kind whose face is only a large circle notched in the middle, reaching up on each side to challenge the sky. He sat where he could broadcast his enchanting melodies to the patients, through their windows.

What astounded me about him was his perseverance in his two daily shifts: the morning one, which began about ten and continued until noon, and the evening one, which began at four and continued until darkness fell. His practiced throat looked more like a hanging sack. He would wake me with short phrases, leave to earn his living, then return at the appointed time.

A small companion might be with him sometimes, adding her tunes to his and learning from him how to sing. But like any young, immature girl, she must have been attracted by many things, for she would absent herself unexpectedly, without affecting his perseverance or the torrent of his melodies.

Al-Shaqra and her flirtatious friend came in, preceded by their adolescent laughter, a mixture of daring and embarrassment. After they took off their face veils, al-Shaqra begged me to forgive her, apologizing for not being able to come before.

I reassured her that I had not thought about the matter; her friend Zainab laughed loudly and sat near my head, while al-Shaqra chose the place facing me. But Zainab loved to joke, and she began to chide al-Shaqra for neglecting me and not visiting me. I didn't know whether it was a play of their own invention or whether the inspiration came from foreign, western elements Zainab was imitating to amuse herself with my feelings, as usually happened in politics and love, so I was as cautious as someone walking through a minefield. Zainab, however, said to her, "Prove that you're in love." I was watching, smiling, when al-Shaqra burst into bitter tears, and I didn't know what to do. I recalled that when we met she had hinted that I had neglected her, especially after her flirtatious friend Zainab had succeeded in bringing down al-Qadiri, and now she began to scold me for neglecting her.

The tears were real and accompanied by deep sobs. Zainab began to retreat, addressing me as "professor"; I chided her, and she returned to calling me "Si l-Sharqi." She assured me that al-Shaqra had been thinking of me constantly since…. She couldn't finish, and I supplied, "Since you met Si l-Qadiri."

She blushed in real embarrassment, until her cheeks became two captivating apples, increasing the charm and allure of her face.

They both belonged to the world of the older high-school girls, together with Zahra Barhu. The three of them would flow in a current which one of them would create, the other two throwing themselves after her into the waves. Zahra had a soft, undulating body and sleepy, honey-colored eyes; and after she succeeded in discovering the way to Si Faiq's house, taking advantage of his wife's trip to Wazarzat to give birth, it happened that Si l-Qadiri had remained in the classroom a few minutes after six in the evening, when the last class ended. He was gathering his things when he discovered that Zainab and al-Shaqra were alone. He joined their laughter as they went out, and the laughter found fertile ground, which Zainab planted and then quickly reaped. She had set her traps: a flow of glances, questions about his health and well-being, and his spending time far from his family. At that point al-Qadiri realized that he had before him easy prey with no fatal consequences, especially as she was at the end of her last year of school. He said that he saw such lust in her eyes that he knew she would not be satisfied even if she slept with all the men in al-Mohammediya. He had to be careful or the pleasure would turn into a scandal, and he was not too dense to stop her at her limit. He went to the last round with her but with great care, fearing to inflate her narrow waist.

Al-Qadiri was among my best friends, so it was to be expected or even certain that al-Shaqra would be with me; the way was prepared and sure. But at the end of the year and for specific personal reasons I had turned down several double dates. That must certainly have affected al-Shaqra, as she began to give me a complete list of the times I had rejected or ignored her. Then she explained to me how she had not been able to come because of his watchfulness, and when I asked her who was watching her, she looked at me in disbelief, raising her eyes. Her tears had ruined her carefully applied eyeliner. She looked as if she had been crying for a long time, the small space around her golden irises mixed with red. She said, "Si l-Hansali."

"Al-Hansali—the security officer?"

The light coming from the garden divided Zainab's face in half, dark and light. "Yes."

His complexion was dark, his stature short and thin, and he had a cold manner. The difference between their bodies, their looks, and their ages was enormous, although all these differences would have disappeared if there were love between them. I used to meet him to renew my residency permit, and he seemed organized, bureaucratic, and stiff, in opposition to the personal freedom his fiancée enjoyed. I began to imagine how she would look after marriage, struggling to retain the kind of behavior she was used to, which would now depend on how her husband reacted to her.

I said, "What are these puzzles?"

Zainab interrupted: "She told me she had told you!"

I looked at al-Shaqra questioningly, and she assured me she had told me in the store the last time we met. Zainab put her hand on my bare forearm, and I had the odd thought that she was going to pinch me. "I'll tell you, Professor." She began to flirt, moving seductively as she usually did. "Do you know why she didn't tell you? Because you hate the police, and she didn't want to shock you."

I shrugged. "I was talking about the police in my country."

Al-Shaqra smiled as she wiped her tears and asked me to forgive her. I assured her again that I bore her no ill will. Then Zainab told me that they had come to Casablanca to shop, and that otherwise they would not have been allowed to come. I asked al-Shaqra seriously, "Do you love him?"

She and Zainab exchanged glances again. There was no need for either of them to say that they had exhausted the topic from A to Z. Zainab said, "What's important is that he's a man."

I looked at al-Shaqra reprovingly and shook my head, for she was expecting an attack from me. Her face darkened again, but I said nothing. She added, "I can't do anything about it. My father says that a girl must marry."

"And love?"

"He says it's worthless."

I continued: "Zainab is better than you."

Zainab smiled, as if she didn't deserve this praise.

"Why?"

"She enjoyed herself at least."

Al-Shaqra again burst into tears. "You're the reason."

Zainab laughed, and her face reddened in embarrassment after she made the mistake of calling me "professor," and she apologized. She said, "I've found work in Tangiers, and I'm leaving at the beginning of next month. As you see, we're splitting up: al-Zahra is in Casablanca, al-Shaqra is getting married, and I'm going to Tangiers."

"You'll be near Si l-Qadiri."

Her face colored again. She extended her hand in pain, as if she were pushing away what I said. "I'll only see him during the vacation—one more month and then he'll return to al-Mohammediya and I'll stay in Tangiers." Then she was silent, and looked at me. "You'll make up for everything you've missed in the future."

I stared at her, as al-Shaqra's eyes beamed happy promises. I said, "I don't understand."

"After marriage, the door is open for you."

The door did open, unexpectedly, cutting off her voice. The opening of the door was the worst possible intervention, stopping a stream of important, interesting words about the most delicate of topics in an absurdly silly way.

A modern woman of forty whom I had not met entered, followed by a short man wearing glasses that magnified his eyes and covered his face; the latter tapered to a sharp point, giving him earnest, fox-like features. A smile floated on his face, hesitant, feminine, and embarrassed, as if he doubted very much that it would be acceptable to others.

His wife strode in, a look of determination on her face, with its pretty features and large eyes. It was as if she were giving him strength by means of an effective control that blocked all roads. I was still astonished.

Then I began to recognize her features—where had I seen her? The door remained open and I nearly signaled to al-Shaqra to close it, but I suddenly remembered the face. I smiled and extended my hand. I shook hands with her and her husband, noticing the great difference between her tender hand and his firm grip.

Since there were only two chairs in the room the girls gave them up, after the refusal required by good manners, and sat near me on the bed. The situation seemed comical, and I hid my laughter several times: my suspended leg was now on the level of their heads, and their left hands had to touch my right, sound leg when they leaned on it as they sat down.

The woman smiled widely, preparing to speak, but I still found it odd and unlikely that they would take the trouble to visit me without a strong acquaintance or solid friendship. There was nothing between us beyond a passing encounter dictated by a dwelling that had been chosen at random.

She was wearing a dress of pink satin that was trimmed with lace, showing her firm forearms and modestly covering her chest. Her hair seemed to be arranged with care, falling to her shoulders. There was a great difference between her and the lady of the vinegar in her bathing suit on the beach; I unconsciously said to myself: What a woman can do! But I could not comprehend the motive that led them to visit me.

"We've come to apologize," she said

It was incomprehensible to me at first. I exchanged glances with al-Shaqra and Zainab, who smiled, and the nightingale began singing for the second time. His tones rose clearly in the few brief moments in which quiet dominated our speech.

"Why?"

Zainab looked at me. "We also apologized when we came in."

The woman began to examine the long nail of her index finger. I said, "You've taken the trouble to come, and I'm grateful to you."

"We are the reason for all of this."

"You are the reason?"

I didn't understand anything. The woman looked at her husband, as if she were permitting him to repeat something memorized, and he said mechanically, "Yes, we're the reason."

I laughed. "I was in a hurry. I don't blame anyone."

"Wait." His voice was husky, clear and strong, as if it were an echo coming from a concealed source I could not place. "Si Muhammad threw a banana peel on the stairs, even though we've told him more than once never to throw anything anywhere but in the garbage. It's a crime, a real crime."

Things were entangled in my mind, memories mixed, and a great perplexity grew in me. His true voice was in complete harmony with the harsh confession of error that he poured out before me. Something I stepped on…. If it weren't for that, I wouldn't be here, in fact. That hateful, slippery thing.

"It was God's grace to you and to him. If anything more than this had happened, God forbid, I would have turned him over to the police. God prevented the worst."

He was clearly determined, and his words came from the heart, but nonetheless I hesitated to believe him. Did such idealism exist? At that point I thought miserably about what would have happened to the boy and not to me, as a hush filled the room, imposed by the seriousness of the speaker. At that moment the voice of the nightingale became clear again, its enchanting tones reverberating around us. The woman continued, her eyes a flag of sorrow above the promise on her face: "You're a good man who fears God; you don't deserve all this pain and suffering."

The man said, "It's bad upbringing."

"You treated us very well," she added.

"And we repaid you badly. Oh, woe betide us!"

It would have been a cause for laughter if that formal expression had appeared in an ordinary conversation, but when he pronounced it I felt the extent of what had happened to me. They were both trying seriously to show me how much they regretted not only my fall but also their child-rearing skills.

I smiled. "I have forgiven him. It was an unintentional mistake. Please forgive him too."

"And his upbringing?" the father interrupted. He took off his glasses, completely altering the appearance of his face, and wiped the lenses, trembling with anger. "Isn't it a lost cause?"

I responded, to lighten matters: "Don't look at it from the viewpoint of loss or gain. I believe it will be an important lesson, and that he won't do anything like that ever again. We all harm one another by our behavior."

"He must be punished. We're keeping him away from the beach for a week."

I replied, "That's a severe punishment."

"You suggest something."

"Forgive him."

"You must suggest something."

"One day away from the beach."

She looked at her husband. "Didn't I tell you he's a good man?"

I felt that the praise was false. I said, "Let's see him first. Where is he?"

The woman laughed. "Behind the door."

I called, "Come in, Si Muhammad."

The woman repeated my summons more than once, before getting up. Then he came in repentant, hanging his head, and shook my hand. I kissed him, as his parents returned to scolding him and warning him against bad behavior in the future. Al-Shaqra and Zainab got up, the latter moving flirtatiously. "We don't want to be late for the bus."

"Go with monsieur and madame, it's the same road."

The man welcomed them: "We'll take you in the car."

I had not introduced them to each other, a bad mistake which I now realized. I hastened to make the introductions with a theatrical movement, which everyone took for the beginning of an expressive speech. I started by how the lady of the vinegar had painted al-Mohammediya and its residents; the two girls unexpectedly felt themselves on firm ground, and let loose more laughter and compliments. At that point they looked like a very harmonious threesome, despite how much older the woman was.

Al-Shaqra insisted on inviting the family to lunch along with Zainab. The lady accepted, but said she'd come by herself, since her husband was going back to Khouribga the next morning; but the husband announced that he would be pleased and happy to meet good people, reassuring himself about leaving his family in their care. Then he ended the conversation in his husky voice, speaking severely: "If it were not for working at Khouribga I would visit you daily. But madame will visit you in my place, from time to time. I must make up for what Si Muhammad did."

I have heard many promises, some of which died immediately after leaving the speaker's lips, like a seed dying in a salty swamp. But when he made that promise I sensed that the seed would grow on the surface of a solid, fertile mountain, unaffected by all the volcanoes and earthquakes in the world.

Al-Shaqra pretended to be busy reattaching her face veil. When she was sure they had gone out she came over and kissed me on the mouth, while Zainab blocked the door with her body, as if she were guarding it against an imaginary demon.

"I'll visit you again."

Zainab signaled with her eyes and smiled broadly, revealing her experience in this area. She opened the door a little for al-Shaqra to pass, and I chided her, jokingly, "If your fiancé agrees."

Zainab laughed, and I added, "Bring him with you."

I waved to her. Her lips had left a new, sweet taste, previously unknown to me. This was the second time during my stay in the hospital in which I kissed a girl without having sought the kiss, and it seemed to me that these two kisses alone made up for all my long years of deprivation and all my burning nights, all throughout my life.

My leg was lowered from its suspended prison after fourteen days. I was given the choice of going home, with a cast and a long list of instructions that I must be careful to follow to the letter, or of remaining for seven more days. I chose to remain in the hospital. The expenses were paid by the mutual aid association, and care was guaranteed with no obligation or fear of future fees. Why wouldn't I stay?

They returned my bed to its original place and provided me with a comfortable chair, and I sat constantly with the window, the nightingale, and the books furnished by Si l-Baqqali. Additionally I would prolong the conversation with my visitors, inventing various topics to make them talk and trying to show them my great care and concern for the delicacy of their feelings, despite a lot of chatter and foolishness.

The only thing that worried me, that tormented me, was that Ruqayya did not visit me again. I thought about ending my stay there just to go to see her. But I forced myself to pass a harsh test, which wore on my nerves and exhausted me.

The head nurse noticed my thinness, my worry, and the change in me, and her sympathy for me grew in an unexpected way: she began to send a new nurse every day, her head full of affectionate expressions, jokes, and stories. One of them—a little older than I, with a tense face and hostile eyes, who aroused my aggression and appetite with her impudence—even offered to smuggle to me any kind of drink. I thought that she was doubtless going through a hard period of loneliness, imagining that she had perhaps ended a relationship with a lover or a friend, and I began to entice her. I presented her with a box of excellent almond candy and a few packages of foreign cigarettes, and asked her to make us each a cup of fresh lemonade. She sat facing me and began to talk about her childhood and her love for Megidish and how he made her suffer, and his adventures. When I told her I was prepared to go to him and reach an understanding when I got out she became angry and left, leaving me in utter confusion.

Other than that there were no visits that had an effect on me. Even al-Shaqra's repeated visits took the form of a one-sided tragedy. She would explain to me every new development in her marriage plans. About a week before I was released she announced that this would be her last visit, because the next day she would be taken to al-Hansali in her formal wedding procession. I blessed the marriage warmly, and tried in vain to keep our farewell simply visual. But she insisted on a real farewell, studding it with long kisses moistened by her tears, as stars are studded in the sky.

chapter 14

About seven in the evening Si l-Habib welcomed me warmly
in his apartment, while Qobb contented himself with a steady
smile as he shook my hand before he left, taking his magic
cane. Seconds later I heard the sound of her feet on the stairs.
She knocked lightly and entered, then embraced me with real
longing and kissed me in front of Si l-Habib.

The room was shaded by white curtains striped with deep
olive green. Si l-Habib's single bed left a large space, not fully
swallowed up by the small table and its four chairs.

She stood near the table, and I stared at her in astonishment. She laughed her usual enchanting laugh, and a wave of
her distinctive perfume wafted to us. In her eyes was the
certainty that I had lost the bet and that she had gotten what
she wanted. I felt a pain I could not identify.

On the table sat a round cake, topped with icing and sugar;
many candles had been set in it, and flowers were arranged
with care. Si l-Habib sat opposite the closed window in his
usual position, as Ruqayya flooded the room with activity, never
settling down. Her white suit clung to her body, showing the

proportions of a model. Her coal-black hair undulated in stormy enchantment. I exclaimed, "Whose birthday is it?"

"Yours."

"Mine?" I broke out laughing. "But I don't know what day I was born."

She and Si l-Habib exchanged looks. On the wall there was a picture of the port of Casablanca crowded with innumerable ships. In the distance there was a white sail on a blue skiff making its way with difficulty through the waves. She began to explain the matter with a sweetness that melted me: "I accidentally scattered your papers and came across your passport. Since the day given happened to be the first of July, we will consider today your birthday; a month doesn't add or subtract anything from a man's life."

I kept laughing. "The first of July is the date for anyone who doesn't know his actual date, in my country."

Si l-Habib cut me off: "All dates are alike, as long as a man is happy."

I sat opposite Si l-Habib and cried, "A celebration without a drink?"

"One bottle of beer only," said Ruqayya, as she filled our glasses. I drank mine down all at once, experiencing the surpassing pleasure of drinking after being cut off from it for a long time. Then I usurped what was in their glasses, and they laughed.

"When I leave you, I'm going to drink until I get drunk."

Ruqayya began to light the candles, bending over our heads like a beloved sky anointed with perfume. Just as she finished it seemed to me that the white sail had reached the port, losing itself in the crowd of ships. Tranquility reigned, and I was caught by surprise, discovering wonderfully peaceful melodies coming from a western radio station. Soon, Ruqayya suggested that we put out the candles, and no one objected. She was acting like a queen who was certain her orders would be accepted. She went to the door just as someone knocked, so she opened it.

The questioner must have been confused, confronting enchantment like that, for we heard no sound during several seconds, which passed like an hour. When he pulled himself together his tongue still stumbled, and he seemed to stutter. "Si... place... al-Habib... house..."

Ruqayya rescued him, making way for him. "Please come in."

He must have been surprised at being invited to enter when he had not expected it. He was shaken again, and fell into a murmur of excuses: "I fear... I'm afraid... I hope I haven't disturbed you... it seems that...."

Matters became confused; Ruqayya withdrew, and the newcomer extended his hands before him to embrace Si l-Habib. But he was surprised that his greeting was returned with Si l-Habib's habitual equanimity, which at first people took for coldness.

"Please come in, Si Idris."

Si l-Habib extended his hand, half standing, preparing to shake hands; but the young man fell on Si l-Habib's hand, kissing it in deep gratitude. Si l-Habib withdrew his hand with difficulty and motioned to him to be seated.

He was thirty-five, a little taller than Si l-Habib, and very elegant. He was looking with embarrassment at the door, which he had left open, so I signaled to Ruqayya to close it. She was standing near me, observing the scene mirthfully. The young man was overcome with joy at meeting Si l-Habib; his eyes began to tear, and he could not stop the stream of greetings and questions. His right hand played with a leather case holding a car key and several others, tightening and loosening with the cadence of the words pouring from his mouth and revealing his pride in ownership

His eyes swept everything with a glance that took in Ruqayya and me, along with the pictures, the bed and its candle, and the lights. The glance was accompanied by a big, oily smile for some reason, a hostile smile that devoured the lower half of his face. Then he sat down, and we took a deep breath. Si l-Habib introduced us to each other, carefully and with modesty.

I noticed that his oily smile returned as his fingers touched our hands. He did not try to kiss our hands as he had Si l-Habib's, confirming the original impression of something deeply personal.

"I heard you were doing well."

Si l-Habib's comment alerted us to the man's unusually sumptuous clothes. His face was shaven and his red hair was arranged with care, parted in the middle. He didn't seem to be much affected by the heat, or perhaps he forced himself to bear it for the sake of a meeting or an evening out, as his expensive silk tie was carefully knotted. He seemed to show good taste in choosing his clothes, which were all in shades of blue. That made me look at his shoes. I was surprised to find that they weren't blue, as I had naively expected, but rather a strange leather that might have been snakeskin. I had been astounded at the price of a similar pair in a store in Casablanca, more than double my salary, and I decided that he must be sitting on a pile of gold. His elegance was exceptional among us three, and only Ruqayya's own elegance approached it. When his voice shook it took on a feminine tone, which appeared clearly when he was moved or when he laughed.

He said, "Yes, I've succeeded, thanks to you. I have not forgotten your favor."

Si l-Habib looked away and smiled deeply, silently. I expected him to respond with some expression dictated by courtesy, "you're welcome," for example, or "not at all." But that smile of his defeated all my expectations, and returned Si Idris to his former confusion. He signed audibly, and threw out a meaningless word: "Eh…"

It seemed like a reaction to Si l-Habib's lack of response. Then he looked around him carefully, and I sensed that he was still living a moment of outstanding success, which made him think he was the center of the world. He rubbed his hands together, making a harsh sound that was unexpected in some-one that elegant. Then his glance spiraled to take in everything again, but with challenge and pride surmounting the previous look.

"I should go. I've interrupted your celebration."

Si l-Habib signaled to him to sit down. "Share it with us."

After he sat down the white sail once again seemed to struggle with the waves. Ruqayya said musically, "Let's begin the celebration."

I cried, "But we've already begun!" Then I added, "I'll bring another bottle from my room."

Ruqayya laughed. "We have another, since our guest has not had any."

I looked at him. He was smiling, his face coated with a greasy layer that shone in the bright light. The beer was of the cheap kind that came in large sizes; Ruqayya filled glasses for the three of us, and brought water to Si l-Habib. They drank a toast to my health, as the western station played a dreamlike symphony. Ruqayya began to sing softly and rhythmically; then, her eyes lost in Si l-Habib's face, she began the familiar song used on such occasions, adding words which I heard for the first time, and which plunged us into deep, unusual melodies. Dancing among the melodies were glimpses of rare moments of childhood happiness, the green of the spring, the delight of a child watching angry rain on the Tigris from the balcony of a distant coffee house, gray clouds shining in peace. She gave every letter the true value for which it was created, in its long journey begun thousands of years ago in the sea of meanings. She followed the line of its development from an abstract signal, until it joined in syllables, then words, then became melodies and strange, warm new meanings, in the inspiration of a unique hour. These meanings were known to those words only at that moment, which would never be repeated in the future. When her voice trembled my heart sank, and tears sprang unconsciously to my eyes. Her voice would rush out, then break, in a sea of delicious yearning. The same thing that had happened at that private party happened here also, though in a smaller way: her enchantment began to radiate, giving eternity to finite moments in time. I had been deprived of singing in my life, except for what I heard on the radio or in the low, vulgar nightclubs common in my country. I had never been to a public or private concert until Ruqayya opened the door for me that shining night, which she repeated now. Those two events enriched my barren desert with eternal songs that could never be erased.

Why did I nearly cry? The question beset me. I, who had suppressed my tears in very sad situations, my father's death for example. Why?

Was it because I had longed for her for a month, or a particular melody? Although the song was directed to Si l-Habib, nonetheless in appearance it related to a special occasion in my life, and that made me believe that it was my property. Perhaps that's what aroused me and made me cry from its effects.

When she said "To you, my dear" during the song, she smiled and looked at him. I witnessed a deep understanding between them, which no doubt expressed many things that had happened in my absence.

Her tender looks were an aged wine that intoxicated a man. Our guest had withdrawn from the circle of the light and begun to pull himself together. He moved his eyes among us as if we were a coin he was examining with an expert's hand and a fearful, piercing eye. Was he trying to understand the unknown that would balance the equation? For the occasion was mine, but the song went to Si l-Habib.

The oily smile died on his lips, and his eyes and face became serious. He looked like a businessman thinking about a major transaction.

When the song ended a deep silence reigned, during which she was the center of our attention. I would have waited for another miracle to take me back to the enchanted world, were it not for her loud, clear laugh, breaking like a rushing waterfall and leaving us in our dream, deeply absorbed.

I shuddered, and applauded. "Bravo, Ruqayya!"

Si l-Habib erupted in sudden laughter, to which Ruqayya responded. Then I joined in, for no reason other than the tremendous happiness that was flooding Si l-Habib for the first time; and the oily smile returned to disfigure the face of Si Idris.

When she began to cut the cake I tried to engage her, as I could not bear to see her silent: "Are we going to eat only cake?"

"Wait."

She offered us icy soft drinks from a cork box, and they lent a special pleasure to the cake in the warm air. As our guest nibbled a little of the cake and sipped the liquid, I caught him stealing glances with a desire he was able to conceal from Ruqayya.

Si Idris got up after he finished his drink, taking leave and inviting us to a lunch of grilled lamb the next day at his farm, which was not far away. We waited for Si l-Habib's answer during an uncomfortable moment, which made him repeat the invitation insistently. But Si l-Habib refused decisively, without dodging or making excuses. We considered the matter closed, dryly and concisely, especially as we were not about to judge something decided by Si l-Habib for what we sensed were valid, though hidden, reasons.

I asked Si l-Habib about him after he left, and he shrugged, as if taking leave of him forever. "I knew him some time ago, and left him five years ago."

"In the glory days."

He laughed shortly. "He was like Si Qobb."

I repeated, disbelieving, "Like Si Qobb?"

"Yes."

His picture came back to me, as he was kissing al-Habib's hand and al-Habib was pulling it away.

"But he was talking about a farm, and—"

"He's become a millionaire."

"In five years?"

Ruqayya broke in: "He seems intelligent."

He nodded. "Yes," he said, looking inscrutably toward the unknown, where contradictions and struggles intertwined. Then he said to me, in an obvious attempt to change a painful subject, "I checked with the hospital daily, and when the nurse told me that you had been released, we prepared this small celebration."

Ruqayya laughed, and hit me on the shoulder. "Open your shirt."

"Why?"

"Open."

I opened the two top buttons of my shirt. She came up to me and began searching my chest with her eyes.

"But what do you want?"

Si l-Habib began to smile.

"Where's the pendant? My gift?"

All the pain and anticipation that never left me in the hospital, as I waited for her, returned. I must have frowned, as I saw Si l-Habib looking at me seriously. I said, "I gave it away."

She laughed. "But you don't give away a gift! Who to?"

"A girl."

"How naughty you are!"

"You must realize that I can't go along with the current fashion."

Ruqayya said musically, "Are you reactionary, or am I liberated?"

I got up, mindful of the time when Si l-Habib's evening ended, as it was after eight o'clock. I asked her, "Where will you spend the evening?"

She continued to laugh. "Here," she said, indicating the apartment.

Si l-Habib's face colored lightly, and he cried, "Stay."

But I believed that Ruqayya had left my ambit forever, so I turned away, stumbling. Everything that had happened began to collide before my eyes, and I could barely see anything.

He spoke again: "I'll give you some good news."

"Tomorrow," I said.

chapter 15

The night was dark but as clear as a plate of glass on which gold and silver points had been scattered by a careless painter's brush. The road was calm, except when the peace was broken by the rush of a car on the distant streets outside the city. The night was long, that first evening out of the hospital, my spirit and all resolution crushed. Al-Baqqali was not at home. Si Sabir was passing through one of his periods of calm that followed his periodic eruptions. There was nothing left but the casino. I set aside what I needed to pay my debts and took the rest of my salary, heading for the broad street, which was aromatic with the odor of the night-blooming cereus. The palm trees adorned the long street in front of the casino. In my country there were millions of dusty, dispirited, dejected trees, but here they were resplendent; even their trunks were washed by the sea spray. Only here did their beauty spring out. Walking was in and of itself a warm pleasure, given to me only then, when I found myself hurrying. I went to the casino.

Then the burden of the night, its oppressiveness, lifted. I had found something to interest me today, after Ruqayya was lost. But what would I do tomorrow, and the day after? And, why was I looking for happiness? Was everyone like me? Those moments of happiness with Ruqayya, were they lost forever? They say that happiness is lost if it is not appreciated fully, like anything valuable when it's not valued sufficiently. I had given those moments more attention than they deserved, trying to live them with my whole being, and yet they had been lost. Only the memory remained.

At the casino, one roulette table served the gamblers for four days running. The patrons were few, no more than thirty in any way, shape, or form. Since the day off was Tuesday, the casino seemed almost deserted for four days. Then on Saturday and Sunday the European tourists crowded in, along with the heads of companies and the property owners, both non-Muslims and Moroccans.

Only a few dozen gamblers surrounded the green table, some of whom preferred to stand behind empty chairs. I had been attracted long before by a stupid idea around which, after exhausting calculation, I had constructed some foolish rules. The essence of them was that red would win after a specific group of numbers, and that black would win after another group; and that my winning during the first moment was a good omen that would produce a good profit in the end, and that the opposite was not necessarily true. Later on I learned that I had become a gambler and that gamblers' habits had taken possession of me, for I would play with all the money I had until I emerged winning or broke, without even the price of cigarettes for the rest of the month. I paid no attention to that, because I found that everything I needed came to me at the end of the month, as regular as clockwork, with a reliability I could never have imagined existing anywhere, before I arrived in Morocco.

For that reason money had lost its value for me. I did not aspire to set aside a certain sum for a major purchase, and books, food, clothing, and entertainment—all that was available without effort. So what did I want for? Thus for me playing, despite the losses, turned into a hobby with a goal that distracted me for a while, which was to discover the specific rule that might one day bring me into the ranks of the rich, those with thousands or even millions.

Those perpetual losses did not lead me to the rule I expected, nor did they affect me to the point of making me quit playing or of changing how I lived my life. Nonetheless they did sometimes place me in difficult predicaments.

I had met a pretty, likable Casablancan girl, who would discuss current political, social, and literary issues with me, smoking and drinking beer until she could barely fight off sleepiness. Sex did not attract her, either because of some coldness in her nature or because reflection dominated her emotions, so our friendship was true and unspoiled; and she had refused to accept any gift from me, despite the happiness she gave me.

It happened once that she came by on the day after I had won a very large sum. When I came back from work I found her waiting, as she had a key to my apartment. She had arrived some time before and begun drinking, so I joined her; then we walked a little, had dinner in a distant restaurant, and returned after eight o'clock. I asked her to accept a simple gift from me, "a few bills"; she refused, but promised me that she would accept a new pair of shoes that she would buy the next day. The time for the casino to open was approaching, and I could not resist the temptation of going, especially since I had won so much the night before. I was afraid to leave part of the money behind, under the influence of a foolish doubt that the money might tempt her when I knew only her first name. In the exuberance of playing I forgot about her, and I forgot about the shoes, and I lost everything. I stayed awake all night consumed by regret, as she slept naked beside me. In the morning I told her what had happened. She looked at me doubtfully and then left, never to return.

The croupier was moving very slowly because the club was so empty. I was looking for an old Frenchman who was very slender, with a thin nose curved like an eagle's beak, whose eyes shone with sharp intelligence behind his glasses. Like me he was the victim of a long list of figures; he would put 350 dirhems on the squares that quadrupled the gain. I had come to model myself on him, for if he won several times I would put my money on the same square where he placed his; if he lost several times I would place my money opposite his. There was no set rule: sometimes he would find a way to win several times in a row, but in one blow the blind mechanism could change any success into loss.

I did not see him, and I took it as a bad omen. That was another gambler's habit I had acquired from playing so much: I would take the most insignificant things as good or bad omens. One of the supervisors smiled at me, however, as if he were asking me about the long time since I had last played, and his smile restored my optimism. I went over to the large windows overlooking the Atlantic, where distant lights were reflected on the surging waves. I had to count to fifty—since I had taken a good omen—while looking toward the distant horizon, toward the fish market and the high cranes of the port. Otherwise I would lose.

There was another man doing the same thing. He looked familiar, but I turned my eyes away. That was because I still didn't have any acquaintances in the casino, even though I had been coming for a long time, because of my ignorance of French.

I discovered that I had left behind the list on which I built my modest rules. I took that as another bad omen and thought that my play, without the thin old man or the list, would be exploring an unknown region, racking my brain, and nothing more. Dreading it, as I always did at such times, I placed twenty-five dirhems on six numbers beginning with four and ending with nine. My pessimism died at a single stroke when the little white ball landed on seven. I kept the money on the same space and it won two more times. It was the first time in my life that I had seen the ball stop on the same number three times in a row, and I expected that it would win again soon. At that point I felt a hand touching my shoulder. I was struck by real fear, since I was very cautious not to arouse the least doubt or dispute about either my money or my winnings, even though now I was sure there had been no confusion because of the small number of gamblers. If that happened, how would I defend my position without knowing French?

I was surprised to see that it was the man who had been staring at the ocean, and who was now shaking my hand warmly. "What are you doing here?"

"Si Idris! What are you doing here?"

His oily smile returned, but this time it did not annoy me. On the contrary, I felt a deep delight; for ever since I had been coming to the casino, this was the first time I had run into someone I knew. I began to play calmly and inattentively, as I chatted with him.

"How did you get in, when the place is closed to Moroccans?"

He went up to the cashier and gave the man 750 dirhems, asking him in French to distribute them among three numbers starting with nine. I placed fifty dirhems on black.

He answered, "I have a German passport."

"Eleven, black, odd, low."

He lost and I won. The operation was repeated several times, and he lost every time. I won nearly a thousand dirhems, while he lost ten times that amount without caring. He reminded me of al-Qadiri when he would eat seeds and spit out the shells.

He asked, "Do you always come here?"

"When I feel lonely."

He laughed foolishly, and sat on a chair near the table. "Say always, then." I smiled, and he asked, "I didn't see you last month."

"I was in the hospital."

He was toying with the large chips that I always dreamed of. It occurred to me that he was not accustomed to leaving his hands at rest: car keys, chips, money, anything. He turned and looked at me as if he were meeting me for the first time. "You said the hospital? Two hundred and fifty on twenty-five."

"Yes."

"Fifteen, black, odd, low."

He kept losing. Then, finally, he won two hundred dirhems, which made his face glow with boyish pleasure. "Look, I won!"

I looked at him reproachfully, and he smiled to justify his joy in the small amount that couldn't be compared to his losses. "What's important is winning. Have you had enough?"

"Yes, but I stay in the casino to watch. I don't have anyone waiting for me."

He asked, speaking from his depths, "Why?" I found the question silly, so I just laughed. He added, "Do you dislike being alone?"

"Do you like it?"

He laughed loudly, annoying a player sitting near him, though it passed over the others like cars passing by shops in a crowded street. He was speaking loudly, as if he owned the place, and did not lower his voice out of consideration for the other players. New arrivals greeted him calmly, in Arabic and French.

"Come with me to Rabat." He stood up and put his hand on my shoulder.

"My leg still troubles me."

He laughed. "People don't go to cities walking."

"And the return?"

"Come on, brother. Hello, Monsieur Ahin, how are you?" He greeted an aged man with sunken eyes, chatted a little with him in French, and then left him.

"He's a Jew. Most of the people here are Jews."

I didn't comment. He pushed me gently on the back to walk ahead of him. He said, "The Jews are really wonderful."

"How so?"

He seemed to be talking to himself. "They know how to make money grow."

"Is it for that reason…?"

He sighed without speaking and turned to face me. The part in his red hair shone, his great nose seemed disproportionate, and I imagined that the nose nearly took over his face. He said, "I come here on Saturday and Sunday to play baccarat."

"Are you running after money?" I made a connection between his remark about Jews and playing.

"Winning is a pleasure, but money isn't important to me. I take pleasure in seeing a man lose something intentionally. What expression appears on the face of the loser?"

I laughed. "But you lost, a while ago!"

He stretched the muscles of his face in an expression of contempt such as I had never seen before. "I have a lot of money. I could lose twice the amount you saw every day and my money wouldn't give out for a hundred years."

"I saw you rejoice when you won!"

"I didn't rejoice over the money; it's only a charm."

"I don't understand."

We were exchanging the chips for money. He said, "I once lost something irreplaceable."

"What was it?"

The casino employee cut in, in French, "Are you going to keep that chip?" He had put a chip worth a thousand in the small upper pocket of his jacket, and it seemed he had forgotten it. He presented it apologetically, and the employee also apologized with great courtesy, including me in his farewell. Si Idris realized that I had asked him about something and that he had not answered. He looked at me inquiringly, as if he had forgotten the question; then he remembered it and repeated, "Something irreplaceable."

He looked haunted, fearful, terrified even, so I did not repeat my question. Suddenly we entered the depths of the clear, open space in front of the vast garden. I took a deep breath, the breeze from the calm ocean refreshing my spirit. He exclaimed, "What a beautiful night!"

His fast American car, air-conditioned, was painted in two colors, a golden yellow and a chocolaty coffee color. In a skilled movement, which he seemed to have spent time practicing in order to master it, he set the car in motion. He said, "Life has lost its meaning for me. I've achieved everything I aspired to."

I laughed in disbelief, and he continued, "I don't know why I play. Money doesn't excite me."

"But you said that others' losses excite you."

"Yes, but I'm afraid I've become sated with them. Maybe my excitement in the future will be anticipating the unknown.

The excitement of anticipation has begun to take over. Now I can do anything—or nothing…"

"What do you mean?"

"I've satisfied my spirit, my stomach and my nerves— money, drink, sex, everything has reached its limit. Nothing matters to me anymore. I've become like the Great Powers in passing the stage of self-sufficiency."

Driving at night in empty streets has a special flavor, spiced with secrets, and it occurred to me that he was driving at random around the streets with their lighted windows, after a bachelor's long homelessness that made him a lonely demon, a suffering soul, yearning for something he could not obtain. Did he believe that behind every window lit at this hour was the kind of family life he had never tasted?

"Have you seen Europe?"

"No."

"You must go. The casinos there?" He gestured toward the outside of the car with his large nose, as if he were pointing at a tree we were passing. "They are huge, and open every day of the week. The waitresses are naked. If you saw them…"

I sensed that my hours of loneliness and suffering had ended for that day, and I was ready to sleep soon, if he left me. Thus I was in his power, for him to take me wherever he chose. He didn't know how to drive slowly. The screech and sway of the car as it turned corners enchanted him, and he smiled the confident smile of a young adolescent controlling a large machine. At that point he stepped on the accelerator and the car took off like an enormous missile.

My eyes were fastened on the speedometer. Because of the big car and its many comforts, at first I had noticed only one thing indicating its tremendous speed: he passed all the cars in front of us. The indicator hardly ever rested on sixty-five, and that was only on the turns. I began to be seriously alarmed. I said to him, "I'm afraid I'll break my leg again."

He answered carelessly, "Use the seatbelt."

After a while I gathered all my strength to shout, "But I'm afraid!"

He laughed, and looked ahead of him. "We've arrived."

I thought he was teasing me or putting me off, but he turned a corner and then slowed down sharply on a small side road. "This is my farm. I bought it two years ago from an old Frenchman, and that was the beginning of the work that you call honorable. Honorable work." He pronounced the two words with great disgust, and then added seriously, "Our Lord has decreed a blessing on all kinds of work—all kinds of work, noble and dirty."

At the time his words were a puzzle. For years afterward I would associate the words with his oily smile, his blue clothes, and his personality.

The gate was of barbed wire surrounded by a wooden frame. I looked around for the guard house and didn't find it, but I found the guard, who appeared before us, as if the earth had split and ejected him.

The Casablanca road was lined by thick walls of trees, but I had not imagined that it contained such secrets. If I had searched long years for the farm I would not have found the gate, despite the air pumps, on which the moon had now begun to pour its pure silver, and which my eye knew well, signposts on the road.

The moon was veiled by the thick shadows of the trees. Si Idris got out and turned on a strong light, which revealed a patio no more than ten yards square, paved in mosaic, also blue. It was surrounded on all sides by iron columns on which grapevines climbed in a hedge, continuing on a trellis overhead. The bunches of grapes hung down as if in the fabled paradise of the saints. The place was very clean and well ordered, and furnished so as to be pleasant at any hour a man might choose to spend time there.

The center was occupied by a broad table on which there was a big green watermelon, with a shiny knife stuck into it; the melon and the knife leaned forward, tempting a hungry person even more. There were more than twenty chairs around it, a chest freezer, and a spacious bar. He exclaimed gaily, "What do you think?"

"It's beautiful."

"Do you want a drink?"

"No. It's lonely, even though it's beautiful."

"Wait, you'll be enchanted."

I sat down, and he opened the freezer. I heard frozen objects colliding, an echo of a familiar, family sound. He exerted great effort to find some things and take them out. Sweat began to pour from his face, and as he took off his jacket a large bundle of bills fell from his pocket and rolled under the freezer, but he did not look at it. The melon tempted me. The air was pleasant, and in my country a melon was like a sponge that soaked up much of the heat from the air. I went up to it and lifted the knife just as he raised his head; his eyes fell on the knife and widened in astonishment at my movement. I heard the sound of rapid feet hurrying toward to me to avert what might happen. I swooped down on the green melon and it split, its center deep red, like blood. I nibbled some of the fiery heart.

"Do you visit the farm every day?"

"Yes."

"Carrying the money?"

"Yes."

"Aren't you afraid of a single stroke that would end it all for you?"

He shrugged. "I'm not afraid of anyone. They all love me. When the old man had the place the workers were forbidden to eat anything the farm produced; they would bring their dry bread crust with them. I allow them to eat anything as long as they're here. I doubled their wages to five dirhems a day, from two and a half. Why would they kill me?"

"Five dirhems! No one will get fat on that, or even be free from hunger."

"But it's a lot for those who have nothing. I would have sold my soul for that, before I went to Europe. They're happy with me."

For some reason that expression made me laugh: "They're happy with me." He looked at me, smiling. Then he changed the subject, the flash in his eyes altering: "Do you know what hurts me?"

"No," I answered.

He continued, "Si l-Habib's humiliating me. I won't forget the humiliation. There was no need for him to cross out his favor at a single stroke and arouse my enmity. They all want to see an end to him."

I was astounded by the words "they all." I asked, "Who do you mean?" An expression of regret stole over his features, as if he had said more than he should. He changed the subject enthusiastically.

"Have you ever seen a larger orange?"

I relaxed since he had moved away from the subject of Si l-Habib, and took one, weighed down by ice.

"No. How much does one weigh?"

"The smallest is more than two pounds. It's a variety we've perfected here on the farm. We've exported more than two thousand pounds of them to France. Eat it, see what it tastes like."

The taste of the melon was still in my mouth, and waiting

for the ice to melt in the orange would take a while, so I returned it to the basket.

"I have to be careful of my throat."

He was looking at the orange lovingly, with pride. Then he looked at the ceiling, where the bunches of grapes hung down. "Look—there are four varieties."

The ceiling presented a unique picture. There were huge grapes the size of walnuts, and others that were small and white with a transparent skin, which would become currants when they were dried. A third kind was broad and flat like a lotus, with the color of pomegranates, and others were thin and long.

"Would you like some?"

"If I came here in the afternoon I would eat some of each. But now, with so much abundance spread out before me, it's a shock to the appetite."

He stood in the middle of the space. "I'll show you a kind of cherries that won the prize at the fair this year for the second time. When we win for the third time, we'll have a famous stock."

He was talking like a peasant, the words pouring from his mouth in the measure of his love for the land and the fruit. But this increasing enthusiasm made me feel that he was a beginner in this profession, not deep-rooted in it. I've spoken with many peasants and never saw this outpouring of enthusiasm in them. They would speak slowly and calmly in a manner that fit their dull, quiet lives, in complete harmony with the slow development of nature. Did he want to perfect a role for which he was never created? Why?

I looked around and was surprised to see the guard standing ready, not far away. I saw him clearly this time. He had wound his turban neatly, allowing the cowl of his jellaba to fall down behind his back. His eyes showed sincere loyalty

to his master, the readiness of an obedient servant to do anything, as well as clear doubts about my intentions, which I
attributed at the time to my having lifted the knife when the
money fell to the ground. I wondered if he had served his
French master with the same loyalty.

Not far away arose a lofty fountain in the Andalusian style,
adorned with colored mosaic tiles. It had stopped a little earlier,
and there were still drops of water on the edges of the basin.

He asked, "Is everything as it should be?"

"Yes, sir."

"Will you have something to drink?"

I thought he was asking the guard so I became aware of
his intention only after he repeated the question. I refused. On
the way to the car I saw hundreds of pairs of cheap rubber
shoes piled up between the car and the bower. He spoke aloud,
his tone sad and regretful. "Why does Si l-Habib hold me in
contempt?" he asked. I was silent, and he added, "Is it because
I owe a lot to him?"

"Si l-Habib never considers things like that."

"There's some reason."

"I don't know."

A feminine tone colored his voice because of his great pain,
and his face contracted. Then he took his place behind the
steering wheel, with a grave look in his eyes.

I asked, "Are we going to keep on brooding over our pain?"

He smiled and looked at me. "What do you mean by
'brooding'?"

"Nothing."

He laughed, turned on the ignition, and started off, as the
guard kissed the back of his hand and his palm, and then lifted
the hand to his forehead.

"I forgot to show you the shoes I bought Monday morning."

"I saw them. Are they for the workers?"

He shrugged, as if he were a union inspector behind the borders of the farm. "There are no workers here, only seasonal laborers."

"From al-Aliya?"

"Most of them are from there. Some of them are from everywhere."

"You must have won a lot at baccarat, last Sunday."

"Yes. How did you know?"

I laughed. "It's obvious."

"I won more than ten thousand dirhems. You were in the hospital, so how did you know?"

"Because you bought the shoes on Monday."

He laughed heartily. "Pretty smart!"

"It doesn't take a lot of intelligence."

He nodded his head seriously. "I was barefoot and poor like them, so I take care of them."

"With rubber shoes?"

He did not choose to hear what I said. "I contributed five thousand dirhems two weeks ago to the Athletic Union team, and a similar sum to the al-Mohammediya Association, and twenty thousand to the orphans' aid association."

"All from your winnings."

"Some of it, not all."

"But winning encourages you."

"That's true. But why is Si l-Habib cutting off his relationship with me? If you saw how beautiful the farm is during the day, with the fountain, and drinks, and grilled lamb, and…"

I imagined all of this. If what he described had happened it would have been an amazing event.

"A man must answer a blow with a blow."

I laughed mockingly. "What will you do?"

"Something."

I was only half paying attention, as his terrifying driving broke my concentration. By now we had entered the city, and he added, in threatening tones, "You'll see."

He stopped the car opposite the casino once more after turning through the narrow streets, and I thought he wanted to go back inside. He was still playing with the keys; however, he headed for the elegant little bar opposite the casino, and signaled to me, so I also got out. It was the first time I had been in the bar, where foreign gamblers recruited their courage before risking their money.

"You run in a circle and come back to the casino."

He laughed loudly, his eyes shining. "The money that pours out on Saturday and Sunday would fill a barrel. What'll you have?"

"A beer."

The waiter brought a double shot of whiskey with a little ice and a good bottle of foreign beer.

"But you said you don't love money."

He laughed again, after taking a large gulp. "It excites me." He stared at me. "Your sharp questions set up roadblocks for me, and I want peace."

"I'll leave, if you like."

He put his hand on my shoulder. "You won't leave. I like danger. Another glass, please."

"You're drinking fast."

"I have to drink before the girls come."

"Girls don't come here."

The waiter came with another double. His behavior with Si Idris showed a long acquaintance. When he gulped down the glass I felt it in my esophagus, and I lifted my delicious, cold glass as if to take away the sting of the whiskey. When he asked for a third glass, I said to him, "I thought you were going to Rabat."

He nodded in agreement. "Yes, we'll spend the evening there."

"How will you drive?"

He patted my shoulder. "You're not the only one who cares about his life. There's a lot I want to do before I die."

"But you said you've become self-sufficient, like the Great Powers, and that you don't care about anything now."

He laughed loudly. "It's an adventure to go out with you."

The alcohol began to affect him, but not the way it did others I knew. He became more open emotionally, as they did, but with a harshness that reminded me of scoundrels who became harder after every sip, then suddenly collapsed.

"You make things difficult. If I were in Europe, I'd order someone to get rid of you."

The alcohol was like rain that washed away a half-dried coat of paint to show the original color. He was becoming more vigorous, a fire lighting his eyes. He even turned his head forcefully, so that a lock of hair fell onto his disdainful, shining face. At first glance he gave you the impression that you were in front of a wax statue painted with a sticky, honey-like liquid that could trap flies.

I don't know why I began to be afraid that he would collapse. I was watching for the appropriate moment, when the negatives of the first meeting would disappear. Then I would look at him again, not only as a mirror reflecting the features, but as a painting whose essential beauty overcame all the external flaws that disfigured it.

"I would gladly have sold myself for a double whiskey five years ago."

Like Qobb, Si l-Habib had said of Idris. Had he really been that deprived?

He continued, looking at me with a concentration in his hard eyes that did not go with his tasteful elegance, "I was poor, wretched, barefoot, ready to do anything. Si l-Habib saved me, he sent me to France. I worked at everything, and did not turn up my nose at any work, honorable or not. Then I happened to find myself in Germany."

His complexion exuded a sticky, glassy sweat that I hoped I would get used to, the way a man gets used to his brother's sores.

"And then?"

The alcohol was a fire that had melted him internally, so he began to say hidden things in the form of deep memories. "I discovered that I have a magic wand that works wonders for pleasure seekers, men or women."

He used a vulgar expression and put his hand on his crotch, laughing. For a moment I believed he was a homosexual, and that I had discovered the reason for Si l-Habib's dryness with him.

"Everyone in existence has a magic wand that will take him to what he wants. For some the wand is creative ideas—politics for example, like Si l-Habib; for some it's golden feet, or a grip of steel. For some it's a cylinder of flesh and blood, like me."

By this time he had consumed more than half the bottle. He paid the check, then stood up and beat his chest, breathing deeply and releasing a long sigh, as he looked toward the city.

"Motherfucking Morocco, so full of pain!"

He turned toward the ocean as if he were getting rid of his pain all at once, and he said in theatrical tones, "Now we will begin the evening."

I was overcome by laughter. "Now?"

"Yes. You've only had two bottles of beer. Are you like me, does it bother you to drink with vile insects?"

I answered, "Who doesn't hate vile insects?"

He punched me on the shoulder, jokingly, with a very heavy hand. It hurt, which I blamed on the long period I had been on my back in the hospital. He continued, "But we see them wherever we go."

"Who?"

"Insects."

"Where are we going?"

"To my house."

"Are there vile insects in your house too?"

He burst into sincere laughter, nodding, "Yes, yes."

I stopped halfway to the car. The moon had lit a large corner of the memorial garden for the victims of the war in front of the casino under the tall, proud palm trees.

"I don't understand."

He paid me no attention, opening the door of his amazing car. He threw the words like stones. "You're lying."

I became angry. It seemed he was drunk. I wanted to insult him but he gave me no chance, adding, "You don't hate women."

"Why would I hate them?"

He spit outside the car as he sat up behind the steering wheel. He argued, "You said a little while ago that you hate vile insects. But I didn't believe you, and now you've admitted it."

I looked at him in the clear moonlight, trying in vain to dispel my anxiety.

"You'll see a lot of women at my place. One of them is bound to appeal to you."

I began to laugh. "Who are you?"

We had just begun to move. He stopped the car and stuck his head out the window, as if he were going to spit. When he did not I thought he would call someone, but he didn't see anyone. He pulled in his head and began to clap, and on his face

I saw an intoxication confined by the car's interior that prevented him from giving it free rein; otherwise he would have started to dance. He cried, "I'm a man like you and like Si l-Habib. But like me, you lied a little while ago. We're equal."

I began to laugh again. Si l-Habib was ignoring his existence, and in response he was expending every effort to seem like everyone else, at least with respect to integrity.

"Do you like Andalusian music?"

"No."

"I thought so. Men who like girls are backward even when it comes to our cultural heritage. You must like western dance music?"

"From time to time."

"I thought so." He stared at me in the darkness. "I'm one of the best dancers, but women like dancing, so I hate it. Do you drink with women?"

"Yes."

He shook his head in annoyance.

I laughed again. Time was passing and there was easy entertainment close to me.

He continued, repeating to himself, "He's like all the others." Then he looked at me. "Go ahead, laugh as much as you want. You think I'm drunk!" He stepped on the gas pedal, and the car took off at great speed. "I'll give you some advice, even if you don't take it. Don't drink with them. I myself don't. They find an opening in you and take advantage of it. They're very smart, they'll use a pin to widen the opening even if it's like the eye of a needle. If it becomes a little wider they'll use a matchstick, then their fingers, then their tongues, then comes the *biiig stiiick.*"

As he finished speaking he pressed down on the gas, and the car took off over Wadi l-Nufaifekh at more than seventy-five miles per hour. Real fear took possession of me, and I extended my arm forward, as a preventive measure that would have been useless if we stopped suddenly. The trees on the slopes were dark in the moonlight, and the heavy, cold air of the valley rushed fiercely into the car. I opened the wing window to curb it, my eyes sweeping the enchanting beauty of the valley, as the moon scattered its precious silver over the branches of the trees.

"Nevertheless she's unique, outstanding."

"Who?"

"Your friend."

"My friend?"

"Yes—the girl who was with you and Si l-Habib."

"She's not my friend."

"She's not likely to be Si l-Habib's friend, I know him. Who is she, then?"

I was silent, as the moonlight took possession of an unstable triangle in front of me in the car. "She's the relative of a friend of ours who lives in the building."

He laughed heartily, and the laugh flew from the car window over the forest in its enchanting, lethal night like a haphazard bomb.

"It's an innocent friendship?"

"Yes."

He made a rude noise and I felt deep disgust. I exclaimed, shaking with anger, "You've gone too far! Take me back to al-Mohammediya!"

"Are you angry?"

He stepped on the brakes and the car stopped all at once on the asphalt. I nearly hit the windshield.

"I didn't mean to insult you. Excuse me." He repeated the phrase in French several times. He realized he had made a mistake and didn't know how to apologize. "To forgive is divine."

"It's okay." But I had lost my capacity for gaiety, and the words came heavy from my mouth.

"Please don't be angry."

"Why?"

"Because there are no clean girls. They're all vile, blinded by materialism."

"Not all of them. Like men, they vary."

"Yes, there are evil men and upright men, but there is no upright woman. They're all vile whores, even my mother and—" He broke off, and I sensed he had swallowed another word intended as another foul curse. He asked, "Why do they yield to temptation?"

"She's different from the others."

"Will you bet?"

I was silent, staring at him. The car started again, using its tremendous power to move freely on a nearly empty road.

"They no sooner hear the jingle of money than they take off their clothes."

I said, annoyed once again, "She's rich, from the family of al-Jaza'iri. Money doesn't tempt her."

"Hmmm. The airline companies."

"Yes."

"What of it? Women are a storehouse of corruption. Do you want to bet?"

"No."

"Why?"

"I feel that a bet is a plot, and I would be your partner in it. In my view there's nothing impossible in love, like politics."

He objected strongly: "There's no such thing as love, only whoring."

The difference between us was great. His experiences had blackened his world, and I had not happened to undergo similar ones: deep, difficult experiences that had made him lose faith in everything. Billboards met us at the entry to Rabat, with their luminous, shining colors. Our huge car had become part of a caravan, in which the cars clumped and separated randomly. He repeated, remembering Ruqayya, "What enchanting beauty. I've never heard a more beautiful voice than hers, even in Germany. But she's a woman—unfortunately."

I laughed. "Would you like to find a man with those characteristics?"

He didn't answer, but asked, "Do you know why I mentioned Germany?"

"No."

"Because it's the center of the world."

I smiled. "Perhaps you're influenced by the new Nazism?"

He acknowledged coldly, "I didn't care about politics even when I was with Si l-Habib. But how can I explain it to you? Take oral sex."

The expression was strange to me and I asked what it meant, but he continued:

"Everyone mistakenly thinks that Sweden and France are the center of sex and prostitution. But only the Germans discovered oral sex. Didn't I tell you?"

chapter 16

Where Wadi l-Rabi meets the ocean a long tongue of land spills out, which a viewer might imagine as an artificial forest blessing the blue waters in an eternal embrace above the golden sands. The choice of the place was not random: someone who possessed a keen insight and an artistic sense must have seen the secret beauty and splendor of the site, and established himself there. Later it turned into a palace, and it must have been renovated countless times. Likewise, title to it must have aroused complicated disputes, swept away by the influence of an arrogant French investor. Si Idris came to own it by means of a convoluted purchase on which he did not elaborate; the heirs received the purchase price abroad.

The huge building gave an aristocratic impression, of a class that was still very influential. It mixed the charm of the old with new art, invigorated by paint that brought out decorated façades shining in imitation of the past. The stone of its corridors had been replaced by something more lustrous, and some of the carvings on the walls had been replaced by mosaics.

The area of the palace must have been huge, as the car passed along a drive to the left of the high wall, which concealed the moonlight for several minutes. I expected to see another servant with a tight turban awaiting his master under the Arab arches, which shone brightly, or perhaps moving to open the door of the car. But I found more than ten cars in the courtyard, where the ancient paving had been covered with pebbles.

"We have guests."

The satisfied tone did not succeed in refining his voice, which still retained a lot of harshness. Since he was now in his property before his assistants and servants, he began to swagger like any bourgeois pleased with the success he had achieved. I noticed that his movements seemed unfeigned, as if he were a true scion of an old aristocratic family.

He looked at me strangely. "As long as you're on Si l-Habib's side, I have to serve you or kill you."

I took no notice of his gloomy expression or fiery eyes, and I laughed. In spite of how much he had drunk he was a firm mountain in his walk, an emperor entering the capital of his empire.

The elegant Andalusian arches surrounded a large courtyard, around which were distributed dozens of rooms, some of whose windows threw light on the periphery of the oblong space under the arches, the corridors of the historic palace. An immense fountain was still playing with the moonlight, its splendor pouring out from seven taps in arches that bowed down to a central, high tap, where water emerged in the form of a wide platter. The palace was very big, and very old. Were it not for the bright lights dissipating the gloom, I would have fled from it.

"Isn't the sight exquisite?"

I was looking at the fountain. I answered, "It is."

He pointed to an extensive garden. "These are the guests."

I didn't see anyone. The garden was divided into interlocking spaces, separated by high walls of green myrtle, trimmed with great care. But I was surprised by two pretty girls wearing loose green dresses that were nearly alike, leaving their backs bare to the belt. They hastened to welcome us, and he greeted them with a harsh frown. "Is supper ready?"

One of them gave a trilling laugh. "Yes, and the table as well, if you would like to play."

The second added, "Everyone is here." She looked at me. "Poker, or baccarat?"

I laughed to dispel the surprise. "I don't play."

Si Idris said, "But you played at the club."

"To pass the time. Here there's something to take its place. Don't mind me, please go ahead."

The girls were beautiful, with obviously suggestive movements. As one of them shook my hand a yawn struggled with her laugh, set to go off at any moment like a spring, and she covered her mouth with her left hand. The other said flirtatiously, "I think he's lonely."

Si Idris insulted her with an obscenity, while the other rebuked her with real anger: "Stupid girl!"

I smiled, and defended her. "She didn't say anything." She withdrew immediately to the rear, without any remorse or embarrassment.

Si Idris drew me by the hand. I was bewildered by the darkness of the place.

I said, "I don't want to meet anyone, unless I bump into someone by chance."

"Fine, if you insist. Come and sit down."

We went down a few steps and were surrounded by a wall of myrtle that concealed us from the world, except for the moonlight tinting the green walls. I thought I heard several people talking behind the walls. The two girls stood behind us ready to fulfill any desire, chatting and laughing. He made a sign with his hand; I was at a loss to know how they understood, but one of them handed me a large glass shaped like a barrel, filled with beer that had an outstanding, sweet taste. I finished it within seconds, and she began to laugh. I wiped my mouth and looked at her in the pale light of the moon and the small colored lanterns, seeing a calm beauty that had been forged under difficult circumstances.

"Do you want to get drunk fast, sir?"

"I never get drunk."

The one with the laugh like a trill chuckled. "They all say that."

Si Idris asked me aloud, in front of them, "Do you like either of them?"

I burst out laughing to dispel the confusion that placed me in a real predicament. I shrugged. "There isn't any girl whom I don't like."

He muttered, "I was expecting that. Which one do you want?"

I looked at him in reproof. "I'll do what I like."

"Scared?"

He was challenging me with obvious childishness so I began to laugh, while he disappeared behind the myrtle walls. I sipped a little of the delicious drink. What did he want with Ruqayya? He had everything.

"I'm Fatima."

"I'm Fatina."

She submerged me once again in her coiled laugh. They were still in their early twenties. I got up to shake their hands when suddenly the space was taken up by a young man, who seemed to spring out of the earth like a demon. He was paunchy, with respectful eyes behind thick glasses and a lower lip that hung down greedily.

"Si Visitor, my husband."

My hand plunged into a mass of flesh.

He said, "Si Idris told me about you."

"Me? What did he say about me?"

"That you were his friend."

"I was? I still am."

His wife's sister handed me the glass and cried, as her glass touched mine, "Here's to your health, Si…"

"Al-Sharqi."

"To everyone's health."

"What do you like, Si l-Sharqi?"

The beer had begun to warm my limbs. The two spouses were absorbed in intimate conversation, looking at each other with love and tenderness, despite everything. The sister repeated her question, and I asked in turn, "What do you mean?"

She gave me a look that tugged at my heartstrings. "This place is a paradise for lovers. Wouldn't you like to look at the sea? Come on."

The neon lights shone on a light violet coat of makeup under her turquoise eyes, which made them pour out magic. I said, "Any effort hurts my broken leg."

"We'll go slowly."

She patted my hand with a studied gentleness. I stood next to her, her bare arm entwining mine; I became silent, enjoying the intimate interplay between her green silk dress and her swelling breasts. She sensed what had engaged my eye and looked at me with understanding, letting loose her laugh, which had begun to seem familiar and dear to me.

The shore stretched far before us, soft and enchanting, embracing the open sea. The choppy waves were lit for a few seconds by a beam of light flashing from atop something, a ship, a skiff, a minaret. The trees behind us shaded us in watchful silence. There were large rocks on the right that had been planted, supremely arbitrarily, as a long tongue within the waves of the ocean. Since that bygone year they had challenged the water, which did not appreciate their presence, so it made them cry in a monotonous melody after each tremendous crash of its censuring waves.

She clung to me, as if we had been close friends since childhood. "What do you think?"

"It's beautiful."

"Beautiful, only!"

I chuckled. "You're right, but there's one thing missing: rain. There's nothing more beautiful than the sight of the ocean under the rain."

"Where are you, Si l-Sharqi?" The ghostly presence of Si Idris appeared like an anxious guard under the pale light. "Are you enjoying yourself?"

"Yes."

He joined us where we stood, then looked at her. I saw only one flash of his eye. "Go away." Then he said to me, "If you want her, she'll comply; there's lots of time. For now, let's talk."

He was talking as if she were a worthless commodity. She must have been used to that, for I could discern no annoyance or anger or rebellion. Nor could I discern any dignity, and I felt that he had succeeded to a great extent in taking his revenge on all the "insects" he controlled.

She turned to go, but suddenly she fell; perhaps she tripped over something. I bent over her, but my leg buckled and began to hurt, so I stiffened in that position like a statue. The girl struggled to her feet and left, and I said to him, "Why do you insist on talking to me? There's nothing in common between a poor man like me and a bourgeois like you!"

"There's no call for anger."

But I was disgusted. I took a second glass of beer, and as I drank I heard Andalusian tunes from speakers planted unobtrusively among the trees, so that the sound came mixed with a charming echo. After I finished the second glass and began a third, I realized that one of the girls was standing behind me to execute my orders, and I felt very uncomfortable. I was unaccustomed to having anyone stand stiffly for my sake, even if it were a slave.

"I'm going to drink this one slowly."

He intervened, looking at her: "Didn't you hear? Leave." Then he looked at the other, and they both left quickly.

He repeated himself: "Any girl who appeals to you, take her to…" He waved toward the inside, where a dim light blinked in some of the rooms.

I had never been in such a situation before, and I cried, "Who are you?"

He began to laugh as a man and woman came into the garden, well dressed, looking like two spouses at the extreme of harmony and intoxication.

"There has to be someone to take vengeance on these insects that are so…"

"Beautiful," I finished, without allowing him to complete his sentence.

He turned his face to the myrtle and I understood that he meant the girl. "In the past her husband was my friend, after I came back. He was proud of her honor, and I made a bet with him about her. I won the bet: she and her sister both fell. A woman is a dirhem. How vile they are!"

The more sedate of the two came and whispered something in his ear. He looked at me as he got up, and said, "I'm going to welcome some guests."

The girl had withdrawn quickly, and he continued, "I've seen every kind of woman except your friend; I've never seen anyone more beautiful than her or her voice. She's a whole, independent world, all by herself. But she's a girl, just another dirhem. I saw that in her eyes, and I've got experience with these things. Only a practiced jeweler knows gold."

My anger broke through the influence of the beer. "I won't listen to this kind of talk."

"Do you want to bet?"

"I hate betting. I told you that before."

He chuckled with obvious mirth, and began to sip from his expensive glass. He said, with great self-confidence, "What will Ruqayya say when she spends the evening in a place like this?"

I sat up in turn and cried out with a strength that I couldn't believe came from my chest. I had been feeling the influence of drinking fast, my tongue had begun to thicken, and my thoughts had become foolish and scattered, but I cried, "I'll kill you if you mention her name again in this place."

He let out a loud laugh, mocking and paternal. The girl, who had begun to walk away, stopped. I finished, "Take me to the nearest hotel. I've had it."

He patted my shoulder to make peace, and I put my hand between his oily face and my own to keep him from coming closer. He stated, as if making a report: "You three seem to work as a unit. That's a good thing." I did not answer, and his eyes flashed. "What can I do to destroy one of you?" His eyes radiated enmity.

"What are you talking about?"

"A lion can't attack three buffaloes unless he isolates them, one by one."

I answered him, the alcohol affecting me like an anesthetic, so he seemed to be talking in a dream. "You're showing your cards."

"That's my way: I show my cards and I challenge, and then we'll see."

The supper was prepared for twelve, when the full moon declined toward the horizon, tiring of its complete control over the universe and ceding its place to the colored neon lights that pierced the darkness. The guests did not gather as a group; each man served himself or was helped by his female companion. Even though I had drunk a lot, I found that Si Idris's remarks about the fruit he grew, which he had made as we talked on the farm, proved true; I saw several delicious varieties I had not seen before. Fatima was beside me, serving me as I ate and choosing for me what she herself preferred, which was in fact good. When Si Idris saw us getting along well together, he came over to me and asked, as if in a whisper, "Don't you want to move up in the world?"

"Teaching attracts me, otherwise…"

"I don't mean teaching."

"What, then?"

"Additional work—during the vacation for example."

"Like what?"

"Ten thousand dirhems for two months and staying for free in the Canary Islands with beautiful Fatima here, what do you say?"

He had moved between us. He put his arms around our shoulders and moved us in front of him until we were next to each other. Then he rested his chin where our shoulders joined. We looked as if we were posing for a photograph.

"Ten thousand dirhems for nothing? What would I be required to do?"

"You would wait for my orders."

The sum was enormous, three years' savings at least. But the task was vague, and I shook my head. "I don't need a sum like that."

"A car."

"I get to school in seconds."

"Think about it."

"There's no need to."

"What do you think of the fruit?"

"Delicious. I was thinking about it before you spoke to me."

We continued taking about the farm and its improved production for five minutes. We didn't speak about the other subject again until the next morning, when he took me around to the farm by the international highway, so that we arrived without passing through al-Mohammediya.

chapter 17

The "happy workers" were hollow-cheeked old men, women, and girls: a strange assembly of hunger, malnutrition, and poor blood, the dregs of humanity. They wore torn clothes so faded by the sun that they seemed almost colorless. I began to walk through rows of tomato plants tied to stakes; the delicate fruit hung down like shiny red lanterns, as large as coconuts, and was collected in new wooden boxes. Si Idris's happiness was overpowering as he walked about, his smile overflowing onto the others as he inspected the unique product. I tried in vain to see any happiness in them.

The sun was very strong. Their sweat had drawn white salt lines on their old, shabby clothes, lines that overlapped like waves on a miserable beach.

I stopped near a girl of ten whose tattered dress had torn on the right side so her body showed through, from under her armpit down to her leg. She was sitting under an awning made of a torn cloak stretched between four little poles. Her leg had been burned by the sun's rays, and three sores the size of hazelnuts festered on it. Near her a nursling was sleeping, protected from the sand by a black rag wet with the sweat that poured from him. Near him a boy of three stretched out, without a scrap of clothes, along with two girls a little older. They were all immersed in a deep sleep, except for one girl who was staring at the holes in the awning where the light shone through like shining threads.

My presence near the girl had kindled terror in her eyes; she twisted her mouth, the tear dried in her eye and her black pupils froze, like the pupils of a terrified mouse. I realized that she would be struck with paralysis if I stood there for long; and the oldest one, who seemed to be taking care of the little ones, began to pull up handfuls of earth in a spasmodic movement, as sweat poured from her. At that point I realized that their presence here was disturbed by many problems and by the real fear from which they suffered, despite their limited understanding.

Suppressed noise, voices giving orders, others singing melancholy songs to lighten the load. Si Idris and I—and the guard, who had a black whip which he cracked with pleasure, like an emperor striding in glory—seemed to be from a distant world, while the others belonged to a second, secret world, not found on the map at that time, a world that had existed hundreds of centuries ago and was still in perpetual misery.

There was a faucet near the arbor where we had stopped yesterday, and which now seemed empty except for its heavy shade. From time to time one of the girls would hurry over, taking advantage of the absence of the overseer's whip, and push her head under the faucet; it would gurgle for a few seconds, enough to soak her head. Then she would hurry back the same way to her "happy" work, her wet clothes sticking to her thin body. I discovered that my standing near the faucet or sitting in the shade of the arbor was enough to strike terror into those who wanted to contain the blaze of the sun. When one of them saw me confusion crept into her movements, and she returned, burning in the sun, to the forest of stakes hung with tomatoes.

I went back to the car and pressed down hard on the horn. Si Idris hurried over, smiling.

"The grilled lamb will arrive soon."

"Bon appétit."

"You won't stay?"

"No."

He stared at me regretfully. "Si 1-Habib also refused. What's the reason?"

"Leave me alone."

"The place will be alive with important men."

"I have nothing to do with them."

"And the suggestion yesterday.... Ten thousand, and..."

I cut him off. "You don't need to repeat it. I won't be bought."

"You're a free man."

chapter 18

I woke up feeling suffocated and foolish and lonely, so al-Qadiri's telegram saved me. It was after ten o'clock when it arrived, and I had only twenty minutes before the train left. I had wanted to bathe, and chat with Si l-Habib, and meet Ruqayya, and share in some adventures with al-Baqqali, but I did nothing of the sort. I was rushing to finish everything in time, somewhat impeded by my leg. Because of my great hurry I even forgot to pack underwear.

I didn't find Si l-Habib in the shop, which was strange; I asked Si Qobb to give him my greetings, and he closed his eyes carelessly. I stared at Bab al-Tarikh as I was passing, as if I would not see it again, and then at the coffee house, at the Chinaman's building enfolded in shade, at the plaza. I did so out of a habit that stayed with me throughout my constant moves, which had given me the pessimistic feeling that a dreadful accident would end my life. As I passed near the fish ponds, I wished with all my heart that I would see al-Baqqali standing at the head of the side street, on the prowl for girls. I was hungry and my temples throbbed from the rays of the sun that came through the gaps in the trees, and my hangover beat on my head like a drum.

I was the only passenger in the station who bought a ticket for Tangiers. Most of the others were going to Rabat, and two to Kenitra. There was no one I knew among the passengers, except for a young teacher, a Frenchwoman, with whom I exchanged the obligatory nod. We stood in the shade, dripping with sweat. The station was devoid of trees and so was an open field for an unusual, scorching wind. But after I sat for a while in the air-conditioned bar car and had some bread and butter along with my café au lait, my serenity returned. I began to enjoy the view of forests swimming in the bright sunlight, and sleepiness began to steal over me.

Si l-Qadiri was waiting for me in Tangiers, where the shade of a drowsy afternoon cheered the heart with a familiar intimacy. He took my arm. "Let's go, we don't have much time."

He was wearing a trim suit and a striped shirt, with a beaming red tie. His eyes shone with happiness that lit up his handsome face. "What's this happy news?" I demanded.

"I'm getting married."

"You?"

He laughed his clear laugh. "Yes, me."

"How strange!"

"It's a surprise, isn't it?"

"It sure is."

"But it comes with difficulties."

"Did I come for the wedding or the difficulties?"

He laughed again. "Figure it out if you can."

The station was flooded with tourists whose white skin had been burned by the fiery Mediterranean sun, so they were heading south to enjoy a sun less blazing. We kept bumping into them as we made our way out to the street.

Al-Qadiri said, "Someone has to stand with me."

"Why?"

"You'll see later on."

"When did you get back from Spain?"

"I didn't go."

I was surprised, He had been deeply in love with a rich Spanish woman, a conservative of the first water, and had agreed to marry her. Out on the sidewalk, I unconsciously stopped still. The noisy street, flooded with light, fascinated me with its amazing mosaic: Spaniards, French, Arabs, Europeans of all regions and nationalities, dozens of languages, shining lights, an amazing throng...

"Are you serious?"

"Yes."

"And love?"

"It's in eclipse for a while."

"I don't understand anything."

He laughed, and patted my shoulder. "Don't get ahead of yourself."

He was walking ahead of me, ignoring the taxis; because of his natural parsimony I thought he was heading for the bus. I didn't pay attention, simply following him, as he was carrying my light suitcase. But we came to a large bus and he ignored that also, and stopped instead near a new car manufactured in Morocco, medium-sized, a shiny silver color. He opened the door.

"Please."

I laughed. "What are all these surprises?"

"All of this is thanks to getting married!"

I repeated, "All of this is thanks to getting married?"

"Yes."

He had failed his driver's test twice in Casablanca, but when he found a car of his own he succeeded in Tangiers, and he attributed that also to the miracle of marriage. The woman was no stranger, a cousin of his, whose husband had died six months earlier. Her father was an old man, and she was five years older than al-Qadiri, but in his view she was charming. Her husband had left her great wealth. The marriage had come about in a nearly miraculous way, for he hadn't seen Bahija for more than ten years, when he was an adolescent and she was a mature young woman. She had come to visit her family, and his father, a poor farmer, had accompanied him from al-Arish to Tangiers in a wooden wagon of a kind that hadn't been made for years. He had nearly died—it was a blazing summer like this one. They were expecting a lot from the uncle but he had greeted them very coldly, and if it hadn't been for his father's insistence he would have refused even the lunch that had been prepared, although he was very hungry; even so, the unexpected harshness of the greeting killed his appetite.

As they were leaving the house Bahija had happened to come down from the second floor. She had been surprised, and cried, "So you're Si Muhammad? How do you do, Cousin?"

He had trembled in a way he still remembered, and he thought he had affected her by his outstanding good looks and his pride; for she suggested they stay and her father agreed, but al-Qadiri had insisted on leaving. They left in a hurry, to catch the wooden wagon before it returned to al-Arish, and before his extremely poor father found a chance to ask his brother for enough money to buy a cow, to replace the one who had died. And even though Si Muhammad hadn't eaten anything to speak of in his uncle's house, he still threw up the little he had eaten.

The incident remained in his memory as a painful wound to his pride. Two months afterwards he was accepted as a resident student in Tangiers, and when his friends would go to visit their relatives in the enchanting big city he would loiter, alone and broke, in the streets thronged with people. Even though he was also hungry, he would often return too late for supper and would starve until morning.

During his bitter wanderings he would pass in front of his uncle's house and see the light escaping from the peephole and the crack of the door. At mealtimes he would smell the aromas of the rich food. In moments of extreme weakness he had almost knocked on the door.

The image of Bahija, as she came down the stairs to welcome him, never left his imagination until he finished his studies and was appointed as a teacher in al-Mohammediya. Then his appointment and the family's increased level of income were sufficient reasons to let down the curtain on that inconsequential relationship.

He said, "But blood is thicker than water."

"How did it happen, Si Muhammad?"

"I heard that her husband had died. But it didn't matter to me anymore, she married the first man who came along when I was far away, and she would doubtless marry another when I was far away. But at the beginning of the vacation when I was going into a store to buy this suit"—he grabbed the collar while he was driving, as if he wanted the fabric to bear witness—"I saw her. I was attracted at first by her white Jellaba, and the sadness and beauty and freshness of her features. She was no longer the elegant girl. She had filled out, but nicely. She recognized me first—imagine, she recognized me after all these years. I was frozen, shocked…"

"And Manuela?"

He repeated, "Ah, Manuela, Manuela!"

"You'll forget her."

"I'll try."

"And Zainab?"

He laughed. "That was just a diversion."

"You'll see Zainab sooner or later. She's found a job in Tangiers and she's coming to start it at the beginning of next month."

"She'll see me in the street with my wife. She'll understand how things are."

I had still not taken in the reason that had summoned me to Tangiers faster than a bird. It seemed to me that Si l-Qadiri was keeping something from me, but I didn't try to find out what.

During my time there I grew close to the two children of al-Qadiri's fiancée. The older was eight. I was astonished by the care that had been taken with their upbringing; they were kind, affectionate children. I also developed a close relationship with his uncle, the old man, who did not want his daughter to become involved in a precarious marriage that would end up costing him thousands of acres and dozens of shops. In order to guarantee everything for the two children and their mother, he had recourse to a friend of his, a lawyer adept in stratagems. His one concern was to bind al-Qadiri by clauses that could not be rescinded.

We would spend most of these family meetings, we four, discussing the most minute details, in order to guarantee the safety of the property until the younger child was able to complete his higher education. I had been thrust into these meeting as a full member with the right to vote, veto, and propose. This had been accomplished with a lot of deception and bluster, for al-Qadiri claimed that I was the only friend he could trust with his private affairs. I didn't see the need for these discussions or for those unreasonable clauses, as in my view no contract can exist between a married couple that cannot be rescinded. Al-Qadiri did not have enough experience to manage property, so the father insisted it be managed by his friend the lawyer; al-Qadiri refused, then agreed reluctantly after the bride intervened. I knew that he dreamed of a large peanut farm that would make him a millionaire in a few years, and the result did not differ from what he wished: he agreed to having the wealth recorded in the names of the two children, with their mother having the right to act as executrix, even though both al-Qadiri and his uncle had opposed this at first.

The stress of the discussions and all the attendant talk had a bad psychological effect on al-Qadiri. He would think about leaving everything and would return to remembering Mauela and Zainab, like two pieces of delicious candy he had eaten in the past and whose taste he still remembered.

After everything was settled I would have liked to spend the vacation with them in Tangiers, surrounded by every sign of respect as the honored guest in the wife's house. But I had not forgotten Ruqayya for a single moment. I deceived myself into thinking that someday, some moment, she would take me to a distant point above the stars where I would find eternal happiness, a point to which I was pulled by my dreams. Thus I found myself at dawn the next day walking toward the Chinaman's building. The small city was bathed in a pleasant, transparent dawn light, caressed by the exhalations of the cold sea. All along the way al-Qadiri's words to me as he saw me off rang in my ears: "I have deceived you. I could choose to never say a word to you and you wouldn't know the truth until you died. But I would rather tell you, because two days before you came to Tangiers I went to Rabat and tendered my resignation. You won't see me in al-Mohammadiya after today. You'll get a letter from me in a few days explaining everything, and I hope you won't despise me."

chapter 19

Qobb alone knew everything that had happened, but he was silent, as always. When I looked into his sad, pale eyes I realized the magnitude of the tragedy. The shop was open. I sat in my usual place, as the sun bathed the sidewalk in its shining morning light, and its reflections pierced through the glass storefront.

He left me in my place, the aroma of the mint tea perfuming the air as its steam rose. The table was clean. Everything was in its place, even the pen was in its place, but not Si l-Habib.

I did not drink the tea. I went out, lost. What would I do? What could I do?

The butcher told me, "On the same day that Si l-Habib came back from visiting his family, four days ago only, he was struck down by a heart attack, and he's still unconscious."

I broke in, "What? He visited his family?"

"Yes."

Si Sabir had a little more information than that, but it still didn't satisfy. Thirteen days before, two days after I left for

Tangiers, the postal worker told him that Si l-Habib had received a telegram informing him that his mother was on her deathbed. The telegraph worker was a good man and believed that Si Sabir sympathized with Si l-Habib's case, so he consulted him before delivering the telegram, fearing the effect of the shock on him. He did that despite the weight of the responsibility, depending on his confidence in Si Sabir and his savoir faire. They talked over the matter and rewrote the telegram with softer words: "You mother would like to see you."

Even so, Si l-Habib's face turned pale, taking it as an evil omen; but he passed through that crisis safely.

The second problem was getting the commissioner and his Moroccan counterpart to consent to Si l-Habib's leaving al-Mohammediya. Si Sabir interceded with the Moroccan administrative *wakil*, who solved this dilemma without any effort to speak of. He showed the telegram to the commissioner as they drank tea after lunch, a lunch always attended by more than ten guests every day, including one of the high officials and anyone who had a relationship with Si l-Wakil, whatever its nature.

My maid added that, when she was coming into the building four days earlier, after Si l-Habib had returned from visiting his family, she saw him coming down the stairs in a very agitated state. She thought I must have returned, but she wondered at his making a visit to me at such an early hour. She thought to greet him, but he had opened the door to his apartment and fallen on his face. She thought he must have stumbled, as had happened to me before, and rushed over to him, but he was in convulsions. She became very upset and didn't know what to do. The design of his room was different from mine, so it took longer to bring him some water. She began to shout for help. Si Qobb came and took him to the clinic of the Spanish doctor, Juaristo, which was only about ten yards from the building.

Oxygen, antiseptics, bottles of nutrition, white walls, flowers, pots of climbing plants, wide windows, cool shade, compulsory polite smiles, great calm, words spoken only in whispers.... But I learned that, in fact, since he had fallen, Si l-Habib had been considered dead bodily. All these measures were only unavoidable arrangements to ease the conscience of the doctor, and to allow loved ones to say goodbye to a patient with nothing left but a miracle, or the end.

A dark-complexioned nurse with a timid, trembling voice told me that his mother and brother visited him daily, that it was almost time for them to arrive, and that they were staying with a friend, she didn't know who.

That was a surprise to me. I cried to Si Sabir as I was leaving, "That means his mother was not on her deathbed—wasn't even sick!"

Si Sabir shrugged without any attempt to explain. My heart began to beat violently. I touched his shoulder and looked into his tired eyes. "You're older than I am and you know more about life," I said. "What do you think of the telegraph worker?"

"What of him?"

"Is it likely that he made up the telegram out of enmity?"

He shook his head firmly in the negative. "Impossible. He's a supporter of Si l-Habib."

"Isn't it possible that they bought him?"

"Impossible!"

"Why did they want him out of al-Mohammediya?"

Si Sabir cried in exasperation, "Who are *they*?" he asked, sharply. "You're talking about a group, a gang, more than one."

I hesitated, remembering what Si l-Arabi had said: "Oufkir won't leave him alive…. Assassination…? There are a thousand new ways." Si Idris's voice also invaded my mind: "Why would he cross out his favor to me at a single stroke? Why would he add to his enemies? They all want to see an end to him." In a weak voice, I said, "Maybe there was more than one."

"Why wear yourself out? It was all fate and divine decree."

"I'm deceiving myself if I believe that."

He said, "You'll see." In spite of everything he frowned, and his eyes were worried, lost in the search for the unknown.

chapter 20

I found his brother, the farmer, and his mother in the house of Si Bayad Ben Bella. They had been surprised when they found Si l-Habib before them, the telegram in his hand. The shock of finding her well had not harmed him, but they were afraid of the telegram's effect on him, since he did not know who had sent it or from where. He didn't say anything to them, in order to reassure them by his silence, but their realization that hidden fingers were pulling strings did not spare them the catastrophe.

The next day I told the doctor what I had heard. He said that these events had further enfeebled a weak heart and prepared the way for the bigger shock that had carried him off.

But what was that shock?

None of those I met knew. That left guessing. He was coming down the stairs, so he had been with Ruqayya, since he knew that I was not home. So what had shocked him?

I left Si Sabir after telling him what had happened to me with al-Qadiri. He laughed, and told me to my amazement that he had seen Si l-Qadiri in al-Mohammediya a day or two before I received his telegram. Since I had spent two days in

Casablanca before I went to Tangiers, I supposed that, when he gave up on seeing me in person, he sent the telegram. But I began to wonder why he had hidden that from me, and to wonder about his admission that he had deceived me. At that point I accepted the darkness shrouding these events, and began to wait for the letter of clarification he had promised me.

I went to Ruqayya's office on the ocean road, but I found it closed. I didn't once close my eyes during the siesta, and in the evening I visited Si l-Habib once again, finding there his mother and brother and Si Bayad's widow. We exchanged a few words amid a sadness as thick as death. I began to drink in my room, leaving the door a little open to hear Ruqayya when she came in; but it was past nine and there was no trace of her. I gave up and went to the movies: a French spy film of which I understood nothing. I nearly went to the casino, but I felt too depressed. The night was dark, with no moon strutting through it, so I went to a bar, where I had two beers. I felt sleepiness stealing over me after the long day, so I went back to my room. I kept the door open again. I stretched out, and I must have slept and had nightmares. I woke up a number of times without being aware of it; I would get up, look at Ruqayya's apartment, and go back to sleep when I saw no light.

I must have experienced an unconscious tremor at two in the morning as I became completely awake. What had happened? My mind was very clear, and if it weren't for the remains of the flavor of the beer in my mouth I would have thought I had just emerged from the sea, I was feeling so energetic.

The copied keys were in the clothes drawer, and I took the key to her apartment. The corridor was very peaceful. There was a pale light shining on the mosaic, and a red light under the door announced her presence. I hesitated before two choices:

knocking on the door, which would wake her, or entering stealthily. Many times my unconscious has acted, and now, before I had decided on either choice, my hands had opened the door as quietly as a first-class professional thief. The red light shone before my eyes, as the sound of Ruqayya's musical laughter gradually increased in my ears, like cymbals reverberating in heavenly tones.

Was there someone with her? There must be. She couldn't be laughing alone!

A man's voice was speaking to her, a voice that was familiar to me! Who was he? Si l-Habib was in the hospital! Who, then? I began trembling in alarm. Why? Perhaps it was the unconscious again. Dread had taken me over, bathing me in a cold sweat. I was nothing but a pile of quivering flesh. I tried vainly to control my nerves. The sweat that poured off me had made me feel that there was a spot of liquid soap under my feet, which would make me fall if I moved, and at that thought I realized I was barefoot. The red light had turned into a fire that was melting me. I made a huge effort to go out after gathering all my courage, but the sweat that enveloped me made it impossible to control the doorknob. I was in turmoil and afraid, and it seemed to me that the doors of the four other apartments were watching me, with their peepholes. At that I withdrew the key without being able to close the door, for fear of their hearing the sound of the tongue of the lock when it clicked in place.

I breathed deeply and stepped back nimbly. I succeeded in crossing the space without making a sound, but still it seemed to me that a huge, ghostly human form had imprinted itself on the shadow at the head of the stairs, and that it was watching me. Panic took hold of me. I walked to the stairwell and went down. I saw no one. I came back and stood in the same place to make sure of the shadow's presence, but I found nothing. Had I imagined it? Perhaps. But if it was a fact, what did the discovery mean for me? The disgrace would ruin my reputation with the Chinaman and the other residents of the building.

I spent the rest of the night drinking and reading, without sleeping or understanding what I read. Ruqayya's laughter with her friend had torn me apart. When dawn began to creep in, coloring the tops of the buildings and the trees with its cool, quiet, white half-light, I stretched out to watch it as I smoked my last cigarette. It burned my fingers, for the first time in life, as sleep had attacked me all at once. I put it out and returned to a deep sleep.

A little before twelve the noon call to prayer invaded my senses, and the sunlight took courage and sent a small ray to strike the window; it became a thousand balls of light, which winked and exploded in every corner. It was impossible to continue sleeping, especially when I heard knocks on the door. I was disappointed; I had been determined to stay awake all night and to be alert in the morning, so I would see Ruqayya when she left with her friend. She must have left by now....

Who could hunt the tigress?

chapter 21

Muhammad's little face looked up at me, his sly eyes smiling. He told me that I was invited to dinner with them, and that I would find someone of interest to me there. I asked him to come in, and he remained standing near the door. I encouraged him to talk. He said that he would wait for me at his house, and when I objected that we lived in the same building he surprised me by saying that they had moved to a house nearby. I gave him a banana and warned him jokingly not to throw the peel on the stairs.

As I was having breakfast and getting ready, he launched into telling me about how he had come to see me there more than once, and how al-Shaqra had found them a little house near hers after she got married, with only a wall of plants between them. He asked me, as he was marveling at my books, if I had read them all. Then he decided that I must be good in written Arabic, and he asked me if I owned the tale of his ancestors. He was greatly astonished, as we walked along the road behind the building, that I did not know who his ancestors were! Especially since they were my ancestors too, the ancestors of all the Arabs. When I insisted on knowing who they were he insisted on imposing the topic on me as a riddle we would amuse ourselves with until we got to the house. I thought he would say I was lucky when I told him I had discovered them—Banu Hilal—but he spoiled my discovery for me: "That's obvious, it doesn't take great intelligence for a man who teaches Arabic!"

He insisted on taking me to his house, but I refused. I asked him to tell his family that I might be late, that I would be there a little after nine.

I thought of a bouquet of flowers, so I strolled to al-Baqqali's house. He wasn't there, but I knew how to open the gate in the hedge. As I was picking the flowers I liked I expected that al-Baqqali would come, from one moment to the next. When I gave up on him I made sure that the door was locked; then I left the little garden, relocking the gate from the outside as it had been. The sun was directly overhead, and tremendous numbers of snails had piled up under the linden leaves, drugged by the heat of the sun high above. There were workers, their shirts wet with sweat, refreshing their bellies with bottles of cold beer in the nearby bar, under the tall trees of the fish pond garden.

At the hospital, the nurse smiled, and her voice quavered when she told me that she had never seen so many flowers rain down on a patient, just as she had never seen this many visitors, of all types and ages and social status and distant cities. They came alone, and in groups. They were postal employees, women, teachers, workers, representatives, wage earners, shop owners, from Casablanca and Rabat and Fez, from Meknes and Marrakesh. She had even seen a railroad engineer among them.

"Imagine, Si l-Sharqi, a railroad engineer! It's the first time in my life that I see a railroad engineer. Ah! A whole world.

Even the French came, even the Spaniards, but you're the only one from the East. Was he your friend? Are you from Egypt or Lebanon?"

I was sitting near her in the hall, far from the doctor's office. That year's calendar was in front of me, with an old oil painting on it by a Dutch artist. The smell of routine daily life rose from the painting, the black and white tiles of the floor reflecting the light from the open wooden door.

The nurse began to fool with her red finger nails and tap the floor with her shoes. I expected them to be white, like her apron and her pretty cap, but they were small and coffee-colored.

"Have you visited Ifran?" she asked.

"No."

"How beautiful it is now, during the summer. Snow and skiing, cedars, you must go see it. I was there last year, I sat in the large coffee house."

The superficial conversation angered me. I got up, and nearly exploded at her.

"The huge owner of the coffee house is an unforgettable person," she went on. "Imagine, he came this morning and began to cry." She hadn't expected such a large person to cry, but he did cry, he really did.

But I did not cry. I asked her about Ruqayya, and she answered me that she had seen dozens of women wearing a jellaba and a face veil. She may have been one of them.

chapter 22

Beautiful Mohammediya had become a prison. Where would I go? My imagination had stopped, reality was transformed. I went into my apartment, agitated. I left the door open a little, to hear her when she came in. Then I decided the idea was silly when I remembered the peephole in the door, and I closed it. But I went back to open it again—the opening was to hear, and the peephole was to see. I went toward the window and leaned on it, and my eyes began to roam over the roof. I saw the pretty Jewess hanging out clothes, and she threw me a suspicious look. I heard the door closing, and my heart beat violently. I almost shouted "Ruqayya!" but it was Qobb. His eyes were blazing with a strange glitter.

I cried, "Are you a cat? How did you come in?"

He shut the door firmly and leaned on it. I knew he preferred to stand. Si Sabir used to joke, claiming that Qobb was the first man in existence to come out of his mother's belly standing, that he was still standing, that he slept standing, and that he would die standing.

I asked him to sit down, and he shook his head. He still had said nothing.

I asked him, "What is it?"

He kept staring at me, but it was a deep, intelligent stare, not the stare of a stupid person, as Si Sabir claimed. "The key." He pointed to the corridor, where al-Jaza'iri's apartment was.

"What?"

"I saw you yesterday going into her apartment and coming out."

It had not been a ghost on the stairs that my fears had shown me. Even though I had witnessed a unique event, as Qobb had said more to me than had ever been heard from him, nonetheless dozens of images crowded into my troubled mind.

"What do you want to do?"

His eyes answered frankly: "That's none of your business." I had begun to understand the nuances of his various looks, as a biologist understands a chimpanzee through his changing expressions; and from these looks I was able to guess what he would do.

"You don't need to speak, just tell me why you want to make a move?"

He extended his hand. It was a strange, bartered transaction. I gave him the key, and he advanced two steps so that he faced the window. He said coldly, "I saw her with him."

"Who?"

"Idris."

I responded, unconsciously, "Then it was his voice yesterday." Had he succeeded in buying her, or had she succeeded in playing him? He had been certain that he would win the bet, something I had considered barely conceivable. I would have liked to know the actual specifics. I insisted, "And after that?"

He did not answer directly. "I knew that if he saw them together after he came back from his family, he would be finished. I wanted to warn him, but I came too late. It's my fault." His lips closed.

I said, "Si l-Habib wanted to tell me something important before my trip to Tangiers. Do you know what it was?"

He thought for a while, looking into the distance. I thought he would remain silent, but after a time he opened his mouth. "He was going to propose to her."

"I expected that. Have you told anyone else about this?"

He did not speak. He returned to his suggestive silence. I expected more, so I stared at him like a worshipper staring at an idol, a worshipper whose future depended on a word. In spite of the tragedy, my curiosity made me a little proud to know something others were unable to find out.

"My papers are complete," he said. "I'll emigrate in a few days."

That was reassuring to me. He embraced me with a warmth that made me believe that he was embracing Si l-Habib, and bidding him farewell for the last time. He turned his face away from me as he was leaving, perhaps because he did not want me to see signs of human weakness in his hard eyes. I remained seated for a period of time, my head between my hands, like a statue.

"A lion can't attack three buffaloes unless he isolates them, one by one." Al-Qadiri had freed him from me, and he got rid of Si l-Habib with the lying telegram about his mother's illness. She remained alone, he isolated her, and he had brought her down.

"Why does he stir up my anger?" "We're equals." "He crossed out his favor." "Will you bet that she's like the others?" I don't know how long I stayed in that state, alone, gathering the scattered pieces of the picture in front of me, but I know how extremely disturbed I was. I trembled. Sweat poured from me, all at once, as had happened the night before. I heard her door open and close. What would I do? Go to her while I was trembling and wet with sweat? Let me calm down first.

I washed my face and hands and stretched out on the bed. After a few moments my door opened, and she burst in. "Si l-Sharqi!"

She came into the room like an impetuous wind. I got up without thinking, and she surged over me, with her reverberating music, melodies of a unique lute flowing down from the summit of a green mountain, with the trees, the nightingales, the brooks, and even the echoes retreating before them. Where had my contempt gone?

She embraced me, gave me a little kiss on the mouth that astonished me, and kissed my cheeks. Then she began to inspect me, my face, my eyes, and my clothes. She pushed me into the chair and put her hand on my mouth. "Let me look at you first, then speak."

She laughed heartily and oh, her grace, her smile! Her teeth, when she smiled and laughed! Her dimples, her coal-black hair that usurped the world! What miracle was before me? Any man would burst all bounds and commit any sin for his dreams, for love. I completely forgot my contempt; I realized that I was weak and unable to resist. A thousand words that I had prepared evaporated, the harshness, the scorn, the insults, expressions I had thought about and studied and which would have brought tears to a stone—nothing remained of them but the blazing life before me, in the form of hair, and music, and dreams.

She patted my hair. "Your hair has gotten long. You've become a little more handsome; even your cheeks are softer. There's suffering in your eyes, and anger. Have you begun to yearn for your family?" She put her hand on my lips. "Don't speak, let me get my fill of you. You've lost a little weight—what did you eat in Tangiers? You haven't fallen in love with some charmer from there, have you? I know everything you want to say, I'm the one who's worn you out."

Then she embraced me again. Her luxuriant breasts and natural scent had an attraction I couldn't ignore, and it paralyzed me. I wished I could stay like that forever.

Her dress was high-necked, appropriate for an office, only her forearms showing. She was a large pink flower like the color of the dress, her perfect body echoing the shapeliness of her head.

She continued, responding to what she read in my eyes: "Don't try to speak. I don't like to hear any blame or scolding. I told you before that I'm free, that I do as I please. I'll welcome anyone I like here, as I please. I'm not afraid of men, so no one ties me down. Even in a friendship I want it to be without strings. Don't ruin my last day in al-Mohammediya with blame and finding fault."

All my arguments and my understanding died at once. I found my voice after a time, wrenching it with difficulty from the flood of my contradictory thoughts. "You're leaving?"

She nodded in confirmation. "Yes." Why did I feel such fear? A painful yearning began to gnaw at my insides, starting now. She sat before me and asked, "Will you come with me?" The upper parts of her breasts were lush under my eyes. She added, in her musical voice, "I'll get you a job at double your salary, with tenure and lifelong insurance."

"And you?"

"I promise nothing. Friendship with no strings attached, also lifelong." She laughed, and I was rent asunder. "Only death will end that, also. What do you say? Think about it, until tomorrow. Don't hurry."

I burned with jealousy. Why wasn't I like Si l-Habib or Idris?

She went into the bathroom. She left the door open a few inches so we could continue our conversation. I heard the rustle of her clothes as she took them off, piece by piece, then the spurting water. She said, "Where are you spending the day?"

"I'm invited somewhere."

"Come with me."

"Where?"

"Don't ask."

"I'm not buying a fish in the water."

"If you agree to come with me, in a few days you'll see the most beautiful tribal celebration—tens of thousands of rifles and horses and singers and clowns and stages in the open air, thousands of dancers and snake charmers and snakes and monkeys....You'll be sorry if you don't come."

She emerged, wrapped in a towel from her breasts to the middle of her thighs. I looked away. I was torn to pieces, in a state of arousal and weakness that left me grieving for myself. She had taken control of my fantasies since I first saw her, and I had been waiting for the miracle that would lift me in a rocket toward the stars, where those orphaned fantasies would unite with her enchanting apparition, in a shivering waterfall from which life would burst forth. And when that happened— I didn't know when!—at that time, after I tasted the sweetness of the promised moment, my weakness would reach its peak, I knew that, I would be her obedient slave. For her I would exchange my life and all the intellectual, ethical, and moral principles I had built.

"No."

"You'll regret it."

"Perhaps. My life is filled with regret. It's become like snow that accumulates so slowly that I get used to it, though in your case it will be a blizzard."

She chuckled, and began unhurriedly to put on her clothes behind a fabric screen between the bed and the closet. That fired my imagination again, which reached its pinnacle when she poured perfume over herself and then rubbed my face with the rest. The room ignited from the flame of her enchanting body. She kissed me, and I bit her lip gently. She laughed, and urged me to come with her.

"The plane leaves in an hour to take us to Marrakesh. Come, my darling…"

She chuckled, mockingly.

chapter 23

I would be lying if I didn't admit that her invitation shook me to my foundations, and that I was trembling like a feather in a storm. For a moment it had enfolded me like a cloak, a moment in which all else seemed foolish: the sea, the trees, people and drink. As for time, it became a chain of flames; there was no escape except in flight.

I took a sleeping pill and stretched out on my bed in my clothes. In a little while the drug began to flow into my limbs, and I sank into an uneasy sleep. I would awake to become conscious of existence for a moment, then plunge again into sleep, trying to chase away her specter with all my strength.

I got up in a gloomy darkness. My head was heavy, but I was thinking calmly by the time the family celebration began, in the house of Umm Muhammad, the "lady of the vinegar."

It was a small garden that reminded me of Si l-Baqqali's, divided from al-Shaqra's garden by a hedge of climbing plants as high as a man. The night was calm, its veil rent by light spilling from the windows of the house's single room. No doubt it had been attached to the other house and then had been separated, so it could be rented out to tourists.

"Si l-Hansali l-Mizwari Maan" was present, and it was the first time in my life that I shared an evening with a member of the security forces. At first I found no common topic of conversation. I yawned and our hostess laughed, believing I must have awakened late in the afternoon; she had not expected that I had gotten up only a little earlier. Al-Hansali commented, laughing, "He's lost the sense of orderly time, like us."

This remark was the beginning of a fundamental transformation in my view of him. The sea breeze was perfumed with the fragrance of the night-blooming cereus, and al-Shaqra chose a middle place, between her husband and our hostess— a hostess who looked ten years younger than she was, with her elegant hair style and her gray dress flowered in yellow stretched tightly over her body and revealing her legs, the color of milk.

I was afraid of being unsettled by the great care with which everyone treated me, for which I saw no reason at the time; so I chose a chair facing Si Ahmad, who sat to the left of al-Hansali. When our hostess arose to bring us more to drink al-Shaqra sat on my right, so without having planned it I ended up between the two women. I became even more unsettled, fearing that al-Shaqra would reveal the inconsequential, blameless secrets between us, by some deliberate or unintended movement. The lady was filling individual glasses when her husband cried, "Let's share a glass, like the common people!"

She said angrily, as if spitting her words: "Do you think you're a bachelor?"

In fact, I considered sharing a common cup repellent despite the pleasure it could give, especially when the group included two loving spouses. The word did not escape al-Hansali's notice: "The poor people, we only mention them in connection with backwardness!"

At that I felt I had before me an unusual man who did not speak arbitrarily, so I became cautious. Si Ahmad laughed and al-Shaqra got up, as if she were fleeing this serious talk on a social evening, using the excuse of helping the hostess.

After three cups of beer for me and Si Ahmad and a similar amount of whiskey for al-Hansali, the atmosphere changed. Many of my reservations disappeared, and a dancing gaiety colored the small garden, mixed with something deeper. Si Ahmad insisted that his wife drink a large glass of beer in a single draft, after which she seemed ready to burst into giggles at every word, creating a distinctly mirthful atmosphere. Against my expectations the sight infected the security officer, but al-Shaqra refused whiskey. I watched her as she drank a beer, which left a few pearls at the corners of her dark mouth.

"Why am I the only one drinking whiskey?" asked al-Hansali.

"Because you're the strongest," said Si Ahmad.

But al-Hansali did not agree with him. He frowned and pointed to al-Shaqra. "She's the strongest."

He made a gesture from which we understood that he meant only her body weight, which at first glance seemed double that of her husband, who was thin and of less than average height. For the first time our eyes met, and we looked at each other deeply. Despite its short duration marriage had made her more mature and glowing, adding greater tenderness to her face and her full breasts.

The lady rubbed her forehead, and complained to her husband in an emotional voice, "You've made me drunk!"

"Never mind—take this." He poured her another glass, and she began to sip it slowly. Al-Shaqra did the same. She reached into the top of her dress and brought out Ruqayya's gift, the pendant with the *shin* I had given her in the hospital, on the occasion of her engagement, rather than keeping it for myself. She tried to make the movement casual; I deliberately ignored it, but our hostess noticed, and gave a small smile that betrayed our simple secrets. I was anxious that it not lead to other adolescent motions, which would dot the *i*'s and cross the *t*'s.

Al-Hansali asked me, alcohol making him talkative, "Why do easterners let their imaginations soar?"

I became absorbed in thinking about whether something had escaped me in our previous meeting, in the police station, that would justify the question. I found nothing, and Si Ahmad interrupted: "Is it a trait found in everyone, so that we can't escape the stereotype?"

He shrugged. "I can assure you that it is."

I cut in, "And me?"

He laughed. "Yes, you in particular. Didn't you imagine you would not need an entry visa, when you came back to Morocco from Spain?

"No."

"What did I say to you? Do you remember?"

"No."

After that the time passed quickly, and better than I would have expected. We played cards and laughed a lot. We caught our hostess cheating; she lost, and al-Hansali won. Al-Shaqra's knee touched mine a number of times, but I was not affected and her expression did not change. We spoke about our favorite foods, about delicious recipes for crabs and other sea foods, about exporting phosphates, about the very poor and the latest tragedy that had happened in al-Mohammediya when a worker hanged himself under the pressure of payments that would cost him his house if he couldn't meet them. I thought of Si Ben Bella's widow, but I didn't utter a word. When we ended our supper it was after one in the morning, and al-Hansali (who had drunk more than I expected) excused himself, saying that he had to get up early to go to Rabat. He did not forget to invite us all to his house the following week, when Si Ahmad would come from Khouribga. Al-Shaqra teased her husband: "So, dear, you're going to leave me alone again tomorrow?"

The host laughed, the hostess pinched my arm, and I caught a meaningful smile from al-Shaqra, as she once again toyed with the pendant on its gold chain. I continued chatting until a short while later, when Si Ahmad surprised me with his intention of going back to Khouribga to arrive in time for work.

I was astonished. "Are you going to drive five hours in this condition?"

"I'm used to it," he said, and struck himself in the chest, as if he were showing me a storehouse of miracles.

chapter 24

I don't know exactly when I heard the scream.

It was the first time, and I don't know if it will be the last, in which I heard agony and terror of such extreme, tragic depth. Just as a deep, understanding smile can restore stability to an anxious man contemplating the eternity of the world, that deep, wretched outburst was a bomb that ruptured the eternity of the world and destroyed it.

I opened my eyes. The morning light flooded everything, and there was a loud buzzing in my head. I wondered if that shout had been the tremor of a dream ending, or a sick fantasy. I tried to return to sleep, but I was defeated by a loud beating on my door, then the sound of feet running. No, it had not been a dream. What I had been expecting had happened. A vision of Si Sabir danced before me: "Qobb is the stupidest man I've seen in my life." I repeated it unconsciously. "How stupid he is. Did he kill her at this hour?"

I began to tremble, just as I had the evening before. Nothing remained in me that worked naturally except for my ears. I heard sounds, and I broke out in sweat. Why had I given him the key? Feet kept ascending and descending. Faint, moaning cries. Gatherings of people. I became tired of remaining alone and motionless, paralyzed with fright. But what should I do?

The voices were rising gradually. I heard a key bursting into the circle of fear. I must look normal, but how can I look normal? I pretended I had just opened my eyes. "What is it?"

The face of the maid was terrified. She cried out, "Blood," and collapsed onto the chair, her bag of groceries spilling onto the table. She closed her eyes after snatching off her face veil. "The poor man... My God, what's going on here?"

I shuddered. "Who?"

"I don't know. A man in al-Jaza'iri's apartment. Horrible blood..."

"A man?"

"Yes."

Thank God! It wasn't Ruqayya, then. She must have been the one who screamed. The maid looked sick from the sight of the blood. I put on the clothes I found within reach and hurried to the door. She held me back with a maternal compassion, and begged, "Don't go, you won't be able to stand it."

The noise increased, and I opened the door. The circle of people had widened to cover more than half the hallway; I was the last of the residents brought out by instinctive curiosity. On tiptoes I saw the Chinamen, his face bloodless; nothing remained to indicate his French half other than graying red hair hanging down over his temples. His eyes were moving in alarm between the head of the room and another point. As he was answering, in French, someone's questions, he lost all his composure. I made my way to him, pushing back the onlookers, who were no sooner hit with the sight of the blood than they retreated.

It was as if I fell from the sky to the Chinaman. His pale features cleared, and he called to the other person whom I didn't see in the crush, not even his head, "Si l-Sharqi."

The three bodies cleared the rest of the path and I crossed the corridor. I reached the Chinaman, and faced the police officer in his military clothes. The late evening had brought out dark circles under his eyes, and in his hand was a small notebook in which he was recording his observations with a blue ballpoint pen. I saw only a dome covered by a white sheet that outlined its contours, and a small thread of blood that had congealed in spurts on the pink sheet under the body but had not reached the edge or spilled onto the floor. It was less than I expected, as I had imagined for a moment that the room was flowing with blood.

"You're his neighbor in the facing apartment?"

It was a foolish question; he must have been as upset as I was. Si Idris's elegant garments were scattered on the floor next to a shoe that had lost its mate in the utter confusion. I remembered that I had been asked a question.

"Yes."

"Didn't you hear anything during the night?"

"I came back late."

"When?"

"Around four. Three-thirty."

He looked at me, his fierce eyes frightening me. "We will have to search your room."

My mouth suddenly became dry. I nodded in agreement, trying not to let my hands tremble. "Let's go."

"Not now. But don't go far from here."

Some of the blood that had drained from the Chinaman's face returned as he saw my name, address, and other information about me recorded beside his in the little notebook.

He began to talk fast and nervously, in an attempt to get rid of the matter all at once, and the officer silenced him with a decisive movement. I felt I would certainly be counted among those under suspicion, who would be summoned for the investigation, so I preferred to withdraw to my room, having lost a little of my fear. I asked the maid for a café au lait, as I watched what was going on in the hallway through my peephole. Suddenly I remembered the copies of the keys in the drawer so I hastily threw them into the toilet, keeping only the copies of the key to my apartment, along with dozens of questions that were beginning to take material form, each with its own essence.

The maid was mopping the floor, asking me innocent questions from time to time that penetrated to the depths. I fled her eyes spontaneously, plunged into obvious agitation that floated on the surface of the truth like a question mark.

I had interpreted the officer's words with great stupidity and chose to wait for the police in my room. It wasn't easy; I didn't know what I should do or what sort of behavior was best. I began to review similar situations I had heard of or read about, in vain; I freely condemned the philosophers and writers whose works did no more than tersely mention a few points or general principles, without any detailed method that could serve as a guide in times of crisis.

Nothing was left but sleep, since memory and books had failed me. I took a sleeping pill and asked the maid to wake me when they came, and to stay near me that day. When she asked me, "Who is it who's going to come?" I said, "I don't know."

It was after four in the afternoon when she wakened me, without difficulty. I remembered I had eaten nothing since the morning, and a dispiriting hunger attacked me. She asked me, her eyes doubtful but expressing a great sympathy, whether I wanted her to stay. I left it up to her and she said, impatiently, her voice shaking, "They moved him this morning, so why are they bothering people?"

I laughed without any real attention, and she whispered that they had come and searched the room without finding anything. I trembled, but I kept my composure and laughed again. I opened the door and shook hands with the civil policeman, who was more than six inches taller than I am and who looked at me in a very superior way. He had a strong build and a long face; the cleft of his chin was a little to the left in an unusual way, which made me believe he must have taken the punch of a lifetime.

We left for the police station, using the back door of the building, as he requested, so that no one I knew saw me. I would not have objected even if we had used the other door, as I had lost my fear of anything. I began to feel that I was different from the way I had been in the morning, and I assumed that this consideration of his was based on orders from al-Hansali, who must have returned from his task in Rabat.

There was obvious tension inside the police station. At first I saw no one other than the guard, who replied to my greeting with a polite nod of his head, while the others looked severe, frowning with tension. Then I was brought into a waiting room filled with several chairs and a table. A small window overlooked a rear garden. On the table was an open package of cigarettes; its owner started to take one, but he was summoned away and left them as they were.

Eventually, I was taken to an official whose face showed not the slightest severity. He gave me a genuine smile, which I had not expected from a policeman. He offered me a cigarette and asked me to sit in a chair near him. I was pessimistic; I hated that he was wrapping himself in affability. But my pessimism was out of place, as he informed me that I was free not to answer any of the questions that I didn't care to. There was no one with us to record what we said, so I forgot myself and began to chatter with great liveliness, and with the ability to face calmly any embarrassment the questions might present.

On his right was the trunk of a large tree that had been notched in the middle and sprouted two branches, surrounded by evergreen plants that framed the window. The fresh moisture of the tree was somehow reassuring.

"Are you in love with Ruqayya?"

It was a trap, wasn't it? I laughed, though my eyes were grave. I was confused to an astonishing degree. In love with her? I didn't know. What could I say?

He smiled. He had a shining, white complexion, for which the residents of Fez are known, and his thick red lips would have suited a girl. He took the journal of my observations from the drawer. Suddenly the maid's words filled my mind: "*They didn't find anything.*" So she didn't notice what they took? I was disturbed. What else had they taken? I couldn't remember who said, "The police have the same skills as thieves."

"Is this yours?"

"Yes."

"Will you permit us to read it together?"

"Why pretend? You've already read it!" He brandished it in his right hand, and I became afraid.

He asked, "Do you object?"

Another trap. "Certainly not."

He opened the journal. "Your observations are precise and brief, like intelligent telegraphs. I'll read them without the dates, the dates aren't important."

"'Si Habib is a genius.'"

He smiled. "I won't ask you about your relationship with Si l-Habib. You know what his role was!"

At that point I realized the great stupidity. I shouldn't have written a word about Si l-Habib, for any connection that could be interpreted badly would be a calamity for Si l-Habib and anyone connected with him. What should I answer, if he asked me? Thank God he turned the page.

"'Si l-Arabi is sincere but his horizon is limited.' What do you mean?"

He saw my dismay and shook his head. "Never mind, don't answer. You'll say that these are general observations, but they are political. I won't ask you about your relationship with a member of the opposition, for those are things that will lead you into a maze. Here's another observation, about Si Sabir." He turned the page, and I heard: "How beautiful Ruqayya is! She's the beauty of the centuries gathered into human form." He looked at me. "Listen: 'I adore her. What's the matter with me? When I hear her coming I lose my mind... I become agitated, my hands shake, my mind is fixed on her motions. If she asked me to do the impossible, anything, even if it were a crime...'"

He looked at me, his eyes sketching a picture of a crime in the air. He smiled, and I was dripping with sweat. He didn't utter a word. He turned the page. "'I'm suffering. I envy the one she loves.' Envy or jealousy? You're truthful with yourself, but a man's feelings change with the speed of light. 'I've met the dirtiest man in Morocco, Si Idris.' 'Al-Qadiri's marriage, a marriage of convenience.' Al-Qadiri doesn't matter to me. Listen: 'He's a cunning snake. He's made off with Ruqayya. I'd like to drink his blood.' The last observation, two days ago. What do you say? Very well, don't answer if you prefer not to, but listen to the opinion of some of the witnesses."

"Witnesses?"

"Yes."

He tapped on the bell, barely audibly. The window intruded on a wide, luxuriant garden, but my eyes were glued to the door. My head was spinning. I repeated, "What witnesses?" I laughed in confusion, and he smiled with unbelievable friendliness.

The guard from the farm came in, with his precise white turban, his upright stature, and his stern eyes. Nothing had changed in him, except that I missed his ever-present whip. "He nearly killed Si Idris with the knife from the watermelon when he dropped his money, but he stopped when he saw me, and said, 'Aren't you afraid of the farm workers?' If I hadn't been there he would have killed him."

I wanted to object, but he stopped me with a movement of his hand and with the same friendly smile. He asked the guard various questions about the workers, their numbers and their problems, which reassured me that he had moved away from the heart of the matter. After the guard left he said to me, as if he were a close friend, "Wait. We'll hear your side later. What's important is to listen, first."

At a signal from him Fatima came in, and I remembered that moonlit Rabat night in the garden of Si Idris. She was different from that heroine of the evening: modest clothes under a long jellaba, eyes worn by tears, hair pulled back like a school headmistress, an angel of purity.

She looked at me with disgust, pointing to me: "He said to Si Idris, 'I'll kill you if you mention her name again.'" Then she stopped, took a deep breath and burst out, "He chose to stay aloof while Si Idris tried all evening to entertain him in every way. He must be a queer."

She had indeed tried to entertain me, but I had been plunged in thought about Ruqayya. Not even her accusation that I was a queer surprised me, for after she had despaired of getting a response from me she had cried, "I'm worn out—are you impotent or queer?" If I had responded to her that night she wouldn't be taking her vengeance on me now!

As she was leaving I felt the absurdity of all existence. Even though he tried again to silence me, I cried, "Everything they said is true."

"And so?"

I shrugged. "How can I convince you? I wish you would help me."

He laughed heartily, and got up. He was of average size and elegant, wearing some kind of scent. He touched my shoulder as if he were leaning on it. "So far you are not accused. You can leave. When we ask you to look for a lawyer, then at that time…"

I remained seated in my place. I was even more disturbed. "I don't understand you."

His eyes shone. "Don't you believe you're innocent?"

"I do. I am innocent, in fact."

He sat near me on the sofa, and I smelled his scent, again. He stared at a picture opposite him, of trees and a boat on the shore of a river, shady and verdant.

"We also found more than six thousand dirhems at your place."

"My winnings yesterday from—"

He cut me off abruptly, killing the words that poured from my mouth. "You are not accused. We will decide when to accuse you, despite your abundant motives. Get your affairs in order; motive is half the crime. And don't leave al-Mohammediya until we contact you."

chapter 25

As far as I know that was no more than an indirect accusation. The officer gave me a strong impression of fairness, and I could not believe the kind of treatment I had witnessed; I did not feel he was trying to intimidate or frighten me. He had simply presented his point of view, as a practiced journalist might present a political issue, in a neutral style. But he had shaken me badly, and when I stood up I felt shattered.

In the hall I encountered al-Hansali carrying papers in his right hand. I smiled, appealing to him for help; but he didn't look at me, and that made me doubt that I had met him, other than in waking dreams. Nonetheless I had gone only a short distance from the station, my gaze held by the evening horizon, when I met Umm Muhammad and another woman, in her gray jellaba and her green face veil. I did not know her at first, because I had not been expecting anyone to wait for me. Si Muhammad was the first to see me, and his cry made me realize who was under the jellabas!

She asked, "What did you say to them?"

Al-Shaqra shook my hand warmly. The cursed face veil

defeated the purpose of conversation, although I felt an indescribable happiness that there was someone who truly cared about me. The joy of Si Muhammad and his mother overflowed. She repeated, threateningly, "Do not confess!"

I burst out laughing: "Confess to what?"

She insisted determinedly, "You were with us until morning. I told Si l-Hansali that, and I telegraphed Si Ahmad and he's now in al-Mohammediya."

At first I didn't understand all the implications of what she said; I had to pull myself together first. I repeated, "What did I do?"

"What's important is that you're innocent. I convinced Si l-Hansali."

Al-Shaqra cut in, "But he's not convinced. The investigation is one thing, and sympathy is another."

I intervened, pain cutting into my soul, "I won't be able to face Si Ahmad. You know it's not the truth."

"Let's go to the house." She cut me off, as if she wanted to impose her will on me for my own good.

"I won't go with you."

Surprise silenced me, for the dusty little Fiat had just stopped and Si Ahmad got out, stretching his legs because of how long he had sat behind the steering wheel. His tired features emitted anxiety, but he smiled as he pressed my hand: "Don't worry." Then he looked at his wife: "I'm nearly paralyzed from hunger." Then clapping me on the shoulder, "And you, Si l-Sharqi?"

"I haven't had anything since morning."

"The food is ready."

It was impossible for me to stay behind, despite my strong need to be alone with myself. Anxiety over future developments curbed our tongues, but the chill of the situation was dispelled by the arrival of al-Hansali. Everyone looked to him to decipher the puzzle of the events, but he jokingly refused to speak until he had finished his meal, adding to my worry. Nevertheless, he reassured me that all doubts about me had evaporated. As the hot couscous and vegetables made our mouths water, Si l-Hansali began to talk about the casino, and I learned that they had obtained precise information about my movements after I had left the house until I returned to the apartment at a quarter to five. The casino workers had also given them information which not only certified the amount of my winnings but also my way of playing and my favorite times. As he was closing the topic he cast a searing look of blame at the lady for having rushed to testify on my behalf, and I was afraid he would expose her kind initiative in front of her husband. We learned, however, that she had told him everything while he was washing after traveling and he had encouraged her in her "gallantry." That made me review my concepts of right and wrong, as I had thought that gallantry was a characteristic of men only. He said, "A friend in need…"

Al-Hansali cut him off: "But it was false witness." Then he produced my diary with a flourish. Al-Shaqra begged, "Let me read it."

"Should I give it to her?" he asked me, and I answered casually, "I have no objection."

But Al-Hansali asked her, "Why do you care? Are you interested in his love life?" So she said she didn't want to see it after all.

As I put it in my pocket along with the money from the casino, the two women occupied themselves with an emotional conversation about the extreme anxiety they had felt throughout the day. The topic turned to an appointment in Casablanca in the morning, and al-Hansali began to talk about the report of the forensic scientist. He had placed the time of death at about eleven-thirty, deducing that there had been more than one killer, as the body bore the traces of numerous punches dissimilar in strength. Robbery was the motive, as only a few dirhems had been found in his pocket. I was agitated, and I don't know if I succeeded in hiding it. When I declared that perhaps he had only been carrying that much, al-Hansali emphatically denied the possibility that someone as rich as Si Idris would move around with only a few dirhems in his pocket.

I was attacked by a nausea unlike any I had ever felt before, along with a sense of depression, despair, and loss. I got up in spite of everyone's protests; Si Ahmad explained that he had taken a week's vacation, and that he did not want to be separated from me during that time because I was alone. I tried to smile naturally, and said that the vacation was for his wife and child. When he insisted, I promised that I would come over if I didn't travel to Tangiers, though I don't know how I happened to say that word! He continued to grip my hand with his, encouraging me with a deep, understanding smile.

I walked around the town aimlessly, and after a while I found myself in front of the hedge of the little hospital. Visiting hours had ended and the door was closed, but I whistled to the nurse who was in the garden, plunged in a sea of thought. She hurried to me in the half-lit corridor. She greeted me in a whisper, intentionally giving her movements a secret appearance, as if for an amorous tryst in the dark. She showed that she was prepared to open the door, so I asked her about Si l-Habib. She assured me he was the same, neither alive nor dead, and my heart sank.

She asked me about the truth of the rumors circulating that I had been charged, and I laughed and denied everything:

would I be in front of her if I had been charged? So she opened the gate to the hedge and invited me in, as she described to me how the workers on the murdered man's farm had gathered in front of the door of the hospital, and how they had blocked traffic on the road. For a moment I thought they had come to throw stones at him, but she assured me they were weeping for him and slapping their cheeks, and the ache in my gut became worse. I looked in briefly at Si l-Habib, and the sight of the intravenous tubes and the oxygen tank increased my feeling of nausea. His face had become paler, his tan color changing to an obvious yellow.

As I looked at him I remembered Si Idris, who had been taken to his grave a little before, and I asked the nurse whether there was any hope of survival. She answered, saying, "God makes miracles."

I answered her, "Hasn't the time of miracles passed?"

She repeated, "God's will has no bounds."

chapter 26

In Si Sabir's opinion I should rejoice rather than being depressed, as long as the case had turned out all right for me. But I had touched the intelligence of the investigating officer and his superior techniques, so I remained convinced that someone like him would not be able to rest until he had discovered all the secrets. When I asked about the truth of the farm workers gathering in front of the hospital he confirmed it, adding that to his knowledge al-Mohammediya, since independence, had not witnessed any gathering like the one in Si Idris's funeral.

When I told him that Si Idris had been exploiting his workers he stared at me mockingly, and cried, "Where will they work now? And not only them—if only you had seen the Mohammediya sports team and its supporters, hundreds of athletes from Casablanca and Rabat, and—"

"He didn't lose anything from his one pocket—a little of what he won at gambling brings him all these people?"

Si Sabir answered, exasperated: "But it's better than nothing."

The waiter was looking closely at me; I whispered, so he wouldn't hear any more: "He thought gold could buy everything." Then I added, "God damn him to hell."

"Why do you hate him?" He looked at me challengingly, sipping his cup. "Don't attack him in front of anyone else. A lot of people love him. And besides, you're bringing suspicion on yourself."

"We've talked about him more than he deserves. Don't you think about Si l-Habib's condition?"

"They're just alike."

I was alarmed even at the comparison. "How?"

"They both reached the summit."

I laughed loudly, drawing the attention of the waiter and two other workers who were drinking on my left. "But one of them was honorable."

Si Sabir smiled to conceal his nervousness as he fished in his pocket for money. "Let's finish up at the Maliki Hotel." Then he chastised me: "Don't speak ill of the dead."

The street was desolate. Bab al-Tarikh was pale and the Casbah was nearly dark. I excused myself by saying I had to rest, and he did not object, but confirmed that he would finish drinking at the hotel.

chapter 27

I hadn't thought that the encounter with the police would terrify me so much, but when I got home and saw a light under the door I began to tremble. I rushed back downstairs. If they were waiting for me, then let them suffer, I thought, trying to talk myself out of my fears. The street was also hostile, there was no way you could walk in it, so I ran toward the hotel, and found Si Sabir coming out. He said, "Did you change your mind?"

"And you?"

"I didn't want to drink alone." We started to go in, and he stopped to impose his usual condition: "Two beers only. My wife is waiting for me."

I laughed. "You always say that, and then two aren't enough."

"They'll be enough today."

The middle-aged French barmaid smiled fondly at us, while her Moroccan husband was praying inside. When she turned away, I said, "What a contradiction!"

Si Sabir shrugged. "There's no contradiction. Here—read

this letter to you from Si l-Qadiri. Your extremist thoughts made me forget it the whole time."

I was thinking about who was in my room, and I opened the letter to dispel my worries. It seemed like an ordinary letter, questions about my health, and an invitation to visit Tangiers again. I was pleased, and took pleasure in the taste of the beer as I lit a cigarette for Si Sabir. He's asking me to forgive him—why? He'll tell me everything, in detail. What's this nonsense? Si Idris gave him a huge sum of money to send me the telegram summoning me…? Why? Al-Qadiri doesn't know anything except that Si Idris convinced him that I was his friend, that I had been released from the hospital, and that I needed to be calm during my convalescence. What convalescence was that? He's repeating his request for forgiveness for not telling me the truth in Tangiers. Then you were fooling me the whole time? Was your marriage to your cousin another lie?

I tore up the letter, and nearly wept. I felt oppressed. I thought: Do you know what the result was, Si l-Qadiri? Two crimes. And you've come out of it with a pile of money.

Si Sabir shook my shoulder. "What's wrong? Is it bad news?"

"No."

"The second bottle's empty, I'm leaving."

"But I'm going to stay."

He laughed heartily. "It's the first time you've done that."

He waved at me as he left, and I ordered another bottle. I began to think the fifty-year-old woman was younger than her age. She spoke to me in Arabic that was half French, and that I didn't understand. Her voice was calm and her face was serious. What if it was just the maid, and she was waiting for me because of something important? I finished my beer in a hurry and got up to leave. The waitress realized I had remembered something

I had forgotten, and she comforted me with a big smile.

Back at my room, I tried to be very quiet, and to surprise the person inside, but in spite of my precautions the key grated in the lock. It seems that the police do away with a man's daring in stages. My legs trembled. The light in the room was dazzling; I couldn't have forgotten to turn it off, and there was no trace of the police. What if someone in Si Idris's family was in the bathroom or the kitchen? It was too late to turn back. I stepped inside.

"I almost lost hope that you would come back."

The voice was still beautiful, resonating musically, but it had lost something. What was it? Maybe it was the power to enchant me. She wore that same tight white dress she had on when she had roamed with me in a world of happiness in Casablanca... The memory shook me. I did not answer, ignoring her as I opened a bottle of beer. I stood at the window. The night was deeply dark, charged with murderous secrets, dispiriting as it spread its sad, black cape over all. With the exception of the first glance, which gave me an initial impression that her eyes were puffy from weeping, I did not try to meet her eyes again. What would I do with her? How would I act with her? Ignoring her like this, didn't that mean I was afraid of her? No, I love her! Then let me throw her out. Can I? Oh, God! I can barely understand anything.

The night was pitch black except for flashes of light exhaled by the small city. Perhaps she too was thinking of me; she respected my silence. Why should I cross-examine her? Suddenly a firm expectation sprang up inside me, contradicting the views over which we had differed before she decided to leave; I never expected anything whatsoever to come from her with respect to her strange explanation of the events. For when we meet people repeatedly it seems to us that we know them, and then we are surprised by odd things that make us hesitate a long time before making harsh judgments, and this happens even in the most complicated secrets of the human mind.

"Look at me. Please."

Ruqayya, begging? What sound did this echo? A piece of ice falling in an expensive crystal glass. She got herself a bottle of beer, and I sat down across from her. The silver buttons of the dress I loved shone, but I still didn't look into her eyes, though I didn't miss her movements across the table as she poured beer into her glass. Her burning flames tortured me. Her voice, when it poured out into the room, ripped my gut. The jingling music of it…. Once more I wanted to cry.

"Now I've discovered the truth."

I didn't answer. I let her subside. Whatever I said, I would find myself far, far away from her! A tomb for two. Two human bodies in perpetual mourning.

"Now I know what I want."

I suppressed the questions raging in my breast. I looked past her to the window where the dark was.

"I looked for the impossible until I found it." Her voice trembled, and she began to weep. She implored, "Answer me."

Her voice was stronger than my will, and I was afraid I would lose my resistance. I shook my head. "How many hearts have you collected, snake that you are?"

She took a cigarette, and her hand shook as she lit the match. The tears in her eyes shone. She sobbed, the match went out, and she threw away the cigarette nervously. "Don't torture me," she said, and took another cigarette. Once again her hand trembled. Her pride and self-confidence had disappeared in true humility. I saw before me only a child who was trying to extract the right expression of what she was feeling from among the thorns.

"I know your love is boundless," she said. "Ever since I was an adolescent men have submitted to me and have been willing to sacrifice, but what you did for me happens to only one girl in a million. Now I know what you're worth."

Even though I knew what she meant, I asked her, "What are you saying?"

"You killed for my sake, because you love me." She became a little more assured as she spoke.

"You're wrong! I didn't kill him, even though I wanted to."

"Why? What did he do?"

I was overcome with anger. "You ask why? It's natural you'd defend him, you slept with him, didn't you? You're nothing but a whore."

She broke down in tears. "You're being unfair to me. Don't you know the truth about him?"

I shrugged and said, imitating her in bitter mockery, "What's the truth about him?"

"He's impotent. Yes, they all know that about him, even the police. What's the difference between your room and my room? Haven't I slept in your room? If you had left the key, I would have let him have my room. Don't you believe it? There was nothing between us!"

She put her hand on mine in reassurance. I closed my eyes for a while, thinking of his boasting to me about his wand which made miracles with women. I went away from her toward the window, where I began to exhale my thoughts into the dark reigning over the expansive depths of the sea. Then all his excess—collecting girls, extreme speed, astounding wealth, castles—all that was compensation for his disappointing wand…

"Didn't I tell you that I discovered the whole truth?"

"The truth about Si Idris?"

"No, your amazing sacrifice for my love."

"But I told you that I didn't kill him."

"I don't want you to deny it or confirm it. I'm convinced. I know that, even if you confessed that you wanted to avenge Si l-Habib, I'm still sure that I've found a great love that I will not lose."

No group of psychological experts could remove this idea from her head, even if they used the most modern methods of brainwashing. Admiration for her beauty had made her extremely free at others' expense, taking advantage of how spoiled she was by those who had everything. In the short years of her life she had discovered what was desired of her from others who, like her, desired but did not give, and what she should look for. So she had stayed in the desert running after a mirage, waiting for the great, tragic miracle that would restore her equilibrium and balance in a harmonious human life. She had found it in what she saw as my sacrifice of my life, and who could wrest away from her the discovery of a lifetime?

I did not try to learn anything about her past, her child-hood, her present, her psychological complexes, anything that might at least let me understand how her thoughts had allowed her to connect things in this way and to produce this conclusion. It was impossible to know now. But she collapsed: she dissolved into meadows, castles, servants, yachts, airplanes, roaring, late nights, and epic luxury. Her tears washed away all the filth left by the poisonous thoughts. Her tears took her beyond the obstacles between us, to make her for me the most beloved of beings. I said, "We cannot be bound by any tie whatsoever."

I was afraid I would also collapse before her seductions, worlds on which the sun did not set. For I knew a little about myself, and part of that little was a great weakness: enslavement to pleasure. Being tied to her would mean no more than losing my freedom.

We dissolved in discussions and unsteadiness, in collapsing and in drink. For how long? What did we do?

There was a fog of happiness in which fantasies floated. But I insisted—in what must have been an extremely drunken state—that this be our last night together. I made threats after we discussed it and I failed to convince her.... And now, after many years have passed, I don't know how that night ended. Perhaps she became certain that I would commit some great stupidity.

Perhaps I did convince her that I was right.

In the afternoon I opened my eyes, which were heavy from exhaustion, to nothing.... Just the remains of her perfume that still pulsed in my depths. She left me nothing else to remember her by, despite how hard I searched. A cigarette butt... a pack of cigarettes...her rings, one of which she would often forget... her clothes... her green Parisian shoes... her scent... Everything had disappeared.

When I once again try to remember the last picture of her in my mind, what stands out is her pale, fascinating face and her fearful, anxious eyes, in a mold of pain and disappointment. What did she do? Where did she go?

A new feeling came over me then. At that time, when I looked long into her eyes, when she begged me, when she covered me with kisses, I would have dissolved in dreams— had she given them to me at any other time. But I was compelled by the idea of not accepting the fruit of a sacrifice I had not made, a fruit which would lead me into slavery.

Basra, 1970

about the author

Mahmoud Saeed, a prominent Iraqi novelist, has written more than 20 novels and short story collections. He was imprisoned several times and left Iraq in 1985 after the authorities banned the publication of some of his novels, including *Ben Barka Lane* (1970), which later won the Ministry of Information Award in 1994. He is an Arabic language instructor and author-in-residence at DePaul University in Chicago. He and his work have been featured in the *Chicago Tribune*, *Al Jazeera*, and the *New Yorker*.

about the translator

Kay Heikkinen teaches Arabic language at the University of Chicago and is the translator of *In the Time of Love* by Naguib Mahfouz. She is the recipient of several fellowships, including Fulbright Fellowships in France and Egypt at the Center for Arabic Study Abroad (CASA).